ASUNDER

ASUNDER

Kathryn Haueisen

Blue Ocotillo Publishing

Austin, Texas

ASUNDER with Discussion Guide

Copyright © 2016 by Kathryn Haueisen

Blue Ocotillo Publishing
Austin, Texas
www.blueocotillo.com

Some of the Scripture quotations contained herein are from the New Revised Standard Version, copyright © 1989 by the Division of Christian Education of the National Council of Churches in the U.S.A., and are used by permission. All rights reserved. Some of the Scripture quotations are from THE HOLY BIBLE, NEW INTERNATIONAL VERSION®, NIV® Copyright © 1973, 1978, 1984, 2011 by Biblica, Inc. ™ Used by permission. All rights reserved worldwide.

LCCN: 2016937147

ISBN: 978-0-692-68089-6

ACKNOWLEDGMENTS

Many and greatly appreciated are the people who have helped bring this book to completion and publication. In the very earliest years there were those who hung in with me through the first daunting adjustment months following the divorce. I shall forever be grateful for those who provided soft shoulders, tea and sympathy, and wise counsel. Special thanks go to Gayle Linke, Nora Otto, Margo Johnson, Janetta Morris, Jerry and Mary Markowich, and Larry Johnson.

Later there were those who waded through the first drafts, making valuable suggestions. Thanks to readers Brad Hanson, Alan Sager, Larry Johnson, Beverly Palmer, Zana Gorman, Rosalie Fontenot, Sonia Solomonson, and the professional services of Andrea Lee at Legacy Editing.

Thank you also to colleague and friend T. Carlos Anderson of Blue Ocotillo for accepting this book to be part of his efforts of publishing books that uplift the common good. The publication of his book, *Just a Little Bit More*, has served as the launch pad for *Asunder.*

A special thanks to those who participated in the Kickstarter campaign to fund the cost of producing *Asunder*. The list is too long to list here, but you know who you are and I hope you also know how very much your encouragement means to me.

Finally, more thanks and appreciation than I know how to express to my family who have lived through this chapter of life with me and still speak to me: My incredibly wonderful daughters Carol Flores and Karen Haueisen Crissinger, my brother Bruce Hieber, and my unbelievably patient and supportive husband, Thomas Brandino.

ACKNOWLEDGMENTS

Dedicated to Gaynell—my cousin by marriage and friend by choice. Thanks for being there—every time.

Weeping may last for the night, but joy comes in the morning.
(Psalm 30:5)

CHAPTER ONE

Call for the wailing women to come; send for the most skillful of them. Let them come quickly and wail over us 'til our eyes overflow with tears and water streams from our eyelids. (Jeremiah 9:17-18)

June 1961

"For as Chester and Eloise have consented together in holy wedlock, and have declared the same before God and in the presence of this company, I pronounce them Man and Wife. What God hath joined together, let no one put asunder."

June 1999

How did I get here?! Ellie wondered for the hundredth, no, more likely the thousandth time. She sat alone at a picnic table along the Atlantic shore. These final few moments by the sea brought to an end her first solo vacation. Coming here alone required more resolve than she realized she had.

She knew *how* she came to be alone on vacation. What she still couldn't accept was *why* she was alone. It started after that kick-in-the-gut conversation with Cat, her oldest child and unofficial spokesperson for the other two. She let her thoughts travel back to three years earlier. Three years had passed and she could still replay that conversation with her daughter verbatim.

"My boss says she'll fire me if I don't take a vacation this year and she wants me to take the time off before mid-September when things get busy again. I was hoping that maybe if I rented a large enough beach house this year we could all spend the whole Labor Day weekend together. The kids are old enough now. They'd have so much fun together. I can afford the beach house if you and the others bring along the food. What do you think?"

Labor Day. The day we used to look forward to every year. Now it's a day to survive. That phone conversation with Cat marked the day her newly divorced reality hit with full force. It gave her an unwanted preview of the single-again life. That day Cat dropped the news that crushed any remnant of hope Ellie clung to that the family life she loved would ever make a come-back.

"Oh, Mom. I shouldn't be the one to tell you this. But someone has to let you know. Dad's already with someone. He introduced us to her at a cookout a couple of weeks ago. They're getting married. Labor Day weekend."

Ellie couldn't breathe. She felt numb and disconnected from herself. A slow ember of anger began to build into a wave of fury that frightened her in its intensity. She clenched the phone tightly and forced herself to remain seated. Every muscle she had was twitching to do something—but do what? She didn't know, but now she felt a surge of energy looking for release.

"Mom, you still there?"

Ellie nodded, and then realized Cat couldn't see her through the phone. "Yes. I'm here." She paused, dreading the answer before she asked the question. "Are *all* of you going?"

The pause seemed like minutes but was in reality only a few seconds. "Yes, we are." Cat started to offer other options for getting the entire family together—less Chet. Chet had left Ellie the previous summer—barely a year ago. *He's getting married and I'm getting left out.* Ellie didn't want to hear it. She felt physically nauseous with waves of humiliation and panic about having to face Labor Day alone.

"I have to go now. Someone just came in." It was a lie, but she didn't want Cat to know how much Chet could still upset her when he wasn't even there. She made a quick exit from her desk at the Caring Assistance and Relief Emergency Center, C.A.R.E., as people in town called it. In the privacy of the bathroom stall she tried to sort out what she'd just learned.

Chet was getting married again. On the weekend that had always been their special family time together. The one weekend of the year that had been nearly sacred was now an emotional land mine to navigate without him. Last year she and the kids had gone through with the annual cookout at the house without him. The adults all acted like something or someone might explode if anyone uttered one inappropriate word. Mercifully, the grandkids seemed oblivious to their missing Grandpa. They were too excited to have the cousins together again to worry about adult issues.

It wasn't just that she'd not have her family to lean on to get through those few days. She had to go it alone knowing that *he would be with all of them.* She felt the fury again at the unfairness of it all. *He left. I stayed. I had to tell the kids. I had to let our parents know. And now he's taking them away on what used to be our time with them.*

Ellie felt like she did in her childhood when she got sent to her room without dinner after a fight with her brother.

When Chet left and filed for divorce, her vacation choices boiled down to:

Skip vacations—too depressing. Besides, her boss, Lynette, would insist on her not being at work for two weeks each summer.

Group travel—exhausting, making small talk with people she barely knew.

Travel with family or friends—all seemed too busy with their own lives.

Or go alone? The idea sent ripples of unidentified fear through her. She had forced herself to do it anyway. Now as it was coming to an end she felt pride and actually did feel more rested. She'd broken up the long drive to the beach condo with stops every few hours. The slow walks around various small towns along the way distracted the relentless pangs of loneliness and dread that had become regular companions.

Last week would have been her and Chet's thirty-eighth anniversary. Technically it still was the thirty-eighth year since they exchanged their "I do's" back in 1961. That date didn't change. But since Chet left, the date transformed from an occasion to celebrate to one to endure. Three years earlier—the first anniversary without Chet—turned out to be torture. That year the anniversary date approached like a stalker in the night. Her dread of facing it alone drove her to call her old college roommate, Amelia. Amelia—Ellie's matron of honor and friend extraordinaire ever since.

Back in Pre-D days (as she now referred to the years before the divorce), she and Chet spent several laughter-filled weekends with Amelia and Thad. Ellie hadn't seen them since her divorce. She broke the news to them—and everyone else she thought needed to know—in a Christmas letter. Amelia phoned to express her shock, dismay, and sympathy. She offered an open invitation to come see them anytime. The first anniversary minus husband, Ellie cashed in on the invitation. She closed her eyes and traveled back to the memory of that desperate call. Though that happened nearly three years ago, she still sometimes felt ashamed of her desperate fear of being alone.

"Ellie, you know we'd love to have you, but Thad's travel schedule has been horrific. I'm not sure we're up for company that weekend. What about later in the summer? The weather will be better then anyway."

"Amelia," Ellie said, trying to squelch her panic about being alone, "I guess this isn't fair, but . . . " The claw of pain creeping up her spine stopped her.

"What is it Ellie? Are you okay?"

Ellie sucked in another deep breath and tried it again. "Our anniversary would have been that weekend. This will be the first one since . . . " The throat lump stopped her again.

Amelia, God bless her, rose to the occasion. "Of course. I was there. I just didn't make the connection. You come. I'll tell Thad you and I need a girls' weekend. He'll be happy to just vege out at home. We can do whatever you want."

People really can be incredibly kind when given a chance, thought Ellie.

Amelia was a social butterfly. Ellie always loved and admired the way Amelia could enter a room of strangers and within minutes add a new friend or two to her large circle of friends. That weekend they checked out every activity available in Amelia's small town. The constant activity didn't erase the overwhelming sense of loss and confusion, but it went a long way toward providing support to endure it. *It is so good to have people around who understand and care. How on earth do people get through this without them?* Ellie wondered.

She spent a lot of time these days wondering. Wondering what went wrong. What she did that drove him away. Why he didn't want the life they'd built together. Wondering what would become of her now. Wondering how to function as a single-again woman in the married world around her. Wondering if the pain would *ever* go away.

When their anniversary date approached for the second time without Chet, Ellie forced herself to tough it out at home alone. Amelia hadn't thought to invite her. She didn't want to make an annual event out of inviting herself to see her roommate. Ellie thought it would be an opportunity to finally put the past behind her and prepare for a new kind of life on her own. At first the time alone looked appealing.

That didn't last long. She could almost see her unwanted roommate, Grief, smirking at her. Grief moved in after Chet moved out. Nearly two years later, Grief still showed no signs of moving out any time soon. Rather, Grief taunted her. "See, no one really cares about you anymore. You're washed up. You really are all on your own now." Ellie couldn't think of a single place she wanted to go or anything she wanted to do. Instead she stayed home to confront Grief on her own terms.

She spent the entire week before and after the anniversary date stuck in what felt like a bottomless dark pit. Grief dredged up memory after memory of happier days when she and Chet would sneak off to rekindle the passion that brought them together their last year in college.

For her third pass through the valley of a mate-less anniversary, Ellie took her first cruise as a divorcée with her college alumni group. It wasn't bad. In fact, some of it had been rather fun. However, the non-stop conversations and lack of any quality alone time exhausted her.

At first Ellie thought she and the random roommate assigned to share the cabin would have much in common. Her roommate was a relatively new widow. They had grandchildren around the same ages. They'd gone to the same university, though at different times. She was a good enough roommate, but she was a nervous non-stop talker. Ellie just couldn't offer the sympathy the woman seemed to expect. Her own wounds were too raw and her emotions too unresolved. She spent most of the free time alone in the library reading her way through light-weight fiction.

Another mate-less anniversary date was approaching. Ellie decided she wasn't in the mood to make conversation with people she didn't know well. She wanted a vacation with her children and their families, but none of them were available. Getting schedules coordinated enough to all take time away together was becoming increasingly difficult with each passing year. And, she had to reluctantly admit that Chet was their father and thus entitled to time with them as well.

Ellie didn't want to pressure her three adult children. But neither did she want to skip going somewhere on vacation. She was determined to learn how to be single again, and this vacation was one of the lessons to master. She decided finally to head to the beach, telling herself she'd like it. The beach always had a soothing effect for her. She never tired of watching the waves meet the shore. She loved it all—the wide horizon, the crashing waves, the salty scent. It was just the thing she needed to provide a welcome change of scenery.

Ellie had friends who did this all the time. They seemed to thrive on it. She feared, though, that it just wouldn't be all that much fun for her. Extroverts crave people contact. Even her terrier, Chipper, shared her high need for people contact.

When another annual anniversary date approached, she packed her suitcase, checked that her neighbor would tend to Chipper, and headed for the shore. Now, at the end of her first week-long solo vacation, she gazed out at the Atlantic and let her thoughts meander wherever they wanted.

What happened so that I end up alone when I really do love people in general and still love Chet in particular? I hate what he did; but God help me, I still love him. Maybe it's time to just savor the moment. I do love the water. No one can take that away from me.

CHAPTER TWO

The Lord will fulfill his purpose for me; your love, O Lord, endures forever—do not abandon the works of your hands.
(Psalm 138:8)

Ellie grew up near Lake Erie, which she guessed was the reason for her deep desire to be near water whenever she was seeking reassurance. She remembered with great fondness the sunny summer afternoons spent drifting aimlessly in an inner tube on the lake—alone or with friends or siblings and cousins. Other times she'd sunbathe on a huge old bedspread at Huntington Beach. There were times when she just needed to be by water. This was especially true whenever she needed to restore her soul.

If there was one thing about Ellie's life that needed restoring right now, it was her soul. She felt like it'd been used as a punching bag for years by the people she loved the most. Her parents had migrated into their elderly years with all the grace and dignity of the proverbial bulls in a china shop. Watching them constantly bickering and competing for her attention on their infrequent visits to her busy household, or her visits to them, drained her.

Though she missed them terribly at times, she had to admit it was a relief to be out of the scrum of their later years, with the constant complaining and competing for scraps of her attention. She did remember with great fondness the happier days spent cruising along the Lake Erie coast line. One of her favorite photos of her parents was them picnicking along the Rocky River that fed into Lake Erie. *I sure inherited their love of water. A nice legacy.*

Next Ellie remembered with bittersweet nostalgia the months after high school when she sat overlooking the lake, watching the rhythms of the waves and wondering what the future would wash ashore for her. She had such high hopes back then. She imagined all the fun being away at college meeting new people—maybe even the man she might marry someday. She hoped she would marry and have children. She hoped she could combine marriage and some kind of work, as her mother had done. It was both an exhilarating and daunting time of transition.

Her first young adulthood years proved to be a time of sorting out competing ideals. She knew what her parents believed. She knew what her closest friends believed. What she did not know with any clarity was what she believed.

She thought of those days as her atheist phase. *I'm glad I had that time to wonder and doubt. It helped me believe beyond any reasonable doubt that the God ideas must all be true. What a difference that's made. I can't imagine going through all that's happened since then without believing there really is a God and that God really does care.*

I owe so much to Chet and his family. They are people of such simple faith. The memories of all the meals spent with Chet's family stirred up yet another round of regret and sorrow. However, unlike previous times when she'd remembered such events, this time there were no tears—only a sigh for all that could have been.

I wonder what healing is supposed to feel like. Maybe I am finally healing from the shock of Chet's decision. I sometimes do feel human again. Sometimes. Well, I'm not going to dwell on it now. I've spent enough tears on him.

Ellie was pleased she'd decided to take this solo vacation to the Delaware shore. Watching the white foam roll again and again onto the sandy shoreline reminded her of the dream seminar she'd taken. It was during that surreal time between when Chet moved out and the Black Wednesday eight months later when the marriage was declared legally dead.

During that time Ellie's dreams were so vivid that it was like watching movies while she slept. Each morning when she woke up she could remember the vivid images. She wrote some of them down, going back over them again searching for some meaning.

The facilitator at the dream seminar explained, "Dreams are how our subconscious minds deliver messages to us. They seem strange to our conscious mind because the subconscious mind is trying to get coded messages through the conscious mind's filtering system." In a quick chat during a break, the leader suggested her many dreams were part of her subconscious trying to help her heal and recover from the shock.

Chet was in most of the dreams. Often she woke up convinced he was there—maybe down in the kitchen making coffee or outside picking up the paper. For months she was both surprised and disappointed to realize he wasn't there. He wasn't there and wasn't going to be ever again.

The dream seminar affected Ellie greatly. She was relieved to learn she wasn't going crazy but rather going through a major life change. A change she didn't want and couldn't stop. The dreams were part of the recovery process. She was surprised when the presenter said, "Beaches are where the spiritual and physical meet. Sand or land represents ground—the physical. Water represents spiritual—God. They meet." It was all fascinating. She vowed to study it more at some future time.

For a while she believed and desperately hoped Chet was trying to connect to her through these dreams. Although the reality was that he'd long since quit connecting with her during waking hours. Whatever world Chet was living in now, it wasn't one where Ellie was wanted or welcome.

Reflecting back on their last few months together, she admitted that trying to stem the tide of Chet's shifting, confusing moods was pointless. It had been as pointless as trying to change the direction of the waves before her now. In her more honest moments she realized her own moods also went up and down like the waves. *I guess our moods quit going up and down together and started clashing against one another. Still . . . I wish. Well "if wishes were fishes the seas would be full." I wonder where that came from—I remember reading it to the kids when they were little. Oh my. So many good memories. I need to dwell on those and fast forward through the painful stuff.*

Here she sat—alone on what could have been their thirty-eighth anniversary. But not really alone. She always felt closer to God by water. Somehow the persistent lapping of water against land helped sand away some of the incredible pain she'd been hosting for the past few years.

It had been four painful, lonely years, and she still missed him. The pain was less year by year, but it still hurt. The two years before the official end had been so odd. They became like strangers sharing the same house. Then the separation and then the divorce. How had they gotten to such a place?

She didn't know how to respond to those who urged her to be angry with him and get some sort of revenge. She was angry—enough that she frightened herself with the intensity of what she thought about doing to him. *Now I understand why some people go berserk and run people over or pull guns.* She realized she could have done serious damage to Chet and was relieved she managed to restrain herself.

Others kept prompting her to forgive him. *For what? Getting depressed? Getting bored? For falling out of love?—whatever that means.*

She knew she had to move on and was trying to do that. She was determined not to become a pathetic older single-again woman whose life had been so centered on what her husband wanted or didn't want that she lost herself long before she lost her husband.

But it was hard. *The thing is—I really miss him. And the life we had together.* Much of it was good. Or was it? Did she only think it was good? She remembered with satisfaction the many long walks and even longer talks. She remembered the fun of family reunions. The evenings out with friends. The houses they painted and papered and landscaped together. "What happened?" She kept asking that, even though there never was a decent answer. "These things just happen" seemed like a copout, but it was the only answer that made any sense.

She remembered the advice from the divorce support group: "Go through the pain. Don't try to go around it. That won't work. People don't die from the pain. They grow." Someone else told her grief is the gift we want to return to sender. She was still waiting to learn how any of this was a gift.

Now—here at a picnic table near the ocean—she thought about how much she had grown. And how much growing up she had needed to do. *My God, no wonder Chet didn't want to stay with me. I was so immature. Well, I'm not now. And maybe that is the gift of grief—it forced me to grow up. Finally. Here I am. Fifty-eight years old, kids grown and gone. Grandchildren that I adore but don't see as much as I'd like. Other family scattered across the country and too busy with their own lives to care much what happens in mine. I really am alone. And I'm not sure I like it very much. But I am. So I guess I better adjust to it and figure out what to do from here.*

Ellie started writing a list of the facts of her current reality:

58-years old.

Married 34 years. Well, six weeks short of the full 34.

Divorced for reasons still trying to sort out.

3 grown children; 3 in-law children.

5 grandchildren.

She sighed. *Five grandchildren whose parents are so busy with their various activities that it's virtually impossible to see them except for major holidays—which have to be shared with other grandparents.* She forced herself to focus on the task at hand.

1 brother & 1 sister living—1 brother deceased.

A niece overseas somewhere. 2 nephews not seen in years.

Cousins somewhere not seen in decades.

Her mind drifted to thoughts about how her monthly expenses exceed monthly income more months than not, but chose not to write it down. She was afraid the frequent raiding of her savings was going to create problems soon. Yet another thing to worry about—on her own.

I had enough savings for a rainy day. I didn't think the rainy day would turn into a monsoon season.

"Okay," Ellie said out loud. "It's time to get a grip here. I need to focus on what I can do and let go of what I can't do anything about anyway."

She turned to a clean piece of paper.

Here we go, she thought as she started a new list. Ellie drew three columns: Assets, Liabilities, and Possibilities.

Under Possibilities she surprised herself by writing down, "write a book." *Write a book!* She repeated the idea over and over again. *I wonder if I could write a book. I'm always joking about how I could write a book. I do like to write, and others tell me I'm a pretty good writer. I wonder if I could do this.* "Whether you think you can or you think you can't, you're right," a little voice whispered in her head.

"I'm going to do this!" she said out loud to herself. "Who cares if it ever gets published? I'll have the satisfaction of writing it. What should I write about?"

"You have to write about what you know about," some English teacher way back when had said.

Now she was smiling. *Well, I know about getting divorced and surviving the experience. Guess I'll write about divorce.*

Ellie looked out over the water again. She packed her things into her beach bag and headed off to put them in her car. *Time for one more walk along the beach before I head back to the condo for the day*, she decided.

Ellie walked for over an hour, not really thinking about anything and yet somehow thinking thoughts too deep for words. She had come to a place of calm, conviction, and determination. It had been a very long, painful journey. A journey she knew wasn't over yet. She had finally arrived at a place where she knew that her future would be a good one. She didn't know how she knew this or any of the details, but she was sure it was so.

I don't really know how I got here, she thought. *But I am here and I am okay. God, it feels good to believe that.* She looked down at the waves washing over her feet and savored the smell of the salty water, the coolness of the breeze, and the birds in the distance flying high and free. It seemed as if her spirits were soaring with them.

Chapter Three

Then they believed his words; they sang his praise.
(Psalm 106:12)

Throughout the long drive home to Rocky River, Ellie thought about the life awaiting her there. She had mixed feelings about returning to her job as Volunteer Coordinator at C.A.R.E. She felt good about all the people she managed to help through her work there. There were now fifteen partner churches supporting the effort. However, her work didn't provide much opportunity for many in-depth conversations. The center was run almost entirely by the dozens of volunteers she had to recruit, train, and keep busy.

Other staff worked equally hard keeping records, answering the phones, fielding questions, and running errands. Her colleagues were too busy to take time out to socialize with her. She didn't want them to anyway. They were there to serve the people who came for help. Nonetheless, it made for some lonely days followed by too many evenings at home alone. Her social life was at an all-time low, but she didn't know what to do about it.

Yet Ellie sensed this job was a big part of how she survived after the divorce. Focusing on something else had freed up some sort of inner healing energy. In retrospect, she also concluded the weekly sessions with Dr. Thorpe had been part of the recovery process. Seeing a counselor had been Elaine's idea. Elaine Forbes was her confidant, friend, and pastor.

"What's the point?" she protested when Elaine suggested she might benefit from some professional emotional health guidance. "All I want is my marriage back, and Chet's made it very clear he's not interested."

"Ellie, it's time to take care of you. If you broke a leg, would you let a doctor set it for you?"

"Well, of course."

"If your car wasn't running right, would you take it to a mechanic?"

"Of course."

"I think you have a heart that's been broken and some emotions that are running away with you. A professional counselor can help you sort that out and get control of your life again."

In the end Ellie reluctantly agreed to see Dr. Thorpe more to appease Elaine than because she expected it to make any difference. She was surprised that after a few sessions she actually looked forward to the time to talk openly about the whole life-sucking emotional stew in which she'd been simmering for too long. She gradually got tired of talking about it and started focusing on other things—like the new job.

Tidbits of peace began to surface to her conscious awareness once she gave up thinking about her own raw pain hour after hour. "It's sort of the watched pot theory of recovery, Ellie." That's what Dr. Thorpe told her as she was discussing whether or not to accept the job at C.A.R.E. "Eventually you have to let go of focusing on the pain and start looking toward the horizon to a better tomorrow you can't see now."

Easy for him to say, she'd thought. But then he'd told her in their first session that he had firsthand experience with divorce. That was part of what encouraged her to commit to talking to him once a week. That and the fact several people she trusted told her she needed his help.

"But everyone tells me I can't run away from this and it's so big I can't see beyond it. Will this ever quit hurting so much?"

Dr. Thorpe nodded sympathetically. "Yes, but probably not for a long time. You have a lot of history to process and re-frame. That's not trying to run away from your pain. It's acknowledging it, but not letting it become the sum total of who you are. You can't outrun grief. Many people make themselves sick trying—emotionally, mentally, spiritually, and even physically. You can't outrun the grief. But you can displace it. Elementary physics, my friend. Two focuses can't occupy the same space at the same time. As you grow stronger and sturdier you have more control over which focus gets your attention."

It had worked. Well, it sort of worked. Day in and day out Ellie saw people who were truly desperate. She gradually came to recognize that she had much for which to be thankful. Seeing the messes some of the C.A.R.E. clients got into following a divorce, she determined to do everything in her power to stay out of some of those traps.

I don't know if God helps those who help themselves or not, but I do ∖
believe God helps those who help others. That had become part of her
"think positive" mantra she repeated to herself when she wasn't sure
she could make it through one more day. *Thank God that part of this
ordeal is behind me.*

Part of her "think positive" plan was to believe she might recover.
She really could start a new and, she hoped, a healthier chapter of
life. She just needed to focus on doing something to help others who
were also struggling. As if on cue, once she came to that conclusion,
Pastor Elaine suggested she take the volunteer coordinator job at the
community relief center. Her qualifications for the position were many
if somewhat nebulous: regional Girl Scout cookie sales coordinator;
director of the Christmas pageants; planner of the 50th anniversary
celebrations for both her and Chet's parents; and primary coordinator
of the church's annual garage sale.

This can't be a coincidence, Ellie thought to herself six months
later when the chair of the board campaigned to make the volunteer
coordinator position full-time. He then encouraged C.A.R.E. Director
Lynette Combs to ask Ellie to take the newly funded full-time position.
Though reluctant to commit to a full time position, she had to admit
the increase in pay was very welcome. Suddenly she was too busy
sorting out the tangled messes of other peoples' lives to have time to
stew in her own pain.

The job wasn't exactly her dream job. *What would be my dream
job?* Ellie sometimes wondered between phone calls and interviews
with potential volunteers, directives to current volunteers, and more
letters requesting more volunteer support. *I don't know* was the usual
answer she gave herself. *I guess I have to take some time to figure that
out before I'm too old to work. For now, thank God, I have this position. I
do like the idea of what we do. And most of the church staff and clients I
work with are pretty decent folks. I miss the life I had. But, I have to build
a bridge and get over this. One day at a time.*

Chapter Four

The Lord is close to the brokenhearted and saves those who are crushed in spirit. (Psalm 34:18)

Ellie pulled into her driveway ten long hours after she left the Delaware beach. It was three-thirty in the afternoon when she parked her aging green-mist Honda Civic in the garage. Pulling her suitcase out of the trunk, she prepared for the onslaught of Chipper's greeting. Paying neighbors to take care of Chipper at home was a luxury she indulged in whenever she left town. She'd gotten Chipper without discussion in the divorce. Chet had quit caring about the dog along with a long list of other people and places they had once shared.

As anticipated, Chipper's enthusiastic welcome nearly knocked her over. "Well, at least you're always glad to see me," she said as she coaxed him outside. By the time she picked up all the flyers and pizza special notices from the front stoop, he was ready to go back in.

She picked up the pile of mail lying below the mail drop and turned the air-conditioner back down from the eighty-five degrees it'd been at while she was gone. Promising Chipper a walk later, she fed him, made herself a glass of iced tea, and sifted through the mail.

Bills, ads, and pleas for money. When was the last time I got a personal piece of mail? If I write a book maybe I'll get some fan mail. Or maybe I'll at least get personalized rejection slips. Even that would be an improvement. When your husband dies, people send cards, casseroles, and sympathy. When your husband leaves you, people don't know what to do. Is it a mortal sin to wish he'd just died instead of deserting me?

For the next half hour Ellie dozed off and on and dreamed about writing a book. She remembered that her mother had won a couple of writing contests when she was in grade school. *I have the gene for it somewhere. How do I get started? I'll go to the library tomorrow and look for some books on how to write a book.*

The nudge to write had been part of her life off and on for decades. Yet, something always sidetracked her. Marriage. Kids. Work. And probably the real reason—fear. As long as writing was only a dream, there was no chance of failing at it. Committing to actually writing meant taking a chance. It was time to take the chance.

Ellie managed to get through the dreaded dinner-alone-again hour by finding an old sitcom rerun to watch while dining on her scrambled eggs, toast, and canned fruit. She had put on a lot of weight during the divorce and now was working diligently to get it back off. Her personal Nagging Trio reminded her often of the virtues and advantages of doing so.

One member of this Trio was her medical doctor who prescribed an anti-depressant when she reluctantly admitted she wasn't sleeping well at all, hadn't for months, and couldn't quit crying. Another was Dr. Thorpe. Elaine Forbes was the third member of the Nagging Trio.

As if they'd rehearsed their lines, all three kept suggesting she eat less and walk more. Grazing aimlessly through the day wouldn't speed the recovery process or prepare her for whatever new life awaited her. Not to mention the possibility of an unwelcome side trip through some major physical problems to match the already huge heartache she'd acquired.

At the end of the show she turned off the TV and put the dishes in the sink. She took Chipper's leash off the hook by the back door. He was instantly on full alert and ran to the door with such hyper energy that she had difficulty clipping the leash to his collar. He practically dragged her out the door.

She was so focused on her thoughts about how to start writing that she was startled several times when neighbors called to her to welcome her back. She was, in fact, surprised anyone had noticed she'd been gone since she'd lived in this community less than a year.

She'd had a financially disastrous year trying to maintain the Lakewood house after Chet left. After a string of expensive home maintenance issues, she admitted the house needed to become another part of her past—along with Chet and a growing list of people and things that used to be. She didn't earn enough to hire the help she needed to keep it up. Besides, it was too depressing to sit in a house full of memories of happier days.

She thought of her new Cape Cod style home here on Laurel Avenue as her personal Recovery House. It had been the seller's dream retirement home. The former resident was an elderly man who'd lived here alone for eighteen years after his wife of forty-five years died. To hear his son tell the story, the old man had supervised the pounding of every nail. He was moving to a nursing home. He wept openly as his shaky hand signed the closing documents.

That signature meant a lot more than letting go of a piece of real estate. He was giving up the place he'd shared with her. He was signing the end of his independent life. It was the beginning of what seemed like a dismal end to him. *And I was thinking he was the lucky one—his wife died. She didn't just decide to end it and walk out.*

Ellie would have felt guilty taking his home from him had she not been so full of her own feelings of regret about giving up the home where she and Chet had raised their family together, the home where they'd celebrated high school and college graduations, hosted out-of-town wedding guests, and rocked their new grandchildren. This was the home where she and Chet had shared their last Christmas and birthdays. She fought back tears long enough to sign the papers. Once she reached the familiar safety of her car she could contain them no more.

Here at her new home the neighbors only knew she was a single woman. Most of them neither knew nor cared about the drama leading to her move to Laurel Avenue. Though Lakewood was only a few miles away, her life there with Chet and the children seemed as far away as the moon.

Back home from the walk, Ellie headed to the phone for her routine Saturday evening calls to her children. She loved hearing their voices and getting the latest updates on their busy lives. She also still had a lifelong habit of checking in with someone about her whereabouts. Her parents were gone, and now so was Chet. She had no one else to let know where she was. Fifty-eight years of checking in with someone was a hard habit to break. She also hoped her weekly routine of checking in with her children would rub off and they'd call her more often than they did.

As she dialed her daughter Cat's number she remembered her resolve: *I will not nag my children about not calling me more often. I hated it when my parents did that to me. Most of our conversations were weather reports and stock market prices anyway. They never went anywhere or did anything worth talking about, and they never seemed to care what I was doing.*

"We're not home right now, but if you leave us a name and a number we promise we'll get back to you asap," chirped Cat's cheerful recorded voice on the answering machine.

"Hi Cat. It's me, Mom. Just back from the beach. Great fun. Hope maybe we can get the kids there sometime. I'll catch up with you later. Love you."

One down. Two to go, she thought as she hit number 2 on the speed dial for Ben, her middle child and older son. She still just loved the sound of her children's names. She loved telling the stories about how they'd chosen them. Catherine Annette Trout—Cat for short, her initials. Though once Cat married Jerry Larkin these weren't technically her initials. Catherine was Ellie's mother's name; Annette was Chet's mother's name.

She and Chet named the next child Benjamin Paul after their fathers. They named their youngest Isaac Wilson because Chet so appreciated the work of Isaac Asimov and Wilson because Ellie's mother insisted they were related to President Woodrow Wilson's family through some distant connection. Though this connection had never been proven to her satisfaction, she thought it good to add the name to the family genealogy in case it was true.

Once again she got a voice mail message.

Two down. One to go. Please, let Ike be home. I'd really like to talk in person to one of my three. No such luck. She heard her youngest son's recorded message. With a sigh she sipped the ice tea and debated what to do next.

The decision was made for her. Cat returned the call. "Hey, Mom! You're home!" Cat greeted her mother with her usual warm affection. Every time Ellie started to think she couldn't count on her children for any more emotional support one of them surprised her with some act of thoughtfulness. *I am fortunate indeed to have these three and their kin. Truly, I am. I need to remember that.*

"Yes. I got back a few hours ago. So, what's new at your place?"

"The usual. Swim lessons for Lucy. You should see her. She's a regular fish. Soccer for Joey. I think we're funding some retail manager's retirement portfolio getting Annie ready for camp next week. Jerry's working too hard, and I'm wondering why I haven't gone back to work yet. How was your trip?"

"Actually, it was good. Very different than what I expected. But good. I was hoping maybe you and I could steal away for some time together soon. Any chance?"

"Well, Mom, it's hard. I'd love to see you and have an adult conversation. Let's try for next week when Annie's at camp. There's a pretty decent little restaurant that's just opened up nearby. Maybe we could do the trick you and Dad used to do with us. You and me at one table. Joey and Lucy at another table. They're old enough now. Can you take off enough time to drive over for lunch so soon after vacation?"

Ellie still felt her stomach clutch whenever Cat mentioned Chet. It was a quick, painful squeeze that still caught her off guard after all this time. Of course Cat would continue to talk about her father. Ellie wanted to be grateful that her children stayed in touch with him. She wasn't grateful, but she'd made it as far as wanting to be and figured that ought to count for something on this long road to recovery. Mostly she wished she didn't have to keep running into reminders of what wasn't anymore. But then, if her children never mentioned Chet she felt the acute loneliness of being cast aside from the family that had been the main focus of her life for all those years. It was a no-win situation—for all of them. She hurt either way and never knew how to respond.

She took in a deep breath and turned her attention back to Cat. "Probably. It's summer. Plenty to do, but it's not nearly as frantic as usual. But dinner would be easier. Any chance Jerry could watch them for a couple of hours?" Ellie constantly tried to balance her almost desperate desire to have her daughter to herself once in a while with her equally passionate conviction that a mother shouldn't put undue stress or demands on a married child's family.

"Maybe. I'll ask him. He's been traveling a lot lately. It would do him and the kids good to spend some time together at the pool and have some less-than-fine dining on their own. I'll check it out and let you know."

An eerie chill swept over Ellie as Cat said, "He's been traveling a lot . . ." *Dear God,* she half prayed and half sighed, *not another generation.* Though she didn't want to believe it, she sometimes wondered if all the traveling Chet did was the reason they'd grown apart. She knew he'd met his new wife Shirley on one of his many trips.

"I'd like that, Cat. It was a good trip, but half the fun of a trip is having someone to tell about it when you get back."

Ellie wondered if that sounded too self-pitying. *God, I hate this. I don't want to be a burden to my children, but sometimes I really just want a long conversation with someone I already know and love*, she thought as she hung up.

That was one insight she'd gotten from her couch time counseling sessions with Dr. Thorpe. At first she was thoroughly annoyed about how Dr. Thorpe wanted to know about her childhood family. Ellie wanted to know why her marriage fell apart. She eventually realized that the death of her older brother right as she was transitioning from childhood into her teen years had effectively blocked all helpful emotional communication with her mother. *Mom just didn't have anything left to give me. It wasn't really her fault . . . but it sure left me in an emotional void.*

To compensate for Chet's frequent long trips, Ellie had thrown herself full tilt into the daily details of her children's lives. In retrospect she could see how this eventually led Chet to conclude he was playing second fiddle to a houseful of noisy kids. The relationship started really getting out of balance a couple of years after Ike was born. The more Ellie focused on the kids, the more Chet had to travel for his work. And the more he traveled, the more she focused on the kids.

Now with Chet permanently gone from the daily equation of her life, she was still trying to focus on her children. Only now they were adults and didn't need so much attention. *I don't want to be a cling-on; but I need to be around people.*

She hung up and gave Chipper another treat. She headed to her desk. *Okay. Writers write. I know that much. Clean screen on the computer. No distractions. No place I have to be until Monday morning. Household chores can all wait until tomorrow. Write!*

Her pep talk to herself didn't work. Nothing came to mind. The blank screen before her seemed to say, "I dare you to fill me." *Okay then. Plan B. If it was good enough for Shakespeare, it's good enough for me. Paper and pen it is.*

Ellie found an almost-empty spiral notebook and her favorite pen. She headed for the sun room. She curled up in her recliner and began.

"It was a dark and stormy night." *No. Think that's been taken. Besides, it lasted a lot longer than one night.* "It was the best of times. It was the worst of times." *Can't copy Dickens. And it wasn't the best of times. I wonder if he had this much trouble getting started. I wonder if "Once upon a time" is copyrighted. I wonder how I find out. My God, there's a lot I don't know. How about "In the beginning"? I probably shouldn't try to plagiarize Scripture. I wonder where I put those notes from that creative writing workshop?*

She stretched and went to her guest room. There she pulled out a storage box from under the bed looking for the notebook saved from a workshop attended years earlier. Soon she was deep in memories as she looked through old letters, photographs, certificates, ticket stubs, and other reminders of the life she'd known, loved, and lost. Lost to what? Always it came back to that. What had gone so terribly wrong between her and Chet that had led her to this place?

She heard the antique clock on the mantel strike ten. Leaving everything where it was, she started her nightly routine. Chipper out. Coffee timer on. Alarm set for seven a.m. in case she needed it. She seldom did. Change into nightgown. Check the doors. Chipper back in. Turn off all but the bedside lamp. Climb into bed.

She picked up one of the three current self-help books she was reading and glanced at the next chapter about "Letting go." *Not tonight. I'm not up for more character development.* She offered a quick prayer of thanksgiving and gratitude that she'd come through her first solitary vacation; had people to call when she got home; had a home to come to; and now had an idea of a major project to tackle. She was soon sound asleep.

CHAPTER FIVE

Turn to me and be gracious to me, for I am lonely and afflicted. The troubles of my heart have multiplied; free me from my anguish.
(Psalm 25:16)

Sunday morning Ellie was up and out for a walk with Chipper by seven. When she got back she scanned the headlines of the *Sunday Plain Dealer* while sipping the first cup of coffee. By nine-thirty she was showered and dressed for church. Once again she'd forgotten to leave time to fix something to eat. She grabbed a banana to eat on the way to St. Luke's.

When Ellie arrived at church, Pastor Elaine motioned for her to wait until she was done shaking hands with the early service people. When the last lingerer finally headed off for the coffee line she walked over to Ellie.

"I'm glad you're here. There are a couple of visitors I spoke with briefly before worship, and I don't have time to properly greet them now. Would you go have some coffee with them and find out more about who they are for me? I think he said he's taking a new position at the community college."

Ellie agreed and soon was trying not to look as stunned as she was feeling when he introduced himself as Dan Chesterfield, a new professor of English at the college. "And this is my wife, Ginny. She's a writer and is trying to line up some freelance work here locally."

"Really?" Ellie managed to respond. "That's a coincidence. I was planning to go to the library this afternoon to get some books on writing. I found out from the internet last night that there's a writer's club in this area. I was thinking about checking it out."

Ginny's eyes lit up. "Oh! I'd love to go to something like that. Maybe we could go together. Dan here is always dashing off articles and chapters of books on his own, but I need someone to nag me along before I can really produce. When does it meet?"

Ellie said she'd find out and get back to her.   They exchanged phone numbers and e-mail addresses before saying good-bye to each other. Later Ellie accused Elaine of setting this whole scenario up. "Not guilty!" Elaine protested. "But I don't believe in coincidences. You want to write. Now you have a club and a new couple in town who already are writing. Maybe you're onto something, Ellie. Keep me posted, gal."

Maybe I should get to know Ginny better before I go to that writer's club, Ellie thought on the way home from church. She decided, however, that the first priority was her traditional Sunday afternoon nap on the couch. When she woke up she debated calling Ginny. Then she chastised herself for her sudden spurt of shyness. *What's gotten into me? I never used to have this much trouble making a decision. It's a phone call to a new person in town for crying out loud. It's not a major commitment. If I were the newcomer I'd want someone to invite me to a meal. Why am I suddenly so insecure? Is it because I've been rejected by the person I thought I'd take my dying breath with—or witness his?*

The internal debate continued a few more minutes before Ellie retrieved the scrap of paper with the Chesterfields' number on it. Five minutes later she was committed to lunch the next day at Pepper's, a local Italian restaurant.

When she called Cat that evening she debated telling her daughter about this. *No. I don't really have anything to report. I think I'll keep this new dream to myself for the time being.* Somehow this new secret life that was developing felt good and solid to Ellie. It felt like when she planted bulbs deep in the earth in the fall. Throughout the long, cold, gray Ohio winters she anticipated the first green sprouts pushing their way through to the warm spring air. *I might jinx whatever is trying to grow in my life if I talk about it too much to too many people too early.*

CHAPTER SIX

I, wisdom, dwell together with prudence; I possess knowledge and discretion. (Proverbs 8:12)

After she hung up she sat on the patio trying to decide what to do next. Her responsible personality suggested laundry and meal prep for the coming week were in order. Her new and enticing writer-in-waiting personality suggested a trip to the library.

Once in the library she paused to consider her options. *Self-help section to read up on divorce? No. Use the computer to look up books on writing? Maybe. I miss the card catalog. I used to love flipping through those. Check out a few of my own favorite authors—Danielle Steele, Rosamunde Pilcher, Nora Roberts, Pearl S. Buck? All women authors. I must have some sub-conscious storehouse of literature to draw on.*

She browsed through the reference area hoping to find books on writing. She pulled *Writer's Market* off the shelf. *The Right to Write* by Julia Cameron caught her attention. She opened it to a random page and read, "The act of writing, the aiming at getting it right, is pure thrill, pure process, as exciting as drawing back a bow." *I wonder if I should take another class in writing.*

Years earlier, when the kids were hardly more than babies, she'd taken a short creative writing course through the community college's continuing education program. She had wanted to spend one evening a week around other adults who were doing interesting things. She'd written a few articles and tried to place them, but nothing came of it. Still, the longing kept returning. The one year spent editing her church newsletter had helped refuel that longing.

Another thing she had given up for Chet. He didn't like having the piles of papers all over the dining room table the one week a month it took her to produce the newsletter in the pre-word processing days. It was tedious work, and she wasn't all that upset to let it go. Still, she wished Chet had appreciated how much it'd meant to her to have something meaningful and helpful to do once the kids were beyond needing her constant attention. He had his work. The kids had their school. *Well, that's water over the dam. Onward and upward.*

Ellie found an open chair in the reading area and sat down to read more from the books she'd selected. When her stomach growled, she looked at her watch. *Oh my gosh! It's quarter after three already and all I've eaten so far today is that banana.* When the librarian saw she was checking out several how-to-write books, she looked up at Ellie and smiled.

"If you're serious about this, we have a writer's group that meets here once a month, you know. I'm sure they'd welcome you."

"I saw something about such a group online," Ellie said. She had never considered such a possibility and now twice in less than twenty-four hours she'd received information about it.

"There's a flyer about it on the bulletin board over there."

West Cleveland Writer's Network

Meets First Monday of the month at 7 p.m.

Lakewood Library

Bring a good idea, an open mind, and a commitment to write

Call Cheri Lawson at 289.5300 for details.

For the first time in a long time Ellie was excited. It'd been so long she almost didn't recognize the sensation. She imagined herself perched at her desk in front of the sunny window with the great view of the street out front. She loved to watch the squirrels chasing up and down the maples. She'd put bird feeders everywhere to attract her fine feathered friends and it was working. On warm days she loved to work with the windows open—drawing in the smells of spring or fall.

She could see herself writing away the otherwise empty evening hours. "I'm going," she announced to no one. What was left of the day passed in a pleasant routine of laundry, stocking the empty refrigerator, and jotting down ideas for meals for the coming week.

The lunch conversation with Ginny started out easily enough. They talked about places they'd lived and traveled. They compared motherhood stories.

"What does your husband do?" Ginny asked innocently. Ginny hadn't noticed the barren left ring finger.

There isn't even a tell-tale light spot where the ring used to be. All the evidence of that life is slipping away. God, here's the part I dread. What do I say? How much do I tell her? I don't want to lie. I don't want to sound pathetic. I certainly don't want to sound angry. Will this EVER end?

"I'm not married," she said with forced calmness. "Long, sad story."

"Divorced?" asked Ginny gently.

"Yeah. After thirty-four years, three kids, and a mountain of challenges we faced and survived together. Just when the going got easier—he got going."

Ginny's hand on top of Ellie's activated her tear ducts again.

"How long ago?"

"A little over four years."

"You're more than half way through it."

"Through what?"

"The recovery stage. It takes a year for every five you were married. You will recover. I know you probably don't believe that. But you will."

"You speak from experience?"

"I do. It was after twenty-five years for me. We were designing a retirement home together. He was going to start a 'Handy Andy' sort of retirement business to finance the projects we wanted to do on our own place. I was going to sit in the second floor writer's den we had designed into the house—with a view of the pond and the fields beyond. I was going to write for the local paper and try to keep selling to some of the magazines I'd written for in the past."

"What happened?"

"The usual. Mid-life melt-down. A younger woman bought the 'my wife doesn't understand me' line. He took off with her when we should have been at his niece's wedding. I went without him. I believed him when he said he couldn't get out of a conference for work. I thought he was pretty pathetic to skip the wedding without even talking to his boss—but I never dreamed that was his alibi. But he'd been out of work for a long time once. I figured he didn't want to risk upsetting the current boss. Never in my wildest imagination did it occur to me he was off with another woman. One almost young enough to be his niece. Color me naïve."

"I sensed something was up when I got to the family brunch before the wedding. A couple of his cousins paid me more attention than usual. Turns out he'd confided in his cousin about his plans to leave me. Attending a wedding was just a bit much for him to handle. That cousin told the rest of the family. They were all waiting for the news to reach me. They say the wife's always the last to know. Sometimes that's true."

"How long ago was that?"

"It ended eight years ago. I've been with Dan for three years now. He was recovering from his wife Sally's decision—after fifteen years and two kids—that her bliss was no longer with Dan but with a woman "friend." Sally had some mental illness issues. Gay folks aren't immune to them. Her new partner left her after a couple years of dealing with the bi-polar issues. Love can get complicated. At least I didn't have to explain to my kids why their father was leaving me for another man. I know it's tough. I really do know. You'll survive this. There may even come the day you look back and see the benefits of it."

Ellie slowly shook her head. "I'll survive. I've got three terrific kids and now five grandkids. I do like my job. But I don't see myself ever being grateful this happened."

"I didn't say you'd ever be grateful. I said you'll be able to see the benefits of it. But it does take a long, long time. Especially for those of us who bought the whole 'a woman's place is beside wherever her man is' school of thinking. The way I see it, we're caught between two generations. Our mothers never had the choices we do. They had very limited options. Plus, the stigma against divorce was so great back then. It wasn't worth fighting it. Most women would put up with almost anything to avoid being labeled a divorced woman. Today's women can pretty much do whatever they want. Divorce is so common it's hardly a scandal.

"You and I—well, we married under one set of rules and we grew into maturity in a world with a different set of them."

"Yeah," Ellie agreed. "I guess you're right. I've been so bowled over by my own pain and grief that I haven't thought much about what's been happening in the rest of the world. Some days I feel like I'm treading water and getting nowhere. I get so weary. All I can see are more waves coming at me. I can't seem to find the bottom. Remember that case in Houston where some woman went nuts and clubbed her husband to death in their own bedroom?"

"Yes, I do remember hearing something about it."

"It happened right after Chet moved out, but before the divorce was finalized. I met one of that woman's neighbors on a trip a year later. When she told me about it I didn't know what she was talking about. I was so out of it, I didn't watch or hear or read any news for months. The world could have blown up, and I would have missed it."

"Not that uncommon, Ellie," said Ginny. "I'm glad I can't remember most of those first weeks. I don't think I'd be very proud of what I said and did back then. Let's look to the future. Tell me about the writing you want to do. Do you have any experience writing?"

"More interest and curiosity than experience. I've edited a couple of newsletters. I wrote a column once upon a time about places to go and things to do with children. I don't know if I can do this or not. But I sure want to try. I guess it's my attempt to prove something—I'm not sure what—or to whom—but I feel myself being pulled toward this idea like the rip tide at the ocean. Something is telling me, swim this way. This is the way out."

"So this is a therapy book for you?"

"I guess you could say that."

"Well, good for you! You know there are a lot of walking wounded out there. The way I see it, in every divorce one person thinks he or she just got a get-out-of-jail-free card. And the other one feels betrayed and ambushed. Maybe the ones who feel emancipated don't need much help. But the poor saps that didn't see it coming are still picking up the emotional debris years later. They can use all the help they can get."

"For sure. I tried some counseling. Pastor Elaine practically carried me into this guy's office. It did help a little, but all that talking didn't change the bottom line. I loved him. He left. It hurt. I went for a while. It was nice to have a safe place to cry. But then after a while I got tired of it all. I decided I could cry for free. I didn't need to pay someone to get me started every week."

"I know what you mean. Some of them are so damn laid back: 'Tell me how that makes you feel.' I felt like I argued with a giant gorilla and lost the battle. I felt black and blue from my unwashed hair to my overgrown toenails. I didn't want to feel anything anymore. It all hurt too much. I wanted a road map out of that suffocating pain. But you know what? It did help. It just took a while to be able to see the progress."

Ellie stared at her new friend. "You were in counseling? You seem so . . . don't take this wrong . . . so normal."

Ginny tilted her head back and let out a long rich laugh. "What's normal?! I was in serious counseling for months. It was a very long, slow climb out of a very dark pit back up to ground level."

Ellie thought about this for a moment before speaking. "Maybe I didn't try it long enough. I might consider trying it again someday. But not now; for now, it's the book. I don't really even care if it ever gets printed. I just want to do something creative and positive—and get out and meet some people."

"Well, good for you," said Ginny. "And I'm just glad I'll have someone to travel with who knows the territory. This opportunity for Dan is a God-send for both of us. When you live in a small town everyone knows what happened. What they don't know is how to respond to you. So you have those who know, but pretend they don't. Then there are those who know and make sure everyone else does too. The best ones are the ones who know and talk to you in private to offer genuine sympathy and support. God bless them. May their numbers increase."

Ellie nodded her head in agreement. "But my favorite ones were the ones who asked me, 'Whose fault was it?' and 'How much did you get in the settlement?' Did you have people who thought you wanted to know where your 'ex' was and what he was doing when last seen?"

"Oh, yes," Ginny sighed. "It wasn't hard for Dan to convince me to move. When Dan was accepted for this position we jumped on it. We love the academic life. And we're really excited about a fresh start. So, how about I drive and you navigate to the writer's club next week? Then I can learn my way around a little with a pro who can keep me from getting too hopelessly lost. Deal?"

"Deal." Ellie agreed.

In her diary that night she wrote, *Okay. I believe. Apparently I'm not the only one on the planet who knows heartache and disillusionment. Thanks for a new friend. Thanks for the opportunity to explore a new network of people. Thanks for the bit of encouragement and potential I am sensing now. Thanks for not abandoning me. Amen.*

CHAPTER SEVEN

Ask and it will be given to you; seek and you will find; knock and the door will be opened to you. (Matthew 7:7)

After lunch Ellie decided to go back to park by the lake where she'd spent so many of her childhood days. The same old forest green bench she'd sat on years earlier was still there overlooking the lake. She sat down and took in a deep breath. The familiar view stirred up memories of her girlhood hopes. Robins and sparrows chirped their welcome songs. In her mind she saw herself pushing the toddler grandchildren on the nearby swings. The memory made her smile. She had nearly burst with pride when people fussed over them. Well, they were cute! But that was such a long time ago. It seemed another life time. The toddlers were busy now with their own plans. The home where she'd rocked them was now occupied by strangers. That chapter had melted away like the last snow fall before spring.

She sighed and turned her thoughts to the present. At last her life seemed to be on a smooth stretch of road. Her life now was so different than she'd anticipated. Surprisingly, she was getting used to the single-again life. She even felt an occasional sensation of gratitude for the freedom to do whatever she wanted.

Meeting Dan and Ginny had been just the power surge her self-esteem needed. *Ginny is great! She's not bitter. She's not pathetic. She's what I want to be like when I get through this. I wonder if I ever will. I wonder how I'll know if I do. Of course, Ginny has Dan in her life. Does she have Dan because she got over it, or did she get over it because she has Dan?*

Ellie caught herself thinking about Chet again—wondering where he was and what he was doing. Her heart felt like a stone when the children talked about him—a stone that pushed her down, making it hard to breathe normally. But then if they didn't talk about him she felt so isolated—knowing they'd probably seen or talked to him recently. Not knowing anything current about him left her feeling like a total stranger in a room full of close friends. *Stop this, Ellie. You can't change the past, but you can sure mess up the future if you don't quit this. Focus on the here and now. Think about what's going right. Surely other older women have lost their husbands to desertion rather than death. Maybe trying to help them will help me move on too.*

Sometimes the silence of the house was as oppressive as a ninety-five degree summer afternoon. There just didn't seem to be any way to get any relief from it. Ellie had gradually acclimated to it, though—as one eventually does to the hot, humid days of August. The loneliness was part of the landscape. It was best managed by not focusing on it. It was just there. She decided maybe she was adjusting.

Like a magnet, she was drawn back to the home she and Chet had remodeled together—the home where she and Chet lived at the end of their marriage. She drove past the house slowly, expecting something she couldn't quite explain. She hoped there might be a new, more positive feeling or some sign telling her what she should do next. She was grateful the piercing pain and panic had diminished at last, yet she felt like a rudderless boat out on the lake on a calm day. The worst of the grief had finally lifted. But she had no destination—no dock to aim for—just time passing by one unplanned day after another.

After she drove past the house, she parked the car at a convenience store a couple of blocks away. She slowly walked the familiar streets where she and Chet had lived those contented years. She was surprised by several things. She didn't encounter a single person she knew well enough to stop and greet; although she did see a couple of familiar faces. *Maybe there's been more turnover here than I realized.* The second surprise was that this didn't hurt. In fact, it felt good, even comforting. *I guess I am healing. Time does heal all wounds. I'm doing alright. Maybe not great. But definitely alright. What a relief!*

She walked back to her car and drove to a coffee shop, where she ordered a tall latte. She took it, then settled into a wing chair in the corner. She wanted to capture this moment but had nothing with her except the small notebook she kept in her purse. She pulled out the notebook and a pen. Across the top of a clean page she wrote: *Anatomy of a Divorce:*

Suspicion all is not well.

Fear of what may be wrong.

Awkwardness replaces trust and openness.

Tension mounts.

Asking questions that don't get answered.

Trying too hard.

Trying too hard again.

Worrying.

The blow.

The shock.

The anger.

The humiliation.

The dismay.

The confusion.

The worries.

The panic.

The begging.

The threatening.

The cajoling.

The rejection.

The suffering.

The rescue.

The relief.

The new hope.

The new reality.

The realization.

The healing.

The decision to go on.

The discovery of new possibilities.

The renewed energy.

She put down her pen and sipped on the latte. *Well, that may mean something to me but it's a long way from a book. I'm clearly not going to get this done this way. The writer's club looks promising, but I think I'm going to need more help than that. Maybe I do need a writer's class. It'll do me good to sacrifice one evening a week of grazing in front of the re-runs to go to class. I'll see if I can find one that starts this fall.*

I'm glad to have Ginny to go with to the writer's club. I still really dread going places alone. I feel like I'm driving up a steep grade on a gravel mountain with no guard rail when I have to enter a room full of strangers by myself. Well, one step at a time. I'm here and it's a beautiful day.

She sipped the latte and let her thoughts wander. She thought back to Dr. Thorpe's office. *I wonder why I'm thinking about this! I remember his big beige leather recliner and the overstuffed olive green chairs and matching love seat.* She laughed to herself recalling her bewilderment about where to sit on her first visit. She had actually worried that he would interpret her choice of a seat as a revelation of some deep, dark horrible secret.

Instead he'd merely said good naturedly, "It's usually too hot over there and too cold over there, so you get to decide which way you want to be uncomfortable," as he pointed to her two options. There was something he'd said that was tiptoeing around the perimeter of her memory. What was it?

Slowly Ellie drifted further and further back into those weekly conversations. Something about pain. His favorite topic. "Bring on the pain," he used to tell her. "It is what motivates us to change." She'd never quite bought into that theory as eagerly as Dr. Thorpe seemed to think she should. He with his tall, thin, muscular body hardly looked like he knew much about pain and suffering. He always smiled warmly and talked so softly, that she had to strain to hear him. He would just sit there silently through her cycles of sobs and fury.

But there was that one day. He must have just gotten back from a conference or something. He was much more animated than usual.

That day he did most of the talking himself. *It was about pain. I remember that much. What else?*

"Ellie," she could almost hear his voice inside her head now. "Pain is both a postlude and a prologue. It signals the end of something familiar and the start of something unfamiliar. What has ended is an era you cherished. There's a new beginning right before you. It wasn't possible for you before this loss. The pain has led you to some serious probing. Probing to dig down to what you want for yourself. You might never have explored your own desires as long as you had the security of your marriage."

Well, now a couple of years later, Ellie had to admit, he had a point. She did do a lot more serious thinking. All the forced hours of solitude had required that of her. *No, she decided, I chose to use the hours for the thinking. I could have just OD'd on TV or started drinking or running up the limits on my plastic. I chose to use this time in this way.*

She startled herself as she remembered the women's retreat she'd attended about a year after the divorce. Pastor Elaine no doubt put Naomi, the retreat leader, up to asking her to go. But it was good. The study on Mary and Martha was really good. For most of her life she'd identified with Martha and the many details required to run a household. She understood Martha's frustration. It was her own frustration when her retired parents would park on the couch, complaining she was too busy. *Well, the food isn't going to cook itself!* She often thought that but never had the courage to say so.

Now was her Mary time. She was free—indeed she was compelled—to sit at the feet of the master as it were and really soak up the thoughts and insights of others.

Maybe I am growing used to this life of solitude. I do see some advantages to it. Maybe Dr. Thorpe, and Elaine, and Ginny are right. This has all been a necessary part of the process.

"Pain drives us deep into the woods of thought in search of a path to another clearing." Who told her that? Did it matter? Not really. The point is this: pain is not wasted on those who will allow themselves to feel it and then reflect on it.

That idea might work for a book! Ellie looked at her watch. *My God, I've been sitting here daydreaming like this for nearly an hour and a half! I need to move.* Feeling optimistic, calm, and focused, she decided to get another latte to drink on the drive home. But first, she would have to write down some of her thoughts before they eluded her.

CHAPTER EIGHT

He heals the brokenhearted and binds up their wounds.
(Psalm 147:3)

As she was putting her notebook and pen in her tote bag she heard a familiar voice calling out to her, "Ellie Trout! Is that really you?"

She turned and was surprised to see Matt Sommers. She hadn't seen him since she dropped out of the early morning water aerobics class at the Community Center's therapy pool. Another thing she let go when the marriage ended.

Matt looked as good as ever. A little less hair now and nearly all of that was grey. On him it looked great. He had a bit more belly than was healthy, but she'd certainly seen worse. He looked tan and healthy, but also weary. *Well, aren't we all a bit weary these days?* She stood to greet him and was instantly engulfed in a hug. She stood back and smiled at him.

"My God, Ellie. You look great! I almost didn't recognize you with your clothes on."

Ellie laughed at the memories of how she and the others from the early bird water aerobics often said that worn-out line whenever they'd meet each other away from the pool.

"What have you been doing with yourself? And where have you been! You just disappeared off the face of the earth. I miss running into you at the pool for our early morning torture sessions with Lindy."

Ellie laughed again at the memory of a dozen middle-aged men and women faithfully doing the stretching and underwater jumping jacks the twenty-something slender young woman commanded three times a week. "Is she still torturing old folks then?"

"Worse than ever!" groaned Matt. "She went off to some conference and came back with all sorts of new torture techniques."

"Well, add that to the list of things I miss."

"What happened, Ellie? Why'd you drop out? "

"You must be among the few who missed the memo, Matt. My husband divorced me four years ago."

"Oh, Ellie. I'm so sorry. And stunned. No, I hadn't heard. Of course, why would anyone think to tell me? We never even crossed paths beyond the pool and occasionally in the post office lobby. But I am sorry. So you moved to escape the memories?"

"Something like that. I couldn't keep up the house by myself. I moved into a less demanding home in Rocky River. I was able to get a job through my church that I really like. It's far enough away that I shop in different stores and see different people when I'm out tending to the details of life. I'm still close to the kids, but I have new neighbors and a new routine. It's been helpful not running into folks who know what happened and don't know what to do or say about it. Chet left town almost immediately after the divorce to start a new life in a new place with a new person."

"Oh my God. He left you for a younger woman?!"

"Apparently so. He claims the decision to leave came first and the woman came second. I don't believe him. It doesn't really matter. What's done is done! I'm picking up the pieces and moving on as best I can."

"So what brings you back today?"

"Actually, I'm trying to re-kindle some of the memories today. I'm going to try to write a book. I thought being back at the scene of the crime, so to speak, might inspire me."

"Really? Well, I think that's terrific. Have you done much writing?"

"Nothing very serious. A few short articles for various newsletters mostly. And I edited our church newsletter once for a year. I liked that. I just found out there's a writer's club that meets at the library. I'm thinking seriously of signing up for a writer's course next fall."

"Well, well. An author. May I be first to get your autograph?"

Ellie giggled. "Sure. But don't hold your breath. So far all I have is a list of words about what it's like to be divorced. I think I have writer's block, and I haven't even written anything yet. Enough about me. What are you doing these days?"

"Well, I've been through some changes too. The company that brought me here folded about five years ago. So I got to experience firsthand the wonderful world of unemployment for six months."

"Oh, I'm so sorry. That's rough. But you stayed here?"

"Sure. All the memories here are good ones for me. Well, most of them. More good ones than bad." Ellie saw a shadow fall across Matt's face. He paused for a moment before continuing. "All the people I most care about are here. Where else would I go? What about you? Who's there for you?"

"The kids—well they're all adults now. And their kids. Five of them! I love them all. They're so wonderful. Did you find another job?"

"Sort of. I'm doing some consulting—which pays pretty well. My network of friends keeps me pretty busy. I'm looking into training to be a medic too. A good friend of mine does that, and he's encouraging me to try it."

Then he asked, "Say, can you stay in town a few more hours and let me take you to dinner? There's a decent new restaurant that just opened up a few months ago. I haven't been there yet, but folks say it's pretty good. I hate eating alone—especially in a restaurant. You'd be doing me a big favor if you'd go with me."

"Oh, Matt. I'm not sure. I'm not very good company these days. I still burst into tears at the silliest things and . . . well . . ."

"This isn't a date, Ellie. It's one lonely guy begging for a little dinner company from someone I hardly know, but would like to know better. It's just dinner. I promise. No ulterior motives. You can drive your own car and I'll drive mine and after dinner—it's adios, sister. Deal?"

"Well, maybe. I do get tired of eating alone. That's one of the disadvantages of being divorced. Dutch treat though, okay?"

"Sure. Okay. It's a deal. I'll meet you back here at five-thirty, and you can follow me out to the restaurant. It's a little tricky to explain how to get there. It's over near Hudson—out in the country. But I hear it's well worth the effort."

"Oh sure. You're going to lure me out onto some back country road and cut me off from any possible chance of getting help."

"Is it that obvious?"

"Isn't dating later in life the pits? Not that this is a date. But you know what I mean. I haven't dated at all. I just don't have the energy to figure out how one goes about dating at this age. It was awkward and confusing enough when I was in my twenties."

Matt's face changed to a somber look Ellie couldn't interpret. It was like a dark cloud passed over him. Then it was gone, and he smiled at her again.

"I know what you mean. Tell me, do your kids try to give you dating tips?"

"All the time! Mostly how I need to start dating someone. I just let it go in one ear and out the other. I guess we will find things to talk about. See you tonight."

Well, well, well. She tried to sort out her feelings and discovered she couldn't. And really didn't want to. She just wanted to savor the moment. *I'm going to dinner with Matt Sommer. But it's NOT a date. It's just dinner. I wish I had something better to wear. Ellie!,* she scolded herself. *It's not a date. It's a casual acquaintance. Chill, sister.*

She decided to go home to let Chipper out and hunt for something better to wear. When she was as ready as she thought she needed to be, she forced herself to read through the writing books she'd checked out. The books didn't really hold her attention, but they did help curb the obsessive clock-watching.

At quarter to five she locked up the house and drove back to the coffee shop. She was amused and amazed at the butterflies taking formation in her stomach. *I can't believe I'm feeling so nervous! My God, I've birthed three kids and watched them birth another five. Yet I feel the same jitters from the 7th grade worrying whether Jeremy Stenson would ask me to dance. Dear God, help!*

She saw Matt walking toward the table where they'd met a few hours earlier. He had taken time to clean up and looked very attractive in his khaki slacks, Dockers, and light yellow golf shirt. As he approached she noticed that he'd also splashed on some kind of cologne.

"Ready?" he asked cheerfully.

"Sure. I guess it's a little silly to drive two cars out there. If you promise you won't pull off to the side of the road and try to paw me, I'll ride with you, if that's okay?"

"No pawing. Scout's honor. Then let's go."

The forty-five minute drive to the new restaurant was filled with Ellie's repeated exclamations, "Holy Moly, I can't believe all the changes! I feel like Rip Van Winkle waking up from a long nap."

Matt laughed good-naturedly. "I know. Some call it progress. Some call it devastation. The shopping areas out this way have totally changed the landscape."

"Well, I guess life really does go on, doesn't it?"

"Indeed, it does," agreed Matt.

CHAPTER NINE

When I called, you answered me; you made me bold and stouthearted.
(Psalm 138:3)

The dinner with Matt was the most fun Ellie had had in months. True to his word, Matt was a perfect gentleman. He delivered her back to her car a few minutes before nine o'clock. They exchanged well wishes and thank you's before Ellie unlocked her car and got in. Matt waited for her to start her car. She headed home smiling and very pleased with how the day had turned out. She wanted to tell someone but didn't know who to tell about this surprise turn of event. In the end she kept it to herself.

The next morning she decided to call her son Ben at the office. She still hadn't heard from him or Ike. She and Cat talked often, but if she wanted to talk to her sons it was usually her phone call to make.

"Mr. Trout's office," said the receptionist at Granger, Trout, and Westerby Accounting Associates.

"Is Ben available, Lil? This is Ellie."

"Hi, Ellie! No, not at the moment. He's got someone with him. But he should be free in a few minutes. You back from your trip?"

"Yes. I got back last Saturday. I don't need to bother him. Just tell him I'll call him this evening at home. Thanks, Lil."

Though no one would openly talk about it, Ellie suspected Lil knew more about her life than she let on. Ellie wondered how much Ben confided in Lil. He rarely talked about his father, but Ben and Chet had been especially close. It bothered Ellie that Ben didn't confide in her. She often wondered about Ben's reaction to his parent's divorce. Was he playing Biff from *Death of a Salesman*—knowing his father had cheated on her and pretending not to know? One more thing to add to the list of things she couldn't control.

Ellie suspected Ben must have talked with Lil. She was like a second mother to him. Lil was always professional, but she was also old enough to be Ben's mother. Ellie saw the way she both served and directed the young men in the office. Ellie smiled remembering some scenes she'd observed while waiting to see Ben. *She's really good. She knows exactly how to let him think something was his idea.* As one mother to another, Ellie really appreciated Lil's presence in her son's life.

As a hurting woman going through pain more intense than all three labor and deliveries combined, Ellie was touched when Lil spent a few minutes talking to her whenever she called or stopped in to see Ben.

Ellie didn't do that often. She respected how busy Ben was with his accounting clients.

Most of Ellie's contact with Lil was while picking up Cat's children from Ben's office, if Cat couldn't pick them up herself. Ben's office served as the drop-off and pick-up place when Cat's children and Ben's children managed to finagle an overnight with their cousins. Being in business for himself in a small firm afforded Ben the chance to help his sister out once in a while when the Larkin household schedule got too insane. Ben loved it when Cat and Jerry's kids came over. The cousins never seemed to tire of being together.

Ben's office staff, many of them mothers and grandmothers themselves, encouraged Ben to bring the kids to the office often. The staff had even cleared out one corner of a storage room to make room for a small table and chairs and child-friendly activities for their honored guests.

Ellie was touched to see how much other people enjoyed her grandchildren whom she adored. The children were a lot of the reason she fought so hard to overcome the depression and anxiety through and after the divorce.

"It must feel like an open wound that will never heal." Dr. Thorpe's words replayed in her mind like the refrain from a song. *I'm not going to let Chet take this away from me, too. I will survive. I will go on. I will treasure the time with the grandkids—even if he doesn't want this chapter himself.* Ellie wanted to be there for them as her grandparents had been there for her.

\---------------------------

"Sure thing, Ellie," said Lil. "How was your trip to the beach?"

"It was good. Great weather—inside—but I braved the hot sun and got a little tan. I look less pathetic than when I left."

"I'll bet you look great. You always do. I'll let Ben know you called and remind him to call his mother. Take care of yourself, Ellie. Glad you're back."

Ellie waited until the late news to hear from Ben before acknowledging to herself she'd have to call him. She sighed in disappointment and started the nightly routines to close up the house for the night. She caught herself blaming Chet for not being there to fill the void she was feeling and picked up a book to distract the negative thoughts starting to seep in like the way moisture seeps into a basement after a heavy rain.

CHAPTER TEN

You, O Lord, keep my lamp burning; my God turns my darkness into light. (Psalm 18:28)

Though it had only been a couple of weeks since she got home from her solo vacation, it already seemed like a distant memory. In spite of the recent new developments in her life, she was still alone more than she wanted to be. One of the current realities was how many meals she ate alone. *Of course, if Chet and I could have really talked over dinner or any other time those last couple of years, we might not be divorced now. I hate eating alone. How do other people do this?!* She caught herself going down the "what if" highway again and put on the brakes. *Enough! What's done is done. Time to move on. I doubt he's sitting around feeling sorry for himself.*

She dined on another uninspired menu of leftovers from the back of the refrigerator. Then the usual evening debate: try to call someone or turn on the television? Calling was a gamble. If she found someone home the conversation was a real mood elevator. If she got voice mail—which she usually did—it was a mood deflator. Though the TV line-ups weren't much—with the push of a couple of remote buttons she could pass the time.

She was truly grateful for her job at C.A.R.E. She knew she was getting into a rut, and needed to find ways to socialize beyond work, but she felt clueless as to where to start. She hated going places by herself and grew weary of all the effort it took to coordinate having someone to go with her. So much of her adult life had centered on tending to others. Deciding what to do for herself felt like wearing clothes a couple of sizes too small—it was possible, but it wasn't comfortable.

She decided to call Elaine at home to see if she needed any help with anything at the church. She knew she was trying to avoid herself until she could return to the familiar comfort of work. Still, she hoped Elaine would find something for her to do.

Elaine and the community at St. Luke's had become a welcome port in Ellie's personal life storms. At first going there alone was yet another root-canal-without-Novocain experience. Going to worship without Chet felt about as comfortable as attending a stranger's wedding reception. Pre-divorce she and Chet had volunteered hundreds of hours together and separately. Catching one another's eye across the sanctuary when he sat with the choir had given her such a sense of contentment and confidence that all was well in the world. At least their world.

In that life she and Chet talked about their plans for when the kids left home. The ideas flowed like skaters on a frozen pond: maybe a year overseas; what about taking in a foster child or two; Habitat for Humanity always needed volunteers; maybe they'd buy land and open a country B&B. All those ideas had fallen through the thin ice of the empty nest years and were dead in the freezing water.

When Chet walked out the door that Saturday, Ellie thought she might die. Looking back she thought perhaps she'd been in shock. She was so stunned she didn't know what to do. She walked for two hours until she could barely put one foot in front of the other. Going into the empty house sent chills of dread up and down her spine like someone playing a xylophone on her back. Halloween haunted houses threatened nothing compared to her growing fear as she approached her own front door that day. Stunned. Too stunned to cry—yet. That would come later.

That day, time seemed to freeze in place. It felt like an eternity had passed. According to the kitchen clock she'd only been back in the empty house an hour. Not knowing what else to do, she'd phoned Pastor Elaine at home. She and Chet had been members of St. Luke's congregation twelve years. Ellie and Chet had become good friends with Elaine and her husband, Kenny. Kenny was killed in a car accident right before Christmas a few years after Elaine became their pastor. Chet and Ellie's kitchen table became one of her main stops along her own path through loss and recovery.

Ellie and Elaine had shared deeply and often, so it was natural to reach out to her. On the other hand, they were perhaps too close. It was hard having her pastor be such a good friend. All during her two-hour walk that Saturday morning, she debated about calling Elaine. Ellie knew Elaine's own loss would help her understand hers now.

Ellie always admired how Elaine seemed to know instinctively when something was wrong in someone's life. She barely managed to feebly tell Elaine, "I think I need to talk to you."

Elaine simply asked, "Are you at home?"

"Yes," Ellie had answered almost in a whisper.

"I'll be there in an hour."

Ellie was relieved she hadn't needed to explain why—yet. True to her word, Elaine arrived an hour later bearing two steaming cups of coffee and the special kind of bagels they both loved.

As soon as Ellie opened the door Elaine took charge of the situation. "Let's go sit at your kitchen table. You look like you've seen a ghost. Here, I brought you some coffee and a bagel."

Elaine sat quietly while Ellie stared into her coffee. Her thoughts were all jumbled up like a child's game of pick-up-sticks. Every thought hurt and none of them made much sense. Ellie wanted Elaine to say something, but she just sat, quietly waiting.

Finally Ellie looked up. She tried but failed to smile. At last she took a deep breath, and on the exhale blurted out, "I guess I'm going to be getting more character soon." Elaine said nothing. Ellie continued, "Chet left this morning."

"On an extended business trip?" asked Elaine.

Ellie shook her head. She looked up with tears beginning to fill her eyes. "No. He left me. He said he just wants to be alone for a while."

Elaine reached out to hold Ellie's hand and waited.

Eventually Ellie told the rest of the story between gulps of coffee and tears.

"The past few months have been really weird. It's like he's here—but he's not. He hardly ever talks when he is here. He doesn't want to do any of the things we used to do—walks after dinner, going to the park, sitting on the patio for after-dinner coffee."

Elaine nodded without saying anything.

"He said we needed to cancel the cruise we had planned with some of my family. We've been talking about that cruise for years. We finally got everyone's schedules to line up, and now he wants to cancel it?!" Her voice had gradually picked up momentum and was heading toward top volume.

Elaine murmured, "That does seem odd."

"His main pastime these days is watching hours of re-runs on television. When he's home. Which he isn't a lot anymore. He disappears for hours. If I ask him where he's been, he just changes the subject or gives some non-answer."

Elaine squeezed Ellie's hand tightly and then let go of it. She sat back in her chair and started twisting a strand of hair on the side of her forehead—a sure sign she was trying to think of something appropriate to say. She sat quietly with Ellie for a long time before she spoke.

"Ellie, I'm too stunned to know how best to respond. What I'm thinking is this: What could you do this afternoon to make yourself feel a little better before you go to bed tonight?"

Ellie just stared at her. Her world had just collapsed. She couldn't imagine ever feeling good again. Especially not as soon as this afternoon. When she didn't answer Elaine prompted her.

"You've had a terrible shock. This must feel like you just went through some kind of time warp or something. Sometimes, when everything seems out of control, it helps to latch on to any little thing to remind ourselves of familiar routines. What might you be doing this afternoon if you weren't telling me about this? What makes you smile when things aren't in such turmoil?"

"Flowers. I like flowers."

"Then let's go get some. Come on. I have to stop by the store anyway to pick up some things for dinner tonight. I'll drive you."

The sight and smell of the fresh flowers did help. Mostly because they were tangible evidence Elaine cared and she wasn't totally alone in the universe even though it sure felt like it.

Somehow Ellie managed to live through the night. She'd started crying shortly after she tried to push down a peanut butter sandwich. The peanut butter stuck in her constricted throat like a lump of clay.

She wasn't hungry anyway. Dinner went down the disposal, and she went to bed. She was still crying at 2 a.m. when she finally took a sleeping aid.

That day was already four years in the past. She was in a new house. She had the job at C.A.R.E. She had met Ginny and Dan. She'd been out to dinner with Matt from the pool crew. And next week she and Ginny were going together to their first meeting of the writing group at the library. This wasn't the life she'd ever imagined for herself, but parts of it were good. Bordering on very good.

CHAPTER ELEVEN

I lift up my eyes to the hills—where does my help come from? My help comes from the Lord, the Maker of heaven and earth. (Psalm 121:1)

The following Monday Ellie rushed home from her day at C.A.R.E. and changed clothes. She put a frozen dinner in the microwave and called Ginny. Twenty minutes later Ginny rang her doorbell.

At the library they settled into seats and started sipping the coffee they'd been offered. A few minutes later a woman Ellie guessed to be in her early fifties welcomed everyone and introduced the speaker for the evening.

The speaker was arrogant, self-absorbed, and not the least interested in helping other people write. The evening proved worth the effort though when a perky red-headed young woman stopped them on their way out. "Hi! I'm Suzy. Is this your first time?"

"Yes. So how does this work?" asked Ginny.

"Well, if you want to join it's $25 per year."

"Do we have to be members to come?" asked Ellie.

"No, not at all. But if you do join, it helps us publish our monthly newsletter. And it covers the expenses of our volunteers who plan the annual writer's conference."

Remembering her decision to just "go with the flow" for a while, Ellie left the decision to her wallet. If she had more than $25 in cash with her, she'd join. If not, she'd pass.

"You're in luck. I have $25 with me. Here you go." She was now the proud owner of a C.O.W.L.—Cleveland Ohio Writer's League— membership card. Ginny also pulled out the necessary cash and got a matching membership card.

They decided to stop for coffee on the way back to Ellie's house. "This move has really got me messed up!" said Ginny. "I can't seem to get into a routine that works for me."

"Yeah, I know," sighed Ellie. "I can get it together for about a day and a half. Then I'm off track again. It's not that I don't know what to do with myself. It's that I don't know what to do to figure it out."

"I hear ya. I've been thinking lately that there are two kinds of people," Ginny suggested.

"Not the two-camp theory again?!"

"Yup. There are those who know what they want in life. They make their plan. They work the plan. They get what they want."

"And then there are the rest of us," added Ellie.

"Right. No matter how hard I try, something always seems to come along to cause me to detour."

Ellie nodded in agreement. "Sometimes it's a whole friggin' train wreck."

Ginny nodded. "Some days I see so clearly what I want. I just don't see any way to get it."

"And sometimes we have exactly what we always wanted, and then it's all gone."

They sat in silence for a few moments.

Ginny broke the silence. "But, we do get to choose what happens next. I think life's a write-your-own-adventure sort of a deal. I choose to dump all the bad stuff from the past and hang onto the good parts. And go explore the future. I'm glad I've met you, Ellie. You've made settling in here much easier."

Ellie smiled at her new friend. "My life got a lot better when you showed up, too."

They clicked their coffee cups and agreed to call it a night.

Tuesday morning Ellie was excited to get back to work. She had to plan a workshop to welcome and train the eight new volunteers who signed on after a series of talks at the member churches. She wanted to ask one of the board members, Trent Dustin, if he'd help with part of the workshop. He sometimes dropped by the center. Ellie was hoping he would today. She wondered if Trent was married or single. He wore no rings and spoke of no family. She knew he'd been a Methodist pastor for fifteen years.

He'd once told Ellie that his passion for social ministry and justice issues got too far ahead of his parishioners. He started hearing fewer compliments about sermons and more complaints about his time at the homeless shelters or forums on immigration and poverty issues. He'd never considered himself a radical or liberal; he was just someone who was no good at pretending not to see the gross imbalances of power and privilege around him.

Now he was the chair of the C.A.R.E. board and on staff at the downtown homeless shelter. Although technically he was no longer a pastor, people still called him "PT" for Pastor Trent—which over time got morphed to "Pete." Trent, or Pete, didn't seem to care what people called him, as long as they kept talking to him. Pete was in his mid-fifties. He had a leathery look from too many hours in the sun without benefit of sunscreen or hat. He was large and jovial with salt and pepper hair and a short, mostly white beard. The very young, the elderly, and all ages in between seemed to warm up to him immediately. Ellie thought he must be what Santa Claus looked like when off duty.

So when Pete stopped in at the C.A.R.E. center Tuesday to inquire of Ellie how it was going, she knew he really wanted to know. Even so, an hour of this perpetually over-committed man's undivided attention was more than she'd expected. She wanted to ask him to help with the workshop, but he kept their conversation focused on Ellie's personal recovery process. How could he give her this much focused time when so many others were clamoring for his attention? She decided to ask.

He smiled and then explained his secret. "I spend a half hour minimum doing nothing every day."

"What do you mean?"

"Some call it prayer. Some call it meditation. I call it my re-charge time. Somehow, doing this gives me time to do things like talk to people I like to spend time with—like you. I seem to get more time after I spend time doing nothing."

"I've tried meditation. It just never works for me. I keep going back over the same old worn-out path that leads to the same dead end," said Ellie.

"What's at that dead end?"

Ellie sighed. *I wonder if it will ever be easier to talk about this. I never know how to explain what happened.*

"Chet. I never quit loving him. He quit believing that I did. Or, he quit loving me and didn't care whether I loved him or not. He left. I was shocked. The path to the future I had imagined would be ours is bricked up and sealed off for good."

Pete was quiet for a full five minutes. When he spoke again his voice was as tender as the first warm spring day after weeks of the biting winter winds. "You'll never get over it, Ellie. I don't think you should. A wise man—a man named Dietrich Bonhoeffer—put it this way. Some people are so important in our lives that God honors their significance by leaving a permanent hole in our hearts where they belong after they're gone from us."

Ellie felt the familiar tide of tears start to rise. After another minute of silence, Pete continued. "I know it hurts. The trick isn't to try to get rid of the pain. The trick is to let it ferment for as long as it takes. Then—when you're ready—and you'll know when that time has come—pour the love for him into others who desperately need to know someone cares about them."

"Is that why you're at the homeless shelter? Are you transferring a lost love in some way?"

"Ah, a wise and perceptive woman. Yes."

"Well, are you going to tell me about it or is this a one-way soul-baring deal?"

"It was a very long time ago. We were very young. In our senior year at Ohio State."

"Were you engaged?"

"Yes. The wedding was set for a month after graduation."

"She called it off?"

Pete was silent now and staring off into space at something he could see that wasn't in the room with them. "No. Not exactly. Mindy was supposed to meet me at one of the many mood-enhancing bars along High Street. We had a date for nine p.m. She never showed. I was frantic.

"I'd asked her a hundred times to please not walk across the campus by herself at night. There were no cell phones back then. She always thought it was too much trouble to find a pay phone to call me. As if she'd ever remembered to carry change with her anyway to make the call. I finally quit asking and just prayed she'd be okay.

"When it got to be nine-thirty I went looking for her. I walked the path between the bar and the library. No Mindy. I went to her dorm. No one had seen her since dinner. I walked back to the library, then back to the bar. No Mindy. I called the campus police and then I just kept walking all night. In the morning I called the campus police again to see if they knew anything. They didn't."

Pete stopped again. His hands were shredding the paper coffee cup he'd drained a few minutes earlier. Ellie thought she saw small beads of perspiration forming on his brow. She wanted to know what happened but sensed she ought not to ask.

He took in a deep breath as if trying to suck in enough oxygen to get through the next part. "A week later her parents called me. The police found her two days after she disappeared. Naked in a ravine near the campus. She'd been badly beaten. It took several days to ID her. Then they called her parents. Her parents called me."

Ellie was speechless. Finally she managed to whisper, "I'm so sorry."

Pete looked as shocked as if he'd just gotten the news a few minutes ago instead of nearly a quarter of a century ago. "They eventually arrested a homeless man who'd been suspected of abducting, raping, and murdering other women in the area. He bragged about it to another homeless guy he was sharing a bottle of something with. That guy told the police."

"Did you finish the semester?"

"Amazingly enough, I did. I often wonder if I really earned my bachelor's degree or if so many of the faculty felt sorry for me that they just pushed me through the system. Her parents came to the graduation. What would have been her wedding dress arrived at their house the week before graduation."

"So that's why you work with the homeless?"

"Yes. There are so many broken people out there, Ellie. And sometimes in their brokenness, they don't know what else to do but to go around breaking other people. It has to stop somewhere."

"Did you ever meet someone else?"

"I tried. But I just couldn't focus on anyone else long enough for a relationship to take root and grow. There aren't a lot of women who list 'hang out at homeless shelters' as one of their dream dates. I went to seminary and became a pastor because I thought maybe I could catch people before they fell that far. That worked for a while. But a lot of people in the pews just don't want to know how rough life is out on the streets. They felt pretty threatened about the time I spent volunteering at the shelters and places like this.

"I was married for a few years. Right after seminary. She was a dear woman, but she got tired of competing with nameless, homeless men for my time. Her biological clock was starting to tick louder. We ended it with little trauma. She's remarried and has several kids. I never tried marriage again.

"A choice had to be made. I chose them—the lost and lonely."

"But . . . ," Ellie struggled to know what to say next. "You seem so . . . so . . ."

"Normal?"

"Well, yes, I guess that's it."

"Ellie, we all have our secrets and quirks. I've learned how to function in the world of acceptability, so I can get the resources I need to go back into the underworld of the beaten and broken people. I'm sort of like a pack animal taking resources from one world into the other world."

"I had no idea."

"I don't tell this to many. I'm not sure why I told you."

"I'm glad you did. It makes my losses seem pretty trivial."

"Not at all. You loved him very much. You lost that. It *is* a tragedy. It sounds like something or someone broke him too. The fact he wasn't abducted and left dead in the woods doesn't mean your loss isn't just as significant. A loss is a loss. And they all hurt."

"I guess you're right. Thank you for this. I don't know what I'll do with this—but thank you for trusting me with this."

"It felt good to let someone know. She's still so real to me. I miss her every single day."

"I do know how that feels."

"I'm sure you do. One more thing. Try the 'do nothing' therapy again. But start with just five minutes at a time." Pete winked at her. "Doing nothing for a few minutes a day is an acquired skill. Few bother to acquire it. But, I promise you, it will make a difference."

With that he got up and moved toward the door of the tiny conference room they'd occupied for the past hour. Ellie stood too. He turned toward her and hesitated. Then he gave her a quick hug and walked out of the room.

She sat a while longer wondering what to make of all the content of the past hour.

CHAPTER TWELVE

Hear my cry, O God, listen to my prayer; from the end of the earth I call to you, when my heart is faint. (Psalm 61:1–2)

Ellie loved her work at C.A.R.E., which always seemed a bit odd. The people who came in were desperate. They covered the range from third-generation-welfare folks to newly-let-go upper level managers. In here advanced degrees formed a matching set with advancing despair. On the other hand, it was encouraging to see how quickly volunteers grasped the concepts she taught them in orientation. She was touched by how sensitive and caring her volunteer team was toward all the clients. Often clients were battered not only by their pressing financial problems, but also the insensitivity of people who were supposed to help them.

"These aren't problem people. They are people with problems too big to manage on their own. Our job is to give them dignity and hope along with groceries and leads on better housing and jobs. In a strange twist of life, the regular poor clients have something to teach the new arrivals. They know how to work the system. They know where to find resources. They know how to be resourceful. They are often among our most generous supporters when life turns a corner for them. Maybe not in actual dollars—but certainly in percentage of their finances they share and their willingness to give back to those who gave to them."

Ellie told the volunteers the newly-broke folk also had something to teach the regulars. They typically had several months of reserves to carry them through the abrupt end of paychecks. It was usually six or more months of treading financial water without an income before they came to C.A.R.E. These folks usually only needed minimal help before they found another job. Most were back to their middle-class life again within months.

Such was the advantage of a decent education, saving some of every check they got, and keeping up with new developments in the fields in which they worked. It also helped that most had family to turn to for housing, encouragement, job leads, and financial assistance.

She thought of the many *Aesop Fables* she'd read at her grandmother's home. Sometimes the old wisdom was the best. Hard work, learning, saving, and networking with people who had jobs was still the ticket out of the grinding humiliation and anxiety of being out of work. *Yet, we rarely get any help from them after we've helped them over a rough patch. I think maybe they're too embarrassed to have needed the help and never want to look back to those days.*

Sadly, the economy seemed to make the number of people needing help grow while the resources were shrinking. Lynette Combs had been managing the center from the beginning. After twelve years of doing this, she was an expert at finding every available nickel of grant funding. Legend had it that whenever she went to thank one of the local churches for helping, she walked out with another check.

It was an odd combination of satisfaction, distraction, gratitude, and fear that swept over Ellie every time she walked through the back door of the center. The center was an old house in a quiet neighborhood. The neighborhood itself was caught in a time warp. The architecture of the 1960's screamed "modern," but after a half century of wear and tear, it no longer was. New small businesses were sprouting up in the strip centers nearby. Only a handful ever lasted more than a few years. It was a mystery to her why some made it and others died trying. She hoped the new bakery made it. She loved the smell of bread baking that greeted her when she got out of her car in the C.A.R.E. parking lot.

Mostly Ellie sensed that her work at the center gave her some sense of being normal again plus the added bonus of a reality check along with a paycheck. Almost daily she muttered to herself, *There but by the grace of God go I.* Every day the waiting room filled to overflowing with people who didn't want to need this help, but could no longer pretend they did not. She realized she herself was only about one more major financial setback away from joining the waiting-room group.

She still remembered the icy fear she experienced every time she checked her bank account the first few months after Chet left. She watched it slowly drain to a dangerously low level. Chet had not fought her about staying in their home. But with that came the full brunt of trying to manage it on her own. It was so odd—the house was as it had been for years. Yet everything about her life—including her home—was different. When she allowed herself to think about it, the contrast always startled her. *I couldn't bring myself to take down the family photos of us. I just couldn't do it. I wonder if he ever even thinks about the good times we shared. Probably not. Shirley probably keeps his mind fully focused on other things.*

Moving away from the house was near the top of her ten hardest-things-I've-had-to-do list. She remembered the conversation with Ginny about physically moving as a symbolic way to move on from the shock and loss.

"You can't unhave the experiences you've had," was Ginny's response. "They're yours to keep forever. You get to decide how often you want to bring them out to consciously remember. Sort of like my great-grandmother's china I inherited. I rarely use it because I don't want to risk breaking a piece. But I know they're all tucked away safe and sound in the corner cupboard. I see them every time I walk through the dining room. Most days I don't even notice them. Every once in a while I pause and really look at them—and remember the stories my grandmother and mother told me about my great grandmother. I wonder how hard her life must have been. I wonder what I inherited from her. I'm told I look very much like her. I don't see it, but my grandmother says I could be her twin if we hadn't been born ninety years apart."

"The harder I try not to remember some things the more I think about them," sighed Ellie.

"Right. I know! Isn't that the truth?"

"So how do you deal with the memories?"

"One at a time. Day by day. I know it sounds corny. But sometimes the old clichés continue to get said because they're true! 'Sufficient unto this day are the troubles thereof.' That's what my grandmother always used to say. I was a married woman with kids before I realized that was her loose interpretation of Scripture. You know that part in . . . I can never remember where it is. But where Jesus talks about the lilies of the field and the birds of the air and how God takes care of them so we shouldn't worry about tomorrow. Tomorrow will take care of itself."

Ellie had heard all that advice many times. Sometimes it helped. A little. Most days it was like trying to remember the feel of the warm summer sun at the beach while shivering through the last remnants of winter. It was hard to imagine being warm and content while scraping ice off the car windshield or waiting for her feet to thaw after walking through the gray lace of semi-melted ice along the sidewalks.

"Thank God for friends," she told Ginny. "How do people get through this without them?"

"I don't know, and I don't care to find out," said Ginny.

"It really is a journey, isn't it? One step forward, two steps back. But somehow, it has gotten easier. I guess I'll never quit thinking about him. Wondering what went wrong. Thinking if only I had done this or not done that."

"Yup. I'm right there with you, sister. But you know what? Do that enough and you're certifiably nuts. What was, was. The past doesn't have to predict the future. Ellie, I understand. You want him to at least tell you he's sorry. He probably can't. Maybe he's not sorry. Maybe he was miserable for years and didn't know what to say or how to say it. Maybe he's only sorry that he isn't sorry. Maybe not even that."

"Yeah, I guess that makes sense. Sort of. But there was all this evidence that he loved me too. I mean, Ginny, just last week I found yet another funny little card he gave me for no special reason. I had it tucked in the back of a book. When I went to get another book near it I knocked it on the floor. The card came out. I read it."

"And probably sat and cried."

"I did."

"That's normal. I think it's even healthy. That's how grief finally goes away. One little encounter like that after another. It's like building up immunity to it. Like the polio vaccines we all had to get when good ol' Doc Salk came up with the vaccine. Remember that?"

"I do! I went with my parents to stand in line at Roosevelt Elementary here in Lakewood and got my dose. And, I never got polio. But I had a roommate in college who did. She had a permanent limp. It was a mild case."

"See? Tragedy comes in many forms."

"Yes, yes. I know. 'Into each life some pain must fall.' Did Shakespeare actually write that?"

Ginny shook her head slowly. "No, I don't think so. But it's true. It's like sorrow and setbacks are the raw materials we get whether we want them or not. Then we get to choose. We can spend the rest of our life staring at them like a lump of clay. Or, we can start working with them to reshape them into something else."

"Another person told me we're like the clay God uses to make something new."

"That's also from the Bible. We are the clay. God is the potter."

Ellie straightened up in her chair. "Okay. This is enough of that. How do you know all this?"

"I actually read and study such things. It gives me great comfort. I also listen to a lot of hymns when I'm in the car alone. Then I can sing as loud and off key as I want and not offend anyone."

Ellie sensed the universe was lining up to deliver her the same message over and over again. Let go of Chet. Let God re-work the story into a happier ending. She wondered how to do that. She wondered if it might actually make any difference. She'd prayed off and on her whole life. Usually short, "Thank you" prayers and what she hoped were polite requests on behalf of others. She didn't really know how to do more. But she sensed learning how was the next step on this strange path she was following.

Chapter Thirteen

Behold, O Lord, for I am in distress, my soul is in tumult, my heart is wrung within me. (Lamentations 1:20)

Ellie felt the old panic seeping in again. Two of her three children said they really needed to go spend the holidays with their other side of the family this time. It was only fair. She knew that. But her daughters-in-law's parents had each other. They didn't need the companionship the way Ellie did. And Cat, good ol' Cat, who had been there in so many ways both little and great—announced it was Chet's turn to spend Christmas with them.

Ellie's child within was about to lie down on the floor and throw a whopper of a tantrum. Ellie, the rational adult, knew these feelings were childish and irrational. That didn't stop them from demanding center stage of her attention. Ellie felt the prickly dread of being the odd one out. She was utterly at a loss for what to do with herself. The twins—betrayal and resentment—were taunting her already. Her tight chest, the urge to pace, the inability to focus her thoughts—all indicators a panic attack wasn't far away. *How on earth will I get through Christmas Eve and Christmas Day alone?*

The idea of spending those two days by herself—or worse in the midst of others who felt sorry for her and invited her into their family gathering out of pity—felt like a sunless bitter cold day.

You've got to get a grip here, woman. Other people do this every year. Look at your Uncle Stan. Never married. Never had any kids. Lived alone out on the farm. Yet he was always ready with a smile and quick to talk about the latest book he'd read or the next trip he planned to take by himself.

Then she'd argue—with herself. *True. But he was a Norwegian introvert who thought a party consisted of a bowl of cold popcorn and an old movie—with or without anyone else in the room watching it with him. I'm not like that.*

No, you're not. But you're not going to die from being alone either. Go ask Elaine if she needs any help. Think of someone besides yourself for a change. The change of scenery might do you good.

Ellie picked up her cell phone and called Elaine.

Elaine's voice perked up when she realized it was Ellie on the phone. She eagerly agreed to breakfast the next morning.

Over omelets and coffee Ellie talked about everything except the purpose of the invitation to breakfast. Elaine asked the opening question.

"Well, Ellie, what are your plans for this Christmas? Are you feeding the flock this year?"

Ellie's face answered the question. She shook her head slowly. She had her mouth open to speak when Elaine jumped in first. "Ellie, I know this is a lot to ask of you, but I was wondering if I could count on you for some help this Christmas. My Dad's taking a turn for the worse with his cancer. I think this may be his last Christmas. So far he looks and acts okay. But it's liver cancer. I've seen enough of that to know this isn't going to go well. I've convinced Mom to bring him here—because cancer or no cancer—I cannot just cancel the six services that week."

Ellie never thought about the Christmas church math. She just picked the most convenient service and went. It seldom occurred to her that it wasn't that way for Elaine. Ellie was thinking about surviving the long, lonely character-testing stretch from Christmas Eve afternoon to when she could again retreat to the familiarity of the C.A.R.E. center. With Christmas Day falling on a Friday, that meant three services Thursday evening, one Christmas Day, a day off to recuperate, and two more on Sunday. What a load.

Elaine continued, "So, I was wondering—I know this is a huge imposition—but I was wondering if you'd come stay with us, too. You're good with people with problems. Dad and Mom will love you. And then I can come and go and not feel like I'm deserting them. Will you think it over and let me know?"

Ellie was speechless. *Maybe there's more to this prayer stuff than I realize.* She'd been praying for a way to not have to go through this emotional land mine alone. She'd imagined one of her children would figure out that she would be alone and come to her rescue. She'd never imagined that the rescue boat might be someone with a more pressing and immediate need than her own emotional drama.

"What about Chipper?"

"Bring him along. He's a great dog and dogs have an uncanny way of knowing when someone's sick or in pain. My Dad will love him, too."

"Okay. I'll do it."

Elaine picked up the check and insisted this one was on the church. "Your benevolence dollars at work," she said. "Thank you, Ellie. I know this isn't what you're used to for the holidays—but it will help me so much. I really appreciate it."

Mel slipped from life into death quietly New Year's Day afternoon. Elaine and her mother had been going about various domestic chores. Mel was in a hospital bed in the living room dozing off and on with the football game on television keeping him company. He'd been so weak by the end of the Christmas marathon of activities that Elaine and her mother agreed he needed to stay there. Hospice had been called in. Everything that could be said had been said in those last days of the year.

Now it was a matter of waiting and praying the suffering would end soon. Ellie had returned to her own home December 26th, so Elaine and her parents could have the privacy they needed. She visited for a bit every afternoon, but felt like an intruder. Yet whenever she suggested it was time to leave both Elaine and her mother insisted she stay a while longer.

Elaine's mother was sitting quietly next to him when Mel slipped away from the pain and morphine-fog into whatever awaited him on the other side.

When Ellie arrived later that afternoon she knew without being told. Even as she hugged Elaine and her mother she thought, *I'm jealous of them. What is wrong with me? I can't help thinking it will be easier for her because he died and she was with him to the end. Have I completely lost my ability to empathize with other people?*

Chapter Fourteen

The Lord is merciful and gracious; slow to anger and abounding in steadfast love. (Psalm 103:8)

Much to her surprise and relief, Ellie survived her fourth holiday season without Chet and her first with no member of her own family. She was grateful that she could be there for Elaine. It was good to be on the giving end of their friendship for a change.

She did more than survive. She actually felt good about herself, her current lot in life, and the way she'd been able to be there for Elaine's family. It felt good to focus on someone else for a while. Not that she enjoyed seeing anyone suffer. But it made her feel useful and hopeful again to just be with them. Somehow learning to go on without Chet had given her insights she'd not had before. She'd always felt sorry for people whose spouses had died, but she'd never before understood the vastness of the loss. Now she did. She remembered Pete's words: "A loss is a loss. They all hurt."

She was grateful she could provide some support to Elaine and glad her father made it into the start of a new year. It felt odd to feel good about someone's death. She wasn't really—but it was obvious that death was going to be the only relief from the pain and deterioration. It was an honor to be with a couple who so loved each other.

Somehow their courage and tenderness with one another gave Ellie hope. She felt like she was in the midst of something sacred. The funeral was a celebration of Mel's life and their until-death-do-we-part love for one another. The fact her own marriage didn't make it to that finish line didn't mean she couldn't appreciate such commitment in those around her. *This has been such a strange chapter in my life. I carry so many opposing feelings all the time. I never know from one moment to the next which ones are going to surface. I think I'm adjusting to not getting over Chet. It's like he belongs to a chapter of life I can revisit anytime I want through my memories but can never experience again.*

Now January was nearly over with the promise of warmer weather almost close enough to touch. Ellie mustered the nerve to call Matt to wish him a belated Merry Christmas and wishes for a good New Year. They'd had a pleasant few minutes of conversation, but Matt made no offer to see her again. She didn't want to appear desperate, so she hung up after a few minutes. *I wonder what that was all about. I thought the night we had dinner went really well. Well, apparently that wasn't his opinion. Oh well. I guess it's good to know what I'm not going to do next.*

Pete stopped by at the C.A.R.E. center several times to inquire about her health and happiness. None of the visits ever lasted as long or had the intensity of the earlier conversation when he talked about his own wounds. Yet he loved to amuse her with his truly ridiculous jokes. He seemed to collect them as a hobby. And, he sometimes chided her about her spiritual health. "How's the do-nothing therapy going?" he'd ask.

"I'm working at it."

"Ah, isn't that exactly the problem. We work at trying to do nothing. We really are an uptight lot, aren't we?" Then he'd wink, pat her on the back, suggest she keep on keeping on, and go back to his work at the homeless shelter.

One gray, drizzly February day Pete arrived bearing a box full of freshly baked cookies and two thermoses of coffee—one regular and one decaf. The center was actually quiet at the moment. It was about a half hour before closing time and all the day's clients had been seen and sent on their way with whatever resources the staff could provide them.

"Party time!" he sang as he headed for the tiny corner of the storage room that doubled as the staff break room.

Lynette followed him to inquire what he was doing.

"As the chair of the board of this august organization, I have made an executive decision."

"Oh. Do tell."

"You all work too hard. You don't relax enough. You don't appreciate all the truly great work you do for so many. You do so much with so little so often that I fear you will all forget how to relax and just enjoy a slice of life."

"So you're here to teach us how?"

"Indeed I am. Fresh out-of-the-oven cookies. They'd be hot if it weren't freezing out there. And guaranteed hot coffee—in two versions."

"Impressive."

"Not as impressive as the story I've got to tell you. I insist on a staff meeting. Round 'em up and bring in whoever's here for a meeting."

A few minutes later the curious staff arrived. It was a small crew: Lynette, Ellie, and Sam, the "fix-anything" guy who stopped by once a day to see what needed his attention next. Plus one very part-time office administrative woman and two volunteers from St. James.

While they cherished the fresh cookies and hot coffee, Pete told them why he was in such a good mood.

"Sometimes, things just go right. Today was one of them. Remember Sol, the crazy new college grad who thought he could turn a bunch of homeless, hopeless men into caterers?"

Lynette nodded her head. "Yes, I do remember. He realized the homeless needed jobs as much or more than the warm bed the local shelter gives them and the food we give them between shelter meals."

"Right," continued Pete. "And he borrowed money to start a catering business—training some of my regulars how to run a commercial kitchen or deliver the goods or keep the books."

"Yes, I do remember that," said Lynette.

"Well, today is their first anniversary. These are the fruits of their labors. I wanted to share them with you to celebrate. With you who wonder if any long-term good comes of your efforts. Behold, proof that the world isn't a completely hopeless place."

With that he started his litany of bad puns and passed around the box of cookies again.

That night Ellie shared dinner with Ginny and Dan. She retold the story about the young man who started the catering business to employ the homeless. Ginny put down her fork and stared at her.

"What?" asked Ellie. "Do I have spinach on my teeth?"

"No, but you do have the making of a great story for your writing assignment for the Literary Legacy Writing class."

"I do?"

"Of course. Remember the assignment? Bring in a story of how hope trumps despair."

"Wow. You're right. That would be a great story. I should have seen that. I'll start on it as soon as I get home."

"Can't wait to read it. Shall I drive this time?"

One of the members of the writers' group the two started attending had distributed information about a creative writing class being offered at a leisure learning program for the next semester. It was an eight-week course that they were both enjoying a great deal. Ellie had confided in Ginny she was also enjoying the weekly encounter with Liam, another of the older adult students in the course.

Age-wise Liam Patrick Malone was somewhere between "Welcome to AARP" and "Here's your Medicare card"—perhaps a bit closer to the Medicare card. His family had brought him from Ireland to Cleveland as a young boy. Thanks to the U.S. Navy, he managed to get a college education along with a global perspective on life. That had led to a long and apparently successful career in the military. His writings for the class were astonishing. He dealt with the dark realities of military action with grace and compassion.

Ellie had cornered him after their class one evening while Ginny was busy talking to another participant.

"I have very limited experience with the military. But you make it all sound so . . . so I don't know . . . necessary."

"'Tis that indeed," he grinned. Though his family had been in Ohio for decades, he still spoke with a light Irish lilt. Ellie found it fascinating.

"Where did you serve?" she asked.

"Ah, I could tell you, but then I'd have to . . ."

"Kill me? Really?"

"No, my dear. Never a lovely lady like you. But I cannot be telling you. Top secret and all that."

"So how are you going to write a memoir about something you aren't allowed to discuss."

"'Twill be a challenge now, won't it?"

"I'd say so."

Ellie didn't know what to make of this man. He was definitely appealing in the physical realm. His six-foot plus eye-catching body was topped with a full head of just-starting-to-gray hair. He had a twinkle in his eye when he spoke. His firm, deep voice suggested he was used to giving orders and having them followed without question.

She knew from walking out to the parking lot with him that he drove a Lexus. He'd written in one of his assignments about growing up on the West Side of Cleveland—and still had some family there. He wore no ring but spoke occasionally of grandchildren. He didn't offer any details of his family or lack of one.

What Ellie observed of herself was that she was thinking about Liam more with each passing week. She also knew that in a few weeks this class would end and if she didn't do something, she'd lose touch with him. She didn't know what to do about that but knew she didn't like the thought of it.

As though she'd been reading her thoughts, Ginny came to her rescue. On their way to the class that evening Ginny said, "You know, the problem with these short courses is that you just start to get to know the other people and it's over. I've really enjoyed hearing everyone's stories. I was particularly drawn to Margaret. I relate to that woman. She reminds me so much of my grandmother."

"I know. I've really enjoyed this, too. I'm surprised how much I'm enjoying doing the assignments. I didn't know what to expect, but they're all really helpful."

Their instructor, a local newspaper columnist and several-times published author herself, coached her students to keep putting bits and pieces of themselves on paper and then sharing that with others. Her years of experience taught her how vulnerable would-be authors could get about sharing their work with others. She kept reminding them their vulnerability made their work authentic and helped it connect with readers.

That evening Ginny and Ellie were driving to session number six out of the eight. After this course, they planned to audit a semester-long course at Baldwin Wallace College, if they'd be allowed to do so.

"I guess we could ask for a class roster or something," suggested Ginny.

"Great idea. Will you do that?"

"I can. But so could you. Or is that too obvious for you?"

"What do you mean?"

"I think there may be a friendship forming between a good friend of mine and a handsome stranger in the class."

Ellie blushed.

"Silence may be golden, but it's also very loud sometimes," said Ginny when Ellie didn't respond. "I'll take your silence as acknowledgement."

Ellie began twiddling her thumbs.

"It's okay, Ellie. It's been, what, five years now since he left? You're allowed to have a male friend. You're hardly betraying anyone here."

"I know. I mean, I . . . I don't know what I know anymore."

"It is scary. Tell you what. Let's take our time leaving tonight, and maybe we can snag both Margaret and tall and handsome to go get some coffee with us after class."

"Okay. Let's do that."

Their instructor grinned when Ginny requested a class roster. "You're getting ahead of me," she said. "I was going to collect contact information tonight and distribute it the last night. I plan to send you each a booklet of the work you've done. I figured you may want to stay in touch with one another after the course ends. The first class I taught formed a writers' group that's still meeting five years later as far as I know."

After class Ellie, Ginny, Margaret, and Liam all crowded into a booth at Jake's, a popular locally-owned coffee shop. Ellie always loved the aroma of the place. Coffee mixed in with dozens of types of teas—all kept in glass jars neatly occupying three shelves. Jakes was the sort of place where you felt part of the group even if you didn't know a single person there.

She was shocked when Margaret announced it was already eleven o'clock. Reluctantly, they agreed to call it a night and headed for the parking lot. But not until they'd exchanged e-mails and cell phone numbers. "We don't have to be given permission to talk to each other, you know," said Liam.

The next morning Ellie's phone rang at seven-fifteen as she was pouring her first cup of coffee for the day.

"Did I wake you?"

"Uh, no, um, who *is* this?"

"I'm shocked. You don't recognize my voice?"

"Is this Liam?"

"'Tis indeed. And the top 'o the morning to you, Darlin'."

Ellie stared at the phone willing her mouth to say something, anything.

Chapter Fifteen

Upon my bed by night I sought him whom my soul loves; I sought him,
but found him not; I called him, but he gave no answer.
(Song of Songs 3:1)

By March Ellie was feeling simultaneously foolish and hopeful. She went to sleep thinking of Liam and woke up with him on her mind. Had she ever felt this way about Chet? She must have, but it was so long ago she really couldn't remember.

Ellie was increasingly distracted. She hoped people wouldn't notice. She hadn't confided in anyone except Ginny about her emerging feelings for Liam. Even so, people were commenting about an elusive something different about her. "You look terrific, Ellie." This was a comment she was hearing a lot these days.

In mid-March Elaine invited Ellie to lunch "to properly thank you for all you did for Dad." Elaine looked wrung out—but also at peace.

She told Ellie that her mother was back in her own home, starting to figure out how to go on alone without Mel. Elaine was back to her over-stuffed schedule trying to catch up from the couple of weeks she took off for the funeral and time with her mother.

After a few minutes, Elaine told Ellie she was noticing some changes in her and asked if there was anything in particular that had changed for her. "I've been so distracted with my Dad's death and then worrying about Mom I'm afraid I've zoned out a bit. How *are* you?"

Though she admitted being distracted, Elaine said she noticed something different—a lightness or more energy or something new about Ellie. Elaine commented the change was subtle—as if Ellie were slowly moving away from some kind of resigned duty-bound determination to go on living even if she wasn't enjoying life much.

"But lately you seem to walk with a bit of a spring to your step," said Elaine.

She continued, "I'm wondering if this has something to do with that writing class I remember you said you were taking. Whatever it is, it seems to agree with you. So, Ellie, you look different. Am I going to be allowed to know the cause of this change I'm witnessing? Or am I going to have to play twenty questions with you?"

Ellie smiled shyly and grinned. "I've started seeing someone."

"Aha! I want more details."

"Liam, the fellow I met in that writers' class Ginny and I took."

"I've heard the name."

"Well, I don't know if it's going anywhere or not. And I don't even know if I want it to go anywhere. But I like having someone call me just because he wants to talk to me. No agenda. No requests."

"Ouch!"

"Not you Elaine. I didn't mean you. I was really glad I could be there with you and your folks. I feel so honored to have been part of . . ." She paused, uncertain how to finish the sentence.

"Our last Christmas. Yes, it was hard. I'm so glad you were there. You helped much more than you'll ever know. Mom talks all the time about how Chipper curled up next to Dad to keep him warm," said Elaine.

"I was amazed. I'll never look at Chipper the same way. In fact, I'm thinking of getting the training to take him on nursing home visits."

"Great idea. But what about Liam. Come on, Ellie. Spill."

"There's nothing to spill yet. He calls. We talk. He invites me to go out to see a movie or a concert or even a basketball game, and I go."

"That's it?"

"So far."

"What's he do for a living?"

"What, are you taking over where my mother left off? I am an adult you know."

"Of course you are. You are perfectly capable of making your own decisions. It's just that, well . . ." Elaine trailed off. "Sometimes it is hard to separate where our friendship ends and where my role as your pastor begins. I know I can trust you to ask for any advice you want and you're not likely to take any you didn't ask for. Sorry. I think I was at least stepping on the line if not over it."

"Well, you caught yourself in time." Ellie smiled at her friend. She was not going to admit to anyone—especially not Elaine, who seemed to possess x-ray-like insights into people's souls—how much she thought about Liam. She was shocked at herself. She felt like she was back in college wondering if Chet would call. Whenever Liam did call, she would force herself not to run to the phone.

The many lectures she gave herself did little to stop the giddiness she felt. Maybe there really was something to the notion that attraction changes a person's chemistry. All she knew for sure was that it was a lot more fun experiencing these mini-emotional highs when she heard from him than facing all those nuke-a-meal dinners in front of television alone.

The next couple of months unfolded day by day in a mix of work at C.A.R.E. and free time spent with Liam. Though they both claimed they needed one another's help to complete writing projects they'd started, Ellie knew this was more than a writing project. She hoped it might blossom into something even more. Then she found herself being close to terrified that it might.

What she feared was too scary to tell anyone—even Elaine or Ginny. Not even Dr. Thorpe who'd held one end of the rope she needed to climb out of the pit when Chet left. This wound was so deep and so painful she could barely allow herself to even think about it. She'd given this fear a name: she called it Miss Fit, by which she meant she felt like a misfit in the world of love making.

She could remember days of total abandonment with Chet—chasing one another around the kitchen or backyard like little kids armed with squirt guns. These inevitably led to long nights of passion and sheer, overwhelming satisfaction as they came together hungry to combine as much of themselves into one as was humanly possible.

In the many long nights post-Chet she tried to recall when and how that had changed. Gradually the moments of pressing their bodies together and rolling over and over in mutual passion and pleasure slowed in frequency. Somehow they became less about passion and pleasure and more about habit and a gnawing sense of obligation.

No one had ever talked openly with Ellie about the female sexual drive, so she didn't know what to expect or how to even form the questions that were starting to spring up where longing had once lodged. There were books to be sure. But the more she read them, the more she concluded they weren't talking about her body and her responses to the slow descent from youth into maturity followed by the unavoidable changes of middle age and beyond. Thus she concluded she was a misfit, a woman who did not fit into the normal patterns of feminine reality.

Miss Fit was a cruel companion. Just as Ellie was starting to feel whole and vibrant again, Miss Fit would point out the sagging breasts or the sprawling belly fat. Ellie would go for a brisk, long walk and come back feeling good from the effort. Miss Fit would whisper undermining messages about being out of shape and no longer attractive.

Ellie had more or less successfully kept Miss Fit at bay by refusing to dwell much on her physical attributes. She gave her body the basic care required for good health and refused to focus on it beyond that.

But now that Liam was becoming a central character in the unfolding script of her life, she was nervous. She realized she didn't look as good as she once did. She was absolutely dead set against any medical or surgical intervention. She wanted to age naturally—the way she'd watched her mother and her grandmothers do. Vitamins, daily quarts of water, long walks, trips to the gym, and plates of vegetables were one thing. Operations and pills were another.

She'd thought it through and decided she'd take whatever nature gave her and manage it as best she could. Her hard-earned money wasn't going to subsidize the vanity business.

Still, Miss Fit had subtle ways of belittling her. Near the end of their time together, Chet had let her conclude that their dwindling nighttime passion was all her responsibility. Once she thought about it, she realized there had been one pivotal night.

It was a few years after Ike, the youngest of the three, left home for college. Both she and Chet had been going fast and furious in a combination of work, socializing, and volunteering. They picked a fall weekend and mutually agreed that neither would make any commitments from Friday after work through Monday morning.

To her surprise, conservative Mr. "We-have-kids-in-college" Trout seconded the idea of going away to a lodge at a state park for the weekend. Ellie was floored and excited. They rented canoes and paddled away that Indian summer afternoon. After a leisurely dinner in the lodge they strolled along a wooded path.

Later they went through their familiar bed time rituals that sometimes led to deeper passion. She waited for her body to respond, but no surge of sexual energy surfaced. Tension built in anticipation of what was waiting for them, but Chet's aging body wasn't responding either. Finally she murmured, "It's okay. I love *you*—all of you—just the way you are." She snuggled up against him in the old familiar way with her head on his shoulder, one arm draped across his chest and the other under the pillow they shared. She fell asleep that way and never mentioned the evening to Chet again.

Months later Chet asked her if she wanted him to take one of the several male testosterone options advertised everywhere. She didn't, but not because she didn't want more of what they used to share in the privacy of their bedroom. But rather, because she didn't want Chet to stress about it. She loved Chet—the whole person—not just the bedroom companion. She was content to just be with him and naively thought he felt the same way.

Apparently he didn't. He became more distant after that. Ellie sensed something had changed and not for the better. But she was unable to understand exactly what. Nor did she know what to do about it. The atmosphere between them changed from a warm sunny afternoon to a cold moonless evening.

Before Chet left, he inflicted deep scars that led Ellie to blame herself for all that had gone wrong. In one of the rare displays of anger he nearly hissed at her, "I learned everything I needed to know when you said you didn't care if I took a pill."

Miss Fit was right there too whispering nasty little lies to her as she wondered if she should have told him to take the pills. What if she'd found the courage to talk to someone about the fact she no longer really cared one way or the other about the passion part of her life with Chet. What if? What if? What if? She nearly drove herself crazy analyzing the end of their union from every possible angle.

It wasn't that she no longer wanted him. She did. He was as much a part of her life as her heart or liver or aching feet. She just didn't want their love to be about trying to stem the tide of encroaching age. She wanted to be with Chet, the man she'd lived with since they were in their twenties. She wanted to embrace the changes they were experiencing and face them together.

Apparently Chet saw it differently. Ellie had not understood his panic about his aging body. Miss Fit's relentless messages about her own inadequacy kept her from talking with Chet about it.

There had been other nights when they were able to experience a more vibrant night life. But from the vantage point of the divorce and years now of being on her own, she understood that maybe there really was nothing she could have done to salvage Chet's shrinking self-esteem. Maybe the whole divorce was really about his disappointment in himself and his need to get away from the one person who reminded him of his diminishing drive.

The fact that he hooked up with Shirley before the final draft of the divorce decree was off the printer began to make sense to Ellie. The adrenalin of the new relationship must have given him a jolt of sexual energy that blocked out any ability to consider the collateral damage this would unleash into their family. And Shirley was so . . . so smug. So sure she understood Chet. So convinced his only problem was that Ellie didn't understand or appreciate him. Miss Fit was quick to remind Ellie that Shirley was younger, firmer, probably still pulsing with pre-menopausal longing and passion.

At times Ellie felt like her constant companion, Mr. Grief, was giving her a multiple choice test she kept flunking. Trying to understand what happened between them was like a recurring nightmare with no morning alarm to end it.

The test went like this—Did Chet leave you because:

A) You were too clingy and demanding of his attention?

B) You could no longer give him the sexual passion he desired?

C) You were too remote and independent and he felt abandoned?

D) All of the above?

Ultimately it didn't matter. She would probably never be allowed to see the test results and know the real reason. And it didn't change the reality anyway. Bottom line: he left; she hurt. He seemed perfectly content to be with Shirley and leave her with Mr. Grief for company.

Chapter Sixteen

Behold, I make all things new. (Revelation 21:5)

Now Ellie was amazed and amused at the physical attraction she was feeling for Liam. *I thought these days were long gone. I feel like a high school girl hoping Mr. Wonderful will look my way in the lunch room.*

Liam poured on charm the way some pour milk on their morning cereal. Sometimes she just got lost in his soft, deep Irish-lilt as he talked to her about the events of his day. He phoned every night right after the early news.

Sometimes he just showed up with a bottle of wine and an offer to skip the excuse of a dinner she had been thinking of preparing. Whenever she ate alone, Ellie rotated through her limited menu selections of some combination of breakfast for dinner, clean out the fridge, or what she called her "nuke a meal." These went from cardboard boxes in the freezer to the microwave to the tray table in front of the television in fifteen minutes or less.

Liam's invitations always seemed a better alternative. "I know another great place to explore. Let's have a glass of wine here and go check it out."

In the beginning she protested. She didn't want him to always pay and her meager budget didn't include meals in places with white linens and a staff hovering around ready to deliver the next item.

Then one evening all that changed. She'd been wondering if and when and how their relationship might shift from regular nights out to more intimate nights in. One evening he came over with two bottles of wine. They never made it to dinner. She was grateful for the slow, warm buzz of the wine. Though she had imagined this might happen, she wasn't at all sure what she felt or thought or wanted as it began to unfold.

It was time. The moment of decision was here. *We go to the next level or call it off. What do I want? It's clear what he wants.* Ellie took in a deep breath. She looked at Liam looking at her. She saw the desire in his eyes. She closed her eyes. She lifted her top over her head, willing herself to stop thinking and savor the moment.

She recalled that moment many times in the nights to come. He was so gentle. He was very experienced. And he was determined. Though he had waited for her to respond, she was sure he'd have just kept asking until their relationship was sealed with the physical connection. If it hadn't been that night, it would have been another. Of that much she was certain.

There was little else she was certain about. She was so confused. She wanted desperately to talk to someone about the confusing emotions accompanying the glorious physical release. But who? Cat? Hardly. Ginny? She tried a couple of times, but she couldn't figure out how to bring up the subject, and besides that, she wasn't even sure what exactly the subject was. Elaine? She just couldn't imagine it.

So her new relationship with Liam was her private secret shared with him, her journal, and her endless daydreaming.

Liam had plans for Memorial Day weekend. "You work too hard. We need to get away. Do you have a passport?"

"Yes, I think so. I mean, I don't think it's expired yet. Why?"

"I have a friend who has a condo in Cancun. I thought I'd take you there for the long weekend."

She hoped her mouth hadn't visibly dropped. Part of her was ready to toss a few things in a suitcase and call the dog sitter. Part of her was frightened. Though she was coming to adore this charming fellow, she still knew so little about him. It was as if his life started only a few months ago. He never talked much about himself or his past. Mostly she was shocked to be in a position to wrestle with such an invitation.

The invitation threw Ellie into a whirlwind of competing thoughts. *I definitely like the attention. It's certainly more fun to be with someone my own age than alone. I can still feel passion. Chet was wrong. Whatever happened—or failed to happen toward the end—wasn't all about me. I wish we could have talked it through. I wish. I wish. I wish. Well, that goes nowhere fast. Wherever this romance is going—I can't believe I'm thinking of this as a romance. At my age! It is romantic. I'm falling in love with him. I like it. Wherever this goes, he's given Miss Fit the heave ho. I'm thankful for that.*

But I'm not sure I'm ready for this. What will people think? What will I tell my kids? What am I doing? The last time I went through this Mom was there for me.

I'm being ridiculous. Older people date and have flings and live together and remarry every day. What is your problem, woman?

The problem was the creeping tide of fear. Seasick-like waves of indecision and worry were rolling around her insides. A virtual teeter totter of high hopes mingled with dread of being hurt and falling flat on the hard ground of rejection—again. Maybe it was better not to love again and not risk the torture of failure. She feared losing control of her future. She feared being alone the rest of her life. She feared being inadequate. The list seemed endless.

I have to talk to someone. Finally she decided on Amelia. *She took me in that first dreadful anniversary post-Chet. She'll know what to do.*

Amelia laughed after Ellie summed up the reason for the phone call with the burning question of the moment. "So, do I go or not? What do you think?"

"Do you want to?"

"Yes. And, no."

"Which one weighs more?"

"Yes. I think. I guess. I don't know. I'm not sure."

"Okay. What's the worse that would happen if you did go?"

"He could turn out to be a serial rapist and they'll never identify my body and I'll never see my kids or grandkids again."

"Well, that would be tragic. What's the next worse thing that could happen?"

"I'll really screw this up. I'll be too desperate, and chase him away or I'll be too distant and he'll drift away on his own."

"Damn, Chet."

"What?!"

"Ol' Chet really left a boatload of his junk behind when he left you. Ellie, listen to me. No woman is ever the perfect wife. There ain't no such animal. And no one really knows what goes on inside someone else's marriage. But I gotta tell you, gal, from my vantage point, you two had as close a shot at the good life as any couple I know. Something happened to—with—in Chet. And rather than man up and figure it out and deal with it, he dumped it all on you and went off with Shirley, who apparently does a more than adequate job of keeping him from dealing with his stuff."

Ellie was silent a long time.

"You still there?"

"Yes. I'm thinking."

"Thought I heard a strange noise."

"So what should I do?"

"Follow your heart. Forget your kids. They're adults. They can run their own lives. You're way too young to let them start running yours. Leave Chet in the past. You'll probably never really get over what happened. But you don't have to let the past predict the future. Liam seems like the future to me. Go, play. Have a little fun. Call me when you get back."

In the end Ellie's kids helped her make the decision. Usually Memorial Day was a relaxed family gathering for all of them. They rotated houses from year to year, but the day's activities were always the same. Burgers on the grill. Water hose fights for anyone foolish or brave enough to go near the kids running around in their new bathing suits. A few beers. A lot of old family favorite stories. The finale of the day was always the season's first s'mores made over a fire pit in the backyard.

Ellie decided to offer Liam a counteroffer to join in the family tradition. Two things happened. He said he absolutely was not interested in spending the day with so many people, so count him out. It was Cancun or nothing for him.

And, then, each of her three family households apologized profusely but insisted they simply could not make it this year. None of the three had consulted with the others. Each assumed the other two families would include Ellie in their plans. When she realized that she would spend another holiday alone or go with Liam to Cancun, the decision was made.

The first evening was enchanted. After they got settled into their room and finished with the room service dinner, they indulged in more tender physical recreation. It was all the more wonderful because it was in such a romantic setting. Saturday they combined relaxed dining with walking the beaches and strolling through the little shops. Liam insisted on buying Ellie several new outfits. He shushed her protests. "I love spoiling beautiful women. Don't deny me this small pleasure."

I've only heard such talk in movies. I didn't realize people really talk like this.

Over exotic drinks later in the afternoon Liam began to tell Ellie bits and pieces of his story. She was stunned.

He began by telling her, "There's a lot I don't know. I've spent some time trying to fill in the gaps, but the trail doesn't go far before I run into a dead end again.

"This is what I do know. I was placed for adoption as a baby. Apparently I am the result of a one-night fling. My parents wanted the romance but not the baby that came with it. The records are sealed. I've never been able find either of my birth parents. My adoptive parents made it from Dublin to Cleveland, and all went well for a few years, apparently. But then my father couldn't hold a job or his liquor. My mother decided to join him, and by the time I was a teenager they were both alcoholics. My father got religion somewhere along the line and sobered up. She didn't. He divorced her, got custody of me, and moved me cross country to Colorado where some friends were offering a fresh start. He remarried. The new woman in his life said she loved children, but apparently not teenage boys," he said pointing to himself.

"A week after high school graduation—and a month after I turned eighteen—I left to join the Navy and never looked back. That's when I started writing. I have box loads of old notebooks full of all kinds of writing. I've never published any of it.

"Dad died two years later while I was stationed overseas in Germany. I didn't make it home for the funeral. His wife—I could never wrap my brain around calling her 'Mom'—never contacted me again after she sent the telegram telling me he died. She made it clear she wasn't interested in my future, and I sure didn't want her in mine."

"What about your adoptive mother? What happened to her?"

"She remarried some rich guy who spent a fortune on rehab programs for her. I got an occasional card from her. I knew every time she was at Step Four of the Twelve again. She'd send me a card full of remorse and promises. The longest she stayed sober as far as I can tell from the collection of cards was six months post-rehab. I saw her once about twenty years ago. By then she was divorced for I think the third time. It was hard to keep track. She looked horrible. She tried to hit me up for money. I gave her a little cash and never saw or heard from her again. Not that I made it easy for her to ever find me."

Ellie couldn't believe what she was hearing. This was like a train derailing one mai tai at a time.

"How'd you come out so . . ."

"Sane?"

"Yeah, I guess that's the word."

"I didn't. But I survived. The Navy really helped. It was the family I didn't have. A lot of folks join the service to find family. The defending the country part is way down the list of real reasons for some of us. We want a group of people to call our own, to eat turkey with on Thanksgiving, to understand the way of life we lead. The paid-for education part is pretty great too."

"Is that why you made a career out of it?"

"That, and the timing. I was in the right place at the right time. It turns out I'm a pretty good EE."

"EE?"

"Electrical Engineer. There were some exciting new projects coming down the line after the Korean War. I did well in my studies. I kept getting promoted. And I made a career out of helping design more sophisticated ships, with all the best weapons."

Ellie shuddered. Just the word "weapons" conjured up thoughts she'd rather not deal with.

Her response didn't go unnoticed. "Ellie. Darlin', every nation has 'em. 'Tis only a matter of who has the best ones. We have the best people deciding when and how and where to use what we have. It's something to be proud of for sure."

Their conversation was interrupted by the waiter offering to bring yet another round of mai tais. They ordered them and decided to order sandwiches to go with them. Liam continued.

"Do you know how close we came to speaking German after World War II? Did you know the Nazis had a plane that could have gotten through the radar and over England so fast the Brits wouldn't have had a chance to fight back. And maybe my Ireland would have been next. I'm proud of what I did for our country."

Not knowing what else to do, Ellie nodded and encouraged him to go on.

"But my dear, I can't talk much about the things I did."

"You mean you could, but then you'd have to kill me?"

"Something like that."

Ellie noticed a shadow cross his face. For a moment it was as though he was no longer across the table from her in Cancun but far away in some place she couldn't go.

After a short pause he resumed his story. "But, I'm rambling. Long story short, I had a career. I did some things I'm pretty damn proud about. And other things, well, not so much."

"And family?"

"Yes. I had one. History repeats itself. My first wife also became an alcoholic. You'd have thought I'd see it coming and dodge it, but I didn't. I was gone too much. Which is probably why she started drinking. Too many lonely nights alone I guess. The life of a Navy wife wasn't for her. But she didn't figure that out until two kids into it."

"And the kids? How old? Where are they now?"

"After my ex got sober for good, she and our sons had a kiss-and-make-up meeting about ten years ago. I wasn't invited. By the end of that weekend, I was public enemy number one. And she was the abused and abandoned damsel in distress. It's not a proud story, but it's the truth."

"But, I saw photos of little children in your den. Are they your grandchildren?"

"Indeed, they are. One of my daughters-in-law is Miss-Why-Can't-We-All-Just-Get-Along? Gracie called me after she and Johnny were married. She insisted he bring her to meet me. It was awkward. Really awkward. But Gracie was well named. She just keeps pouring on the charm and the grace. One letter and photo at a time. She always has the kids send me cards for father's day, my birthday, that sort of thing."

"Do you ever see them?"

"Maybe every other year or so. I'm not really welcome there. Gracie is always gracious. But Johnny, well, like father like son, I guess. He grew up and went his way and we hardly ever see each other. Pretty much the same with my other son, Mickey."

Ellie sighed and let out a long deep breath she hadn't realized she'd been holding.

"No pity expected or wanted," said Liam in response.

"I don't know what to say."

"Then try saying nothing," he said with an edge to his voice she hadn't heard before.

"Look. I told you. Some of my past I'm pretty damn impressed with. I've done things that have made a huge difference in your security, little lady. But on the personal level—not so much. You asked. If you can't take the answers, don't ask the questions."

Ellie was baffled. What was happening to the romantic little getaway Liam had promised? She was watching him morph from the charming Irishman with the twinkle in his eyes and the irresistible grin into a cantankerous, gloomy stranger.

"There's more, but that's it for tonight. Stay tuned for the next exciting adventure in the life of Liam Malone. Bottoms up. Let's go."

That night their entertainment consisted of watching a very old and not very good movie on their in-room television. Liam was sound asleep long before the closing credits.

Ellie turned off the TV and sat staring out over the water for a long time. *What am I doing here? What indeed.* With that she prayed the prayer she so often used to end the day, "Into your hands, O Lord, into your hands I commend this day."

When she woke up Sunday morning Liam was next to her, still wearing most of what he'd had on the evening before. Her offer to go in search of coffee and something to eat was gratefully accepted. By the time she returned a half hour later he was showered, re-dressed in a bathing suit and loud sports shirt, and reading the paper left by their door.

The day passed quickly with more browsing through the shops, lounging on the beach, and a short tour of some of the older points of interest in the area. Liam made no reference to either the conversation or the sudden change in mood from the previous evening. Ellie began to wonder if she'd just imagined it.

That night they shared a bottle of wine and a light, but truly delicious meal in a little restaurant a half-mile walk from the hotel. Whenever Ellie tried to get Liam talking more about his career or his past life, he'd give a shrug and tell her, "That was yesterday. Today, I'm with you and I want to enjoy every moment of it."

Liam swallowed the last bit of wine in his glass and claimed the last bite of the chocolate delight they'd shared for dessert. With that he signaled for the bartender to tally up the total and stood up. "C'mon. The moon's working overtime tonight, Darlin'. It'd be a sin to not enjoy it. Let me take my lady for a stroll along the beach. Then we'll see what we can find to entertain ourselves for our last night here in paradise." He gave her one of his winks that melted away any and all resistance she might have had and took her hand.

As they walked toward the beach she sighed again. This time it was a sigh of contentment.

He's right. All that stuff he told me yesterday was the past. Right now is the present. And it's lovely. Truly lovely. I had no idea there could be moments like this after all the losses.

Later that night they gave themselves over to the passion that had been slowly building all evening.

The next morning Liam woke her up with a cup of steaming coffee and a grin that covered his whole face. "I have a brilliant idea for how we'll spend today."

"And that idea is?"

"For me to know and you to find out soon enough."

"Does it involve having to get out of bed?"

"Well, eventually. But if you're not ready..." He touched her shoulder and winked to indicate he'd be perfectly happy to postpone his plans.

"No, no. I can't. Not again! Not so soon. I'm not a kid anymore."

"You surely could have fooled me. You sure acted like one last night."

Ellie blushed and cursed whatever ancestors gave her the gene that made her blush so easily.

"What's the surprise?"

"I told you. You'll have to wait."

"How long? Please, pretty please, tell me."

"Better than that. I'll show you. Put on some clothes. I am not willing to share this incredible view with anyone else."

A half hour later they were walking toward the shopping area. Liam stopped at a jewelry store. "This is it."

"This is what? Liam, I can't let you keep buying me things. It's just not right. There's no way I can do this for you."

"Well, I know how to fix that."

"How?"

"Marry me."

Ellie stood statue still and gawked at Liam. *Is he serious? Is he joking? Is he mocking me?*

"Ahem, ma'am. I cannot interpret your response. Is that a yes? I do hope so."

"It's a ... a ... I don't know what to say."

"Then say 'yes,' please."

"Don't you think we need to talk about this a bit more?"

"What's there to talk about? I'm crazy about you. You said you miss being a wife. I happen to be in need of a good wife. You are good. You are decent. You are loving. You are everything I had hoped to find in a woman but never thought I would. I do not want you to ever leave me. Just say 'yes.'"

"But what about our families?"

"What about them? Mine don't seem to care if they ever see me again. And from what you've told me about yours, they'll be thrilled that you've found someone who will treat you with the love and respect you deserve."

"Well, I suppose that's true."

"So, will you marry me?"

"Liam, I don't know what to say. I mean, there are so many things to consider. Where will we live?"

"Wherever you want to live."

"What about your career?"

"Finished. I'm down to writing my memoirs."

"And my work?"

"Can't someone else feed the hungry for a while? Long enough for you to get married?"

"This is all so sudden."

"Maybe to you it is. I've been thinking about it since the third night in that writing class."

"You have?"

"Absolutely. Okay. If you're not convinced, let's go find a quiet place where I can try harder to convince you."

They walked over to a fountain surrounded by a low wall and sat facing each other. They sat in silence for a few minutes. Ellie tried to capture every detail in her memory for future reference. The sound of the water cascading down the fountain. The lights shimmering on the water gathered in the pool. The breeze coming in from the ocean. The smell of salt and surf.

Then Liam took Ellie's hands in his own. "I'm not good with the romantic talk. I'm a man of action."

"You do pretty well in *that* department," she said as the dreaded blush started creeping up her neck again.

"Well, thank you. You're not so bad yourself. But what I'm trying to say is, I've made a mess of my personal life. But you don't seem threatened by that. And I know you've been hurt too. So I thought that maybe we could join forces and see if we can't get it right this time. I put up a brave front, but Ellie, I'm tired of being alone. I want to be with someone. And you're the someone I want to be with."

Her eyes began to fill. The fountain behind her wasn't the only source of falling water. *Is this really the second chance I didn't dare hope for? Answer him, woman, before you blow this chance. She thought back to the beach she'd been on less than a year ago—how alone she'd felt then and now this invitation to end the loneliness.*

"Okay."

"Okay? That means yes? Right?"

"Yes. It means yes."

He grabbed her into such a tight hug that she thought she might have a broken rib.

Hand in hand they walked back to the jewelry shop. A half hour and no small amount of American greenbacks later they walked back to the fountain where the new engagement ring caught the sun, sending shoots of colors off in all directions.

CHAPTER SEVENTEEN

These all look to you, to give them their food in due season.
(Psalm 104:27)

The flight back to Cleveland was like a dream. Ellie felt as if she'd been drinking way too much and was trying to push herself through an alcoholic fog—trying to comprehend something just out of range of clear thinking. But she hadn't had anything alcoholic since before dinner last night. This wasn't a bad feeling; indeed, she felt warm and cozy—a bit like being snuggled under a thick comforter on a sub-zero morning.

That sensation dissolved about the time the landing gear came down on the plane. She was suddenly overwhelmed with thoughts about how she'd tell this to her kids. What would they think?! Was she crazy?

As painful as the years since the divorce had been, she'd gradually adjusted to traveling alone on the journey of her life. She'd gotten used to making all the major decisions on her own. She was comfortable now with the easy give-and-take relationships she had with all her children and their families. Marrying Liam would change everything. Everything! Liam liked the idea of just the two of them—that was obvious. How would this work for holidays? Would she ever be able to take a vacation with all her family and Liam? Would she continue her regular long lunches with Cat?

She looked past Liam through the small window at the runway coming closer. He squeezed her hand as the tires hit the tarmac. "Thank you, Ellie," he whispered. "Thank you. We're going to have such good times together."

She smiled back at him but couldn't think of anything to say.

It was an hour before they finally cleared customs, claimed their baggage, and made their way to the parking lot. The closer they got to the front of the line the more jumbled her feelings and thoughts got. Her concerns about the next steps began to grow. *Now what?* she asked herself.

"Liam, I need some time to tell my children. I mean they hardly even know you. And I haven't met any of your family."

"And you probably never will. Take your time. Do you want me to be with you when you tell them?"

"No, I need to do this myself."

"Well, don't dally. I was hoping we could be married by the Fourth of July. I was thinkin' the fireworks would be appropriate," he said with a twinkle in his eyes and a huge grin.

She didn't know if he was joking or serious. His wink indicated he was joking, but his tone of voice said otherwise. "I really want you to come live with me. Or I'll come live with you. Which one do you want? We don't have to wait for the wedding."

Ellie hadn't really thought this through. No matter how many movies and novels declared it normal now for couples to live together without benefit of marriage, she wasn't sure she wanted to try it. For one thing, she didn't want her grandchildren to see her caving in to popular conventions.

Then there was her home. It was *her* home and she loved it. She considered it her recovery house. She'd only lived there a few years, and it was much smaller than the house she gave up after the divorce. But she felt safe there. Lonely—yes—but also safe. She longed for a companion to share the space, but she also treasured the freedom to be completely on her own schedule when she was home alone. She'd added many little touches and now loved coming home to this place. She'd chosen bright, bold shades of green and pink to accent the practical earth-tone walls and floors. Silk flowers in a rainbow of colors filled vases of all sizes and shapes in every room. Live green plants complemented them. The effect gave her a sense of being in a garden while in the comfort of the climate-controlled indoors.

Her backyard was filled with perennials and flowering shrubs. Usually a fragrant aroma greeted her whenever she took her coffee and latest book out to the patio. She didn't want to give this up. Would Liam understand? Could they really share this space?

So she tried to imagine Liam living there too. Her home with its bright colors and many personal mementos artfully displayed throughout was much different than his home. His was a stark, sparsely furnished condo. Liam collected few reminders of his past life. The few things that he did have were mostly professional awards collected through his military career, a few mugs given him by office mates over the years, and a small assortment of photos of his grandchildren. There were no photos of his sons or any of the people who had raised him. Take out the personal photos and items on the "brag wall" and the condo could have been a model waiting for potential buyers to inspect.

"Let me gather my kids together next weekend, and I'll tell them then. I want them all at the wedding. I'll ask them to keep the weekend before the Fourth open."

"Well, Darlin', we can't wait on them. If it works, that's great. I know your family is important to you. But you can't live your life around their calendars. One week, Ellie. And then we set the date, call the preacher, and prepare for our future."

She was puzzled by her feelings. She felt almost like a child again being told by her father what time to get home from a date. *I'm being silly. He's just excited, and he doesn't have any experience with the kind of family life I've known.*

She nodded in agreement before she wrapped her arms around him to move closer for a good-bye-for-now kiss.

"Mmmm. That's more like it," he sighed after they broke away from each other. "Ellie, this will all work out. You'll see. My goal is your complete happiness."

He gave her a quick kiss on the cheek and with a wink he was gone—leaving her standing alone in her living room wondering where this new road would take her.

CHAPTER EIGHTEEN

O give thanks to the Lord, for he is good; for his steadfast love endures forever! (Psalm 107:1)

Evidently her tone of voice when she called each of her children convinced them this was a command appearance. She was up early the next Saturday. The day was devoted to preparing all their favorite foods and inspecting every nook and cranny of her small but comfortable home. She wanted it looking like a featured home in *Better Homes & Gardens* for them. She'd set dinner for five p.m. Her plan was to feed them a good dinner, get them relaxed and comfortable, and then casually over dessert announce she had something important to tell them.

As she sliced and diced her way through the afternoon she wondered why she felt so nervous. *Am I that dependent on their approval?* She realized that perhaps she was. Her family was familiar. Liam was uncharted territory. She loved her family, but they were so busy with their own lives she only got to savor them in bits and pieces. It was like sampling the buffet line but seldom ever really going away satisfied.

Liam seemed prepared to chase the word "lonely" out of her vocabulary. Yet, he had so few happy memories of either the families that raised him or the one he attempted to create as an adult. He seemed to have a "good riddance" attitude toward the people in his family. She treasured everyone in hers. Even, she reluctantly admitted to herself, Chet. Even after all this time, she sometimes still missed him and wished she could find a re-wind button for their lives over the past years since Chet made his big announcement about wanting out. She wished she could send Shirley on a long trip somewhere and talk with Chet about what really happened. She wanted an academy-award-worthy "good-bye" scene with Chet. After all, he had been her leading man for most of her adult life. *Are you trying to fix this again?* She heard both Elaine and Dr. Thorpe's voices in her head, trying to lead her away from the past and push her forward into the future.

She sighed as her many confusing and conflicting thoughts permeated the kitchen along with the smell of the pot roast roasting in the oven. Liam was offering a second chance at love and a settled home life. He'd be a built-in travel companion, and someone to discuss the contents of the daily paper. All the things she missed and wanted more than anything else. Yet, there was this nagging doubt. *It's because I haven't been in this situation for so many years. I don't know how to handle myself.* She finally ran out of time for tossing the pros and cons of a future with Liam back and forth like an endless ping-pong match.

The first car pulled into the driveway. Cat, Jerry and the kids charged through the front door and hugged her. Jerry whistled when he saw the elaborate table set for dinner. "Wow. Is it Thanksgiving?"

"No. Just a mom thrilled to have everyone here together again."

The kids went off to the guest room to see if there were any new treasures for them in the old trunk Ellie had converted into a toy chest. Cat and Jerry helped themselves to the canned drinks in the fridge.

A few minutes later Ike and Jodi arrived with more hugs all around. Almost immediately the kids came out of the guest room to announce they were hungry and bored. As if on cue, Jerry opened the back door and commanded, "Go outside and play until we call you."

A few more minutes passed before Ben, Missy and their family arrived. More hugs all around. More drinks pulled from the fridge. Two more children chased outside.

Ellie dropped the bowl she was carrying to the stove for the rice. Three people tried to grab paper towels to pick up the shattered pieces. Ellie stood there watching as though she were in a trance. Cat gave up her place on the floor and stood up to survey the scene.

"Mom, are you okay? You look, I don't know, sort of weird or something."

"Oh, all of you. Just stop. I need to talk to you. All of you. Right now."

That got their attention. They lined up around the counters of the kitchen and waited. Ellie took in a deep breath and let her jumbled-up thoughts fly out.

"I'm engaged. To Liam. Last weekend. We're getting married the weekend before the Fourth. I want all of you there."

There. She'd said it. The first reaction was total silence. Then awkward glances from one person to another. Finally Ben took the plunge. "Well, this is certainly news! Congratulations. I guess, I mean, we hardly know the man. Are you sure?"

Next Cat ventured an opinion. "Mom, don't you think this is a little quick? What's the rush? You aren't pregnant, are you?"

That got a round of nervous laughs.

"No, I'm quite sure of that. That's about all I'm sure about. And no, I'm not sure at all. But I like the way I feel when I'm with him. I like all the attention he lavishes on me. And I like the idea of having someone my own age to go places with and do things with and cook for and . . . Well, I'm not ready to discuss the rest of this with my *children,* for God's sake."

Cat moved closer to Ellie and gave her a big hug. "Mom, if this is what you want, then of course we'll support you. What do you need from us?"

Ellie started to cry. "I don't know. I guess most of all your approval. I mean, you all mean the world to me. I don't know what I'd have done without you when . . ."

Though she couldn't finish the sentence they all knew she referred to those difficult first months after the divorce.

Ike chimed in, "This calls for a celebration! Is there any champagne in the house?"

"No. I didn't think of that."

Jerry spoke next. "Not to worry. I happen to have several bottles of very good wine in the car. I stocked up this morning and forgot to take it into the house when I got home. Back in a flash."

"So where's the lucky man?" asked Cat. "Shouldn't he be here?"

"I wanted to tell you all first. I wasn't sure how you'd react. I can call him."

"Do that. He's got to take the plunge and dive into the pool of this family life sooner or later," agreed Missy.

A half hour later a freshly showered and shaved Liam arrived at the door, with a bottle of champagne. Dinner went well. Everyone was in a good mood. The food was perfect. The children were happy to be with their cousins. After dinner they were sent off to watch a movie in the guest room.

The adults decided the best way to handle the situation was to talk about everything except the reason they were gathered together. Over the next couple of hours they covered sports—Liam rooted for teams the rest of them rooted against. They discussed politics enough to decide that topic needed to stay off the table. They discussed religion. Liam pledged his support of Ellie's traditions, given he had none of his own. Before Liam arrived, Ellie had given them the head-line version of his childhood and failed previous marriage. So they knew to steer clear of talk about his family.

Finally they landed on stories about places they'd traveled and the interesting people they'd met along the way. Liam could name two exotic places for any one place anyone else discussed. And, he said several times, he planned to take Ellie around the world. It was his dream to get to every continent and now that he had Ellie to go with him, he was ready for the journey to begin.

The evening finally ended when two of the cousins started fighting. Cat announced it was already nine-thirty and time to start shuffling kids home and to bed. A half hour later the last family unit left.

Liam spoke first. "I can't leave you with this mess. Let me help you clean up." A half hour later he took her hand and led her to the couch. Ellie settled in against him, relaxed, relieved, exhausted, and hopeful for the future.

CHAPTER NINETEEN

She opens her mouth with wisdom, and the teaching of kindness is on her tongue. (Proverbs 31:26)

Four days later Cat called to set up a lunch date with Ellie. She minced no words. "Mom, we're all worried about you."

"Oh?"

"We talked after the dinner last Saturday. What do you know, really about Liam? He seems too eager to us."

"How so?"

"Well, you've known him now for how long? Four or five months?"

"Something like that."

"You've not met any of his family."

"I know. His life's been a train wreck. Well, his personal life. But he's done a lot professionally. You should see all the awards he's gotten. He's had his photo taken with some very high-ranking people in the service. And government too. He was a speaker at some White House panel once. And he has a photo of him and the Governor of Virginia where he lived for a while."

"Have you met any of these people?"

"No, but I've seen the photographs. He was even interviewed once by Tom Clancy for one of his books."

"Clancy told you this."

"No, of course not. Liam did."

"And you believed him?"

"Yes, I did. Do you want me to have the FBI do a background check on him? Did you know he's been interviewed by the FBI—and passed—to work on some secret project he was involved in during his Navy career?"

"Okay, Mom. I don't mean to give you the third degree. It's just that, well, we're worried about you."

"And your brothers appointed you the guardian angel to protect me from myself?" Ellie felt her anger starting to build. She didn't want to have to defend her decisions when she wasn't even sure herself. Cat was hitting too close for comfort.

"Not exactly. But we did talk. Look, I've tried to stay neutral about whatever happened between you and Dad. And I appreciate how you've never tried to drive a wedge between us and Dad. But, it certainly looks to me like you got the short end of that stick. I was just sick about all the pain I saw you go through when he left. And I really felt for you when Shirley showed up and sat where you should have been when Grampy died. That was one of the most awkward moments of my life."

"It surely was. I felt like such an outsider—after all those years of sitting at their table for nearly every major holiday every year—to sit in the back pew. Shirley hardly even knew Grampy. I wish I hadn't gone at all. But your Grammy was there for me so many times when your Dad was out of town. After my mother died, she really filled a gaping hole in my life."

Ellie straightened up in her chair and started nibbling at the corn chips and salsa that had appeared on the table. "So, what is it that concerns you so much?"

"Well, as I was saying, I've tried to stay neutral on what happened between you and Dad, but I can't help but think maybe Liam is just a major distraction for you. Maybe the loneliness has been worse than any of us realized. You always seem so confident and cheerful. We thought you were doing really great."

"I was. I am. But that doesn't mean I don't miss having someone in my life. Someone my own age. Someone I can count on."

"That's just it, Mom. How do you know you can count on Liam?"

"I can't. But I thought I could count on your Dad. I trusted him with everything I had. I believed we'd retire together and spend our early retirement years traveling. I was in it for keeps. I'll never understand why he wanted to throw all that away and spend his holidays now with someone else's family. What's wrong with the family we grew together?"

Ellie's voice began to rise. She realized she was clenching her fist under the table.

Cat backed down. "It's okay, Mom. We want you to be happy. Really, we do. And you're an adult. You can certainly make your own decisions. We'll be there for you. We just don't want you hurt any more than you've already been."

"I appreciate that, Cat. I really do. I'm not sure about anything anymore. Once your Dad left me the whole world turned inside out and nothing made any sense any more. I know people end marriages every day—but I never thought mine would be one of them short of a funeral for one of us. But, I can't undo what's been done. I can't stay stuck in this endless limbo.

"I know Liam's a bit odd. I know he's a bit too loud. I know he hogs the conversation. You haven't seen him at his best. He's good to me. He dotes on me. He lavishes attention on me. And, actually, I like that."

Cat grinned. "Okay. Then I guess we have a wedding to plan. Shall we go shopping?"

"I'd like that very much."

CHAPTER TWENTY

Wives, be subject to your husbands, as is fitting in the Lord. Husbands,
love your wives, and do not be harsh with them.
(Colossians 3:18)

Saturday, July 1st, was a beautiful summer day. True to his word, Liam had been a trooper. He'd willingly gone through a short-cut version of premarital counseling with Pastor Elaine. He dodged all conversations about his previous relationships by insisting that was the past and he was ready to forge ahead into the future with Ellie. She thought it was charming and wise. Elaine was restrained through their conversations, which Ellie attributed to her not knowing Liam very well and not wanting to scare him off before he even got started in this new chapter of life.

"I think I'm ready for whatever is to come. And with time and patience—and some time with our family, I think it'll all work out." That's what Ellie told Elaine in their final breakfast before the ceremony.

"I pray you are right," Elaine said. Ellie couldn't quite interpret the tone of her voice—but it wasn't enthusiasm.

The ceremony was brief, but meaningful. All Ellie's family was in attendance. Liam invited several of his friends and two of his neighbors. They all celebrated together at a restaurant after the ceremony. By late afternoon they were headed for the airport for a two-week honeymoon in Hawaii. Liam started each day with a list of options for things they might do and asked Ellie which one she preferred. Each evening they relaxed over some combination of cocktails she'd never tried before. Then they ate in a different restaurant in the resort area of Maui. And each evening they rejoiced in their new life unfolding day by day.

On the last day Liam told Ellie there was something he wanted to discuss with her.

"You don't really need that job at C.A.R.E., do you? I have plenty for both of us. I hate to see you have to work and I don't like how you get so caught up in everyone else's problems. Most of the people you help should be helping themselves. Some of them are just lazy. The rest of them just need to go finish their educations and get a job."

Ellie was stunned. She didn't know what to say or think. Finally she suggested a compromise. "I see your point. But you still like to go back to consult on projects with the Navy and you spend so much time organizing your memoirs. I guess I don't need to work full-time any more. I could talk to Lynette about cutting back to part-time and training another person to fill in when I'm not there."

"That's a start. We'll try it and see how it goes. But I want you available to travel with me. I didn't get married to watch you go to work. I don't intend to schedule our trips around some rinky-dink little do-gooder agency."

"Liam! That is so unfair!"

"What? We're married. We have to come first in each other's lives. You agree with that don't you?"

"Well, yes, but. . ."

"But what?"

"I don't think your attitude toward C.A.R.E. is fair. We do a lot of good for a lot of people."

"For people who ought to be able to do for themselves."

"Like you did?"

"You're damn right. No one gave me anything. I worked for what I have. I worked hard."

"You did indeed. And you've accomplished a great deal. Let's not end our last day here like this. I'll talk to Lynette as soon as we get back. And, we need to move your things into my—er—our house."

"That's another thing, Ellie. Your house is too much upkeep for us. We're going to be traveling a lot. My condo is easier to lock and leave. I think we should sell the house and you should move into the condo."

"What happened to the Liam Patrick Malone I married two weeks ago? Where's this coming from? I thought we agreed we'd live in my house and sell the condo."

"I never agreed. I said I'd think about it. I have thought about it. I don't think it will work."

Ellie felt a heavy, sinking sensation in the pit of her stomach. An icy finger of fear began crawling up her spine. She tried to push away the doubts that were buzzing her like flies at a picnic.

"I don't want to move out of my house. I've been there four years now. I've just gotten the flower beds where I want them. I've re-done the inside. I love that little house. There are neighbors you haven't even met yet who will watch the place while we're gone. Including Chipper."

"I'm not cutting grass in my retirement years. And I don't want to hire someone to do it. We can use that money for our travels."

"Liam. This is unreal. I feel like I'm at a time-share sales meeting with a bait-and-switch scam. I can't talk about this anymore right now. I have to think it over."

"Well, while you're thinking it over, remember what you just promised me two weeks ago. For better or worse. In sickness and in health. To love, honor, and obey. Remember who's the husband here and who's the wife."

Ellie stood up. She grabbed the room key off the shelf by the door and turned to Liam. "I guess we're having our first fight. I'm going for a walk to sort things out. I'll be back in a few minutes."

Liam got up too and started for the door. Ellie put her arm out full length and her hand up at a ninety-degree angle in front of him like a traffic officer might have: "Do not follow me. I'll be back."

With that she walked out the door and down the path that led around the pool and beyond it to the beach. If he had just hauled off and hit her across the face, she couldn't have been more shocked or confused.

She desperately wanted to talk to someone—anyone—but there was no one available. She thought about calling Elaine. Or Ginny. She even considered Cat, but decided she'd have to deal with this one on her own. As she walked down the beach she rehearsed what she wanted to say when she went back. When she thought she'd come up with the right balance of firmness and compassion, she turned and headed back to their unit.

When she walked back in almost exactly an hour after she'd walked out, she found Liam reading a paper and sipping the first drink of the afternoon. Before she could open her mouth, he spoke. "Ellie, I'm so sorry. I don't know what got into me. I guess it's all the excitement of the past few months. My life today is so different than it was a year ago. I just have so many hopes for us, and I'm so eager to get started on them."

"I understand. I do. Let's take this one step at a time. I'll see about reducing my work to part-time. You try living at my house for a while. If it works, we'll sell your condo. If it doesn't work, we'll come up with Plan B. Fair?"

"Sure, whatever you want, Darlin'. I just want you to be happy. I want us to be happy."

CHAPTER TWENTY-ONE

Therefore a man leaves his father and his mother and cleaves to his wife, and they become one flesh. (Genesis 2:24)

A week after their return from Maui, Liam had moved most of his clothes and grooming items into Ellie's closets and bathroom. He had staked a claim in the guest room as his home office. His favorite cooking gadgets cluttered every available inch of counter space, leaving a clear space about the size of an open monopoly board for actual food preparation. He had assembled new metal shelving in the garage for his "guy toys," as he referred to his collection of items Ellie could not identify. He bought a new $1,500 storage unit and had it delivered and assembled in the back yard. When Ellie came home to find the workers finishing up the project, he smiled and told her, "to make more room for the new man in your life."

Ellie grinned and thanked him for agreeing to try living at the house. But she wasn't really sure how she felt about all the changes coming at her so fast. *You can't have it both ways, woman,* she chided herself. *If you want everything just the way you want it, then settle for living alone.* Ultimately she decided the changes were a small price to pay for the new central focal point in her life.

Chipper seemed thrilled to have an extra human around. Liam and Chipper had become good friends. Ellie suspected that was the result of how often she found Liam sneaking forbidden treats to Chipper when he thought Ellie wasn't looking. Whenever she commented on it, Liam would suggest she lighten up a bit and let the dog and his new master have a little fun. "You've done a great job with this dog. He's amazing. I'm just adding a little zest to his life."

Liam was an eager companion on the regular after-dinner-walks Ellie took with Chipper. She had to admit, it was a lot more fun having a human walking companion. They tried a different route every evening. Life seemed to be settling in.

Lynette had quickly agreed that Ellie could reduce her time to three days a week as soon as she trained one of their regular volunteers to take the other two days. They anticipated accomplishing the switchover by the end of August.

The rest of the summer went by in a pleasant mix of work, short day trips with Liam to various sites around the area, and leisurely hours at home. They saw various members of Ellie's family but only in response to Ellie's requests to do so. None of them ever called with an invitation. It was as though they had launched their mother on a journey, anticipating her now being gone from their lives.

Sometimes this bothered Ellie. Most of the time she was too busy keeping up with Liam to think about it. As promised, he started going to worship with her at St. Luke's. However, given that he had virtually no positive contact with any church in his past, he practically paced around the coffee fellowship area until they were out of the building and safely back in the car. She introduced him to others, but Liam seemed to suddenly go shy. Liam! Liam could chat with a stone wall and get a response. Now he was suddenly incapable of finding one thing to contribute to a conversation with others.

Ellie thought he just needed more time to get used to it all. After all, it was very different from the life he'd led. *Time, patience, and lots of TLC, that's the ticket,* Ellie told herself whenever she had one of those nagging second thoughts that maybe marrying Liam hadn't been such a wise decision. *Love conquers all. Who said that? I'm not sure. But we teach and preach all the time that love is the most powerful force on earth. And I do love him.*

Ellie pushed for an all-family gathering Labor Day weekend. This time everyone agreed to gather at her—now their—house Monday for the traditional burgers and trimmings. Liam eagerly agreed and promptly went out and bought enough food to feed three times the number of people anticipated. Ellie kept quiet. She was just grateful to have everyone together again.

The day was pleasant. It was warm, but not hot. The kids were excited to be together with cousins. Ike and Jodi were full of stories about life behind the curtain at the local little theatre. Jodi had a minor role in an up-coming production. She was as excited as if she'd been cast in a Broadway Across America production. She eagerly passed out flyers to everyone. Liam gave her a hug and a peck on the cheek and promised to be at opening night.

Cat and Jerry talked about the fall schedule for their growing family. Ellie was tired just listening to the complicated schedule. She was in awe at all they managed to cram into each hour of every day. But she was also proud of them. They looked healthy and happy, and their children were thriving.

Ben and Missy were their usual relaxed, jovial selves. Little Tony and Erika charmed Liam. So did Cat and Jerry's three: Lucy, Joey, and Annie. Liam had purchased five flavors of ice cream and all sorts of toppings to make them ice cream sundaes. They followed him around like the Pied Piper. From his permanent grin it seemed obvious he was enjoying this new role as winner-of-children's affection.

All in all Ellie thought it was one of the best days of her life. She went to bed that night as content as she could ever remember being. She was safely snuggled against Liam. Just before she dropped into a happy sleep she whispered her current prayer, "Thank you, Lord, for all this. Thank you."

CHAPTER TWENTY-TWO

*O Lord my God, in thee do I take refuge; save me from all my pursuers,
and deliver me. (Psalm 7:1)*

One evening near the end of September she and Liam were carrying
the dinner dishes to the kitchen sink when the phone rang.

"Mom, thank God you're home." It was Ben and he sounded awful.

"Ben, what is it?"

"Mom, we're all at the hospital. There was an accident."

"Oh, my God. What happened?"

"Tony lost his balance on his bike and fell in front of a car."

"Is he okay? What happened to him?"

"No, Mom. He's not okay. Please come."

"Of course. Right away. Which hospital?"

"Lakewood. ER."

"I'm on my way."

Liam could see she was shaken. "Tell me what happened." She told
him what Ben had just told her. "I need to go."

"I'll take you."

"Are you sure?"

"Of course. If you drive, there's likely to be another accident. Let's go."

It was a very long and difficult night for all of them. Little Tony was
breathing with the help of the respirator they'd hooked up to him. His

pulse was weak. His color was about that of the sheets tucked around his frail little body. He had gashes and bruises all over.

After the initial shock of the news began to subside, Ellie looked around at the many staff people coming and going. *Is that Matt?! What's he doing here?*

Matt saw her too. He was wearing the navy blue EMT uniform and had a stethoscope hung around his neck. "Ellie? Why are you here?"

"Tony, my grandson—"

Before she could finish Matt interrupted. "The kid in the bike accident is your grandson?"

"Yes. You know him?"

"No, but I was on the team that brought him in. Oh, Ellie, I am so sorry."

"What can you tell me? Please. I have to know."

"Not much. It's bad. But I've seen kids with worse injuries come through okay. You'll just have to wait for the team to evaluate him. You've got the best there is."

Liam walked up to them. "You two know each other?" he asked with a confused look on his face.

"Matt, this is my husband, Liam Malone. Liam, this is Matt. A friend from another chapter of life." The men shook hands, each eying the other to assess one another's character.

The awkward encounter ended when Matt's partner called for him to get in the ambulance for another call. Now there was nothing to do but settle in to wait. Liam wanted to know more about Matt and his history with Ellie. Ellie wasn't sure she wanted to tell him. She wasn't sure she understood it anyway. In the end she told Liam they'd been in water aerobics class together. "He told me once he might study to be a medic. I forgot about that. This is news to me too." Liam frowned, but didn't say anything more about Matt.

They waited agonizing hours in the waiting room for any shred of new information. Liam went out and came back with bags of burgers and fries no one had the stomach to eat. Cat had called Chet. Around

10 o'clock he and Shirley showed up in the emergency room. Ben and Missy were keeping vigil at Tony's bedside. Cat had gone home to relieve the babysitter and take the kids to her in-laws for the night, since she and Jerry planned to park themselves at the hospital until they knew more. Ike and Jodi were taking a break in the hospital cafeteria when Chet and Shirley showed.

Chet glared at Liam. Ellie averted her eyes from everyone. Shirley finally broke the awkward silence by chirping her thoughts on the situation. Ellie wanted to throttle her when she said, "Well, things like this happen for a reason. God probably needed to teach someone something important."

If Liam hadn't been holding her hand, she might have used it to slug Shirley. Chet sat doing a good imitation of a stone statue. Finally Ellie composed herself enough to take charge of the awkward foursome. "I guess introductions are in order. It looks like we're going to be here for a while. Chet, this is Liam. Liam, this is Chet and his wife, Shirley."

Three people muttered, "Nice to meetcha," like robots in response. They apparently all agreed the silence was superior to the forced civility. Ellie picked up a magazine and turned the pages without absorbing a single word in front of her. Liam took out his iPhone and started downloading sports scores. Chet and Shirley wove their hands together and stared at the floor.

Cat and Jerry returned to the awkward reunion first. "Any word from the doctor?" she asked as if this were a normal gathering of family and not the meeting of the estranged spouses in the middle of a medical emergency.

"No, 'fraid not." They settled in to wait—for what they waited they did not know.

Finally Ben came out into the waiting room. He looked as bad as if he'd been in the accident instead of his son.

They all looked to him in anticipation. "It's not good. He's got a concussion. Several broken bones. A punctured lung. And maybe a kidney that will never work again." With that he fell into a chair and buried his head in his hands. Ellie and Cat sat on either side of him. Soon both were also crying.

Eventually Ben stood up. He looked as if he'd aged ten years in the past few hours. Deep circles had formed under his bloodshot eyes. His amber shaggy hair was strewn every which way.

When Missy came into the waiting room she looked even worse than Ben. She'd done her crying over Tony's bed. She walked toward them as if in a trance. Jerry decided it fell to him to try to organize the family. He suggested they all go home and get some sleep. Ben and Missy agreed everyone should leave and then sat down where they intended to camp out for the night.

Missy's mother tried to get her to leave as well, but she was adamant that she needed to stay there. "What if he wakes up and I'm not here? I'd never forgive myself. You go. I'll call you as soon as we know anything else."

Reluctantly they all moved slowly from the room toward the parking lot. It was one a.m. and still. The moon was nearly full, casting an eerie light on the cars. Ellie thought about the myth she'd often heard about bad things happening during a full moon. She prayed it was just a myth.

She wondered what it meant that even at this moment she was thinking she should be with Chet; Shirley and Liam shouldn't even be there. She pushed the thought aside and reluctantly got into the passenger side of Liam's car. She tried to think if she'd ever had a darker moment in her life; then she decided this one was in line for first place.

Neither she nor Liam knew what to say, so they drove back to the house in silence. They went through the motions of getting ready for bed and dropped into bed next to each other. Liam whispered a quick, "Good night. Sleep tight. Or try to." Before turning off the lamp on the nightstand, Ellie nodded and said, "You too." Liam was sound asleep within a few minutes. Ellie forced herself to lay still and try to sleep. But when she heard the clock on the mantle strike three she gave up the idea of sleep.

She made herself a cup of Chamomile tea, hoping it might help her sleep. She suspected it wouldn't. She thought about calling Elaine. She knew Elaine wouldn't mind . . . but she didn't have the energy to tell her all that had happened over the past few hours. At three-thirty a.m. she was looking for something—anything to read. At four a.m. she remembered she had some over-the-counter sleep aids and went in search of the bottle. At four-thirty a.m. she was back in bed and could feel the effects of the long night and the pill start to pull her under into the sweet release of sleep.

When she woke up it was already eight-thirty. She heard Liam doing something in the kitchen. The smell of coffee motivated her to slip into slippers and wrap a robe around herself. She felt groggy and dazed but couldn't quite figure out why. Then it came back to her.

Tony. Maybe it was a nightmare.

Liam was busy cracking eggs into a mixing bowl when she got to the kitchen. "Liam, I had the worst nightmare last night. I dreamed Tony. . ."

Liam cut her off. "It wasn't a dream. He's in a coma at Lakewood Hospital. We were there ourselves until after midnight. Don't you remember?"

She plopped down in the chair and reached out for the coffee Liam was handing her. "I remember. I was just hoping it was a dream."

"I suppose you'll want to go back to the hospital."

"Yes, of course. But you don't have to go."

"You're in no shape to drive yourself. I'll take you, and then come back to get you when you call me. I hate hospitals."

"No one likes them."

"No, I suppose not. But I really hate them. Besides they'll all like it better if I'm not there. I don't think your family likes me."

"Liam, what are you talking about?"

"You don't see it, but I do. They barely tolerate me. They only do because I'm with you. But I can sense their intense dislike for me."

"Liam, that is ridiculous. And, really, can't we talk about this later?"

"Sure. Later. That's your favorite time to discuss anything. Are there any more former men in your life to meet? That was interesting."

"Can't you see how stressful this is for all of us? Chet is Tony's grandfather. The divorce didn't end that. It was awkward for me too. And I already told you about Matt."

"I'm sorry about Tony, really I am. But think about me—spending hour after hour in a hospital with people who barely acknowledge I exist. I'm sorry he got hurt, but if . . ."

It was Ellie's turn to cut him off. "If what, Liam? Are you suggesting that this was somehow Tony's fault? He lost his balance. He fell. Kids do that, you know."

"If Missy had been watching him better."

"Oh for God's sake, Liam. Please. Don't do this."

"Don't do what? Point out the obvious truth? None of you ever want to deal with reality. You think life is just like one of those TV family sitcoms that have happy endings after an hour. Well, life ain't like that, Ellie."

"Liam, I don't know what's bugging you, but I'm asking you, I'm begging you, please, not now. I'm going to get dressed."

She stood under the shower letting the warm water ease some of the tenseness out of her neck and back. She turned the water off and leaned against the wall, too exhausted, hurt, and confused to make the effort to get out and get on with the day. Not until she began to shiver did she finally step out to grab a towel. She went through the usual morning rituals and finally emerged dressed and a bit calmer.

Liam was eating scrambled eggs and toast. His next words shocked her even more. "I think you owe me an apology."

She stared at him for a full minute before she slowly asked, "For what?"

"We're supposed to be a team now. You're my wife. You're putting all of them ahead of me. I'm your husband. You're not treating me with the respect you should. I think you should apologize to me."

More out of weariness than any sense of regret she murmured, "I'm sorry Liam. It's been a rough few hours. Why don't you stay here and relax. I'm okay to go to the hospital myself. I won't stay long. Maybe I can get Missy to leave for an hour or two if I stay there with Tony. I'll be home in time for lunch. Okay?"

He reached for her and pulled her into his lap. "Okay. That's more like it. I'll have a little surprise for you when you come back."

She had no idea what surprise he might have in mind and didn't really care. She just wanted to get to the hospital and be with her family. And at the moment, away from Liam. She couldn't believe the way he was responding. Like a jealous little boy who just didn't grasp what the rest of the family had to face.

Tony's condition had improved a little in the hours Ellie had been gone. Though Missy wouldn't leave the hospital, she did agree to go with Ben to the cafeteria to eat a decent meal. They hadn't eaten anything that didn't come in a wrapper from a vending machine since lunch the day before.

Ellie was nearly asleep with her head against the wall when she sensed someone sitting down next to her. She turned to see Elaine. Instinctively, she reached out to hug her friend. "How'd you know?"

"Why, it's my job to know these things," she said. Then added, "Cat called me. She was worried about you as much as Tony. I've checked in with the nurse's station. He's had a tough time of it, but they say youth and all of you are on his side. I've already put your family on the St. Luke's prayer chain. And I brought you something."

She reached into the over-sized bag she used as a purse and pulled out a small knit afghan.

"What's this?" asked Ellie as she felt the soft wool.

"A prayer shawl. We have a group of women who get together once a week to make them. I have a supply on hand to distribute as needed. This one's for you. We have one for Tony too, when he gets into a room.

"Thank you."

They talked quietly for a few minutes. When Ben and Missy came back, Elaine gave each of them a hug. She told them about being on the prayer chain and asked if they'd like to let people start bringing food to the house. The offer was declined. Elaine gave Ben her card and told both of them to call anytime they wanted to talk or they changed their mind about the food brigade.

"I can tell you from firsthand experience when my late husband was dying that these people can cook. Do you mind if I drag your Mom away for a bit? I suspect, she hasn't eaten anything for a while either."

By then Cat was coming into the waiting room. Ben, Missy, and Cat all agreed Ellie needed time to talk to Elaine and eat something more than she needed to sit and wait.

Elaine was never one to drop subtle hints and today would be no exception. She suggested they stop by the chapel to have a little privacy so she could pray for the family, and especially Tony. Ellie was amazed how much lighter she felt by this simple gesture. She immediately felt less helpless and hopeless. She wished her children would avail themselves of this opportunity, but knew better than to push it on them. Especially, not now. She and Elaine had talked about that too, many times. "Sometimes when we say we pray for someone that means we pray in their place because for whatever reason, they aren't able to pray for themselves. You keep praying for all of them. Just remember, there's one prayer in particular that God likes to hear: 'Your will be done.' God's will is always that all the children would come home and gather round the table."

After the stopover in the chapel they headed to the cafeteria. The smell of the bacon frying on the grill made Ellie aware of how hungry she was. It seemed wrong to be hungry when Tony was unconscious and in serious condition. At least he'd been upgraded from critical to serious.

They'd barely gotten seated in a booth in the far corner of the café when Elaine jumped in. "Ellie, are you okay? I mean with Liam. Of course you're not okay about Tony. But there's nothing more we can do about him for the moment. I'm just wondering how life in the newlywed game is going for you."

Ellie didn't say anything. Partly out of loyalty to Liam, who was after all, now her dearly beloved husband. And partly because she honestly didn't know if she was okay or not. The little spurts of anger she had experienced confused her. But she thought they were all part of two older adults adjusting to a new relationship. Finally she asked, "What makes you ask?"

"Well, he seems, I don't know, maybe a bit demanding? Or determined to get his way. I know you haven't been married very long and I know it takes time to adjust to a new marriage. But when I see you together, you both seem a little—tense or something."

Ellie didn't say anything. Instead she pushed her omelet around the plate.

"I don't really think that needs any more mixing. Looks pretty cooked to me," said Elaine. "Look, I'd like to consider myself a safe place for you to say anything. I know it gets confusing sometimes sorting out if I'm your friend or your pastor. I should probably send you off to some other pastor for these sorts of conversations. But the bottom line is I care about you. Deeply. You have been there for me so many times in my life. Let me return the favor."

Ellie sighed and took in a deep breath. "The bottom line is: I'm not sure. I have come to really love him. He does the most remarkable things for me. He spoils me and you know what? I have discovered I *like* being spoiled once in a while. We really do have fun together. But sometimes, well, he didn't have much of a childhood. His marriage fizzled. His kids hardly ever contact him. So I think all the together time I have with Cat, Ben, Isaac, and their kids overwhelms him. He's included, of course. And he and the grandkids have hit it off okay. But it is awkward with my kids. They are polite. But that's as far as it's gotten. Maybe too polite. Liam thinks they don't like him."

"Understandable."

When Elaine didn't say anything else, Ellie continued. "It's like he's jealous or something. I thought he'd enjoy having a family around. But he seems to only tolerate them. It's like he just wants me to be with him all the time. He always seems nervous about having any of them around."

"Uh huh."

Ellie debated how much more to say. It felt good to confide in someone. At the same time she felt like she was betraying Liam.

"Ellie, it's only been a few months. May I make a suggestion?"

"Sure. What?"

"First, try not to decide anything one way or another until you know what's going to happen with Tony. That's a huge deal right there. Then, keep a notebook. Day by day rank how you feel about married life on a 1 to 10 point scale. 1 being the pits. 10 being pure bliss. Warning, no marriage I ever heard about ever gets to 10 more than once in a blue moon. But 7's and 8's are pretty common in good marriages. And jot down a word or two about what made each day whatever number you assigned it."

"Seems a little cold to me."

"Not really. It's hard to trust our feelings. They are so fickle. Up one day. Down the next. But over time patterns emerge. Those patterns are very helpful when it comes time to decide what to do next. Don't try to analyze too much. Just track for a while. Give it a month. Think of it like tracking your internal weather system. Sunny on Tuesday. Overcast on Wednesday. Stormy on Thursday and so on."

"And what exactly am I supposed to do with this weather report?"

"Nothing for now. Just track it. We'll talk again in a month. Of course, you can call me any time between now and then—and I expect you to do so as we wait for Tony to heal."

Ellie returned to find that Tony had been moved from the ER to a bed in ICU. The nurse who told her this said if she hurried she'd be allowed to see him for a few minutes during family visiting hours.

Ellie was unprepared for the sight that greeted her. Tony lay still and very white under a thin blanket. Machines hummed all around him. There seemed to be tubes from every part of his frail little body connecting him to monitors. She had to clench her teeth to keep from gasping.

It was hard to even see Tony for the ring of people surrounding him. Ben and Missy stood on either side at the head of the bed. Next to them were Missy's parents, also on each side of the bed. Tony's sister, Erika, was next to her other grandmother. Ellie took her place across from Erika and gently patted Tony's still hand.

After a few minutes of hushed comments back and forth about how he looked they heard a soft moan. Instinctively Ellie put two fingers inside Tony's loose fist. She nearly jumped when she felt pressure against her fingers. "I think he's squeezing my hand!" she exclaimed.

The family quickly rearranged themselves so that Ben and Missy were each holding one of Tony's hands. They kept whispering, "We love you, Tony. Come back to us. Tony, we love you. Please, baby, come back." There was no further response from Tony. Soon a nurse appeared in the room to check his vitals and record the data from the machines. "I'm sorry, but you'll need to go now. He needs his rest. I suspect all of you do too. He's stable. Still not out of the woods. But stable. He's going to be sleeping for a long time. We'll let him just rest today. Tomorrow we'll start doing mild physical therapy with him, so he doesn't get bed sores, and his muscles don't forget how to work."

Erika asked the question the adults were afraid to ask, "You mean he'll be awake tomorrow?"

"Maybe. Maybe not. Or he might be a bit of both. But we'll make him move even if he's still asleep." She smiled at Erika. "I see too many accidents like this that could have been avoided. Or at least the injuries reduced if only the kids had been wearing helmets. Considering he wasn't wearing one, he came through pretty well. I wish I had a way to make kids wear helmets." With that she shooed them out of the room and went about checking on her patient.

Chapter Twenty-Three

For with much wisdom comes much sorrow; the more knowledge, the more grief. (Ecclesiastes 1:18)

Ellie decided she might as well head home, hoping maybe Liam would be pleased if she came back earlier than she'd planned. It would be several hours before they'd be allowed to see Tony again.

As she walked past the nurse's station, she overheard one of the staff tell Chet he'd missed visiting hours and would have to come back later. She noticed he didn't have Shirley with him.

They had to cross paths to get to the elevator. Chet spoke first.

"Do you want to get some coffee? Get away from all this for a while?" Ellie blinked rapidly and noticed her breath seemed stuck at this unexpected invitation.

"Shirley won't give you grief?"

"Do you really care? Or are you being sarcastic? Anyway, she's not here and I wanted to talk to you alone."

Ellie felt the familiar stones collecting in her gut and the heat rising up her neck toward her ears. *I hate this. I never know what to say. Or if I should say anything.* "You caught me off guard. Last I knew you never wanted to see me again."

Chet's focus shifted from Ellie's face to her feet. "I know. I said some awful stuff. You didn't deserve it."

They looked at each other again as he continued, "Consider this a white flag. I thought maybe we could try a normal conversation while we're in the midst of this rotten situation."

Ellie conceded. "We're both really worried about Tony. I guess Ben and Missy have enough to worry about without us adding to the stress." She still felt tight like a bow before it released the arrow, but at least he was being civil to her for a change.

Chet's jaw relaxed as he said, "You're right about that. Ben and Missy look like the car ran over them instead of Tony. So, coffee? I'll treat."

Fifteen minutes later they sat across from each other at a tiny table in the hospital's busy cafeteria. Each stared into a Styrofoam cup of coffee. Ellie busied herself carving notches along the rim of her cup. Chet cupped his hands around his while shifting through several positions in his chair. Finally he took in a long breath and started their first private conversation in over four years. The last one had only escalated the tensions between them. "Ellie. I'm sorry. That's really all I have to say. I'm sorry it didn't work out."

Ellie squeezed her eyes, trying to contain the tears that threatened to overflow onto her cheeks. She listened to the clatter of dishes on trays and the muffled sound of a hundred conversations all around her. Her heart was racing. Her chest felt too full like it might pop. She felt light headed as she finally spoke. "I've—that is—you see—"

Chet tightened his grip on his cup, but said nothing. A full minute passed before Ellie found the courage to forge ahead. "I've wanted this conversation for such a long time. I still don't know what happened between us. But I know I'll always wish whatever it was didn't happen. But—and this is a big but . . ."

Chet grinned a little and Ellie gave in to a tentative smile at the corny line they had so often bantered back and forth in their happily married days. "But I think I understand now some things I didn't before. I can see how often I failed to let you know how much I appreciated your sacrifices for me and the children. I can see how you might think I wasn't interested or never satisfied." She clasped her hands together on her lap under the table to rein in her sudden impulse to reach out for his. "I regret that. Very much."

Silence sat between them like a heavy morning fog. They sat inches away from each other, staring at the table top like some Impressionist scene titled, "Impasse."

Ellie broke the silence. "It's too late to go back. I'm not sure I would even if we could. I never knew I could cry that much. I lost a year of my life when you left. I didn't think I'd survive. For a long time I didn't know if I wanted to." Ellie looked up and saw a glimpse of the old Chet—the one who used to make her feel settled and at home.

"I wasn't thinking we'd ever get back together. I was just sorta hoping. Maybe this was a bad idea. It's just that—well, now with Tony and all —well, not speaking seems pretty petty and stupid. You're here without Liam. Shirley's not here. I sort of thought maybe . . ."

Ellie interrupted. "I've hated how awkward it is when we're thrown together at family things. I hate it too when you don't come to something because you think I'm going to be there. She paused, gripped her hands together even tighter, drew in a deep breath and finally gave wings to the words she'd played over and over in her head for years. "I want you to know—I never quit loving you. I guess you just quit believing that—or you quit caring." *There. I finally got to say it.*

More silence. But this silence felt more like a quiet pre-dawn summer morning. Finally Chet spoke. "I think I know that now. I didn't back then. I felt so far away from you. Being in the house but not really being with you—well, being alone was better. I didn't expect anything from an empty apartment, so I wasn't disappointed when I came home at night to nothing. I know I hurt you. I'm sorry."

The silence settled over them now like a warm blanket on a chilly evening. Ellie crumpled her empty coffee cup and looked up at Chet. "We did have a lot of good years together. I try to focus on those and fast forward through those last few."

Chet tapped his cup on the table. Ellie knew from years of experience he was as nervous as she was. "For a long time I was really pissed at you. I hated everything about you and everything that reminded me of you."

I figured out that much. I never did understand why. She asked, "What changed?"

"Shirley. Well, rather, her reaction. Her jealousy and resentment of you were contagious. I caught it. But I finally figured out you weren't so bad. You did a great job with our kids. You really did. I won't leave Shirley, but I no longer listen to her when she starts railing against you. I wanted you to know that."

More silence.

Chet continued. "That's what I wanted to tell you—I want to call off the cold war between us. I want us to not be enemies anymore."

Ellie's face was streaked with the tears she could no longer hold back. The pain of what they had and lost hit again nearly as deeply as the day he drove away. "I don't know. This seems too weird. It's what I thought I wanted. But now that you're offering it to me, I don't know if I can accept it. I don't know what I want or how I feel. I would like it to be a lot less awkward between us."

Chet nodded. Ellie continued. "Maybe we just have to settle for admitting there's a big wound that's never going to go away so we have to learn to live around it. Maybe it's enough if we both admit we held the knife that slashed what we used to have."

"Yeah, I guess that's right."

They sat in silence a few more minutes. Then Ellie said, "I think it's time to go back upstairs. Whatever else we did or failed to do, now it's about Tony. You were a good father, Chet. Really. I'm grateful for that. And—I'm glad you're here now."

Chet nodded and stood up. "Ellie?"

She turned to face him. "Yes?"

"Thanks. I know that's not much—but thanks."

"You're welcome. I think we should go our separate ways now. It'll be less awkward, don't you think? If Shirley or Liam came in while we've been down here."

"Yeah, I suppose so. I'm glad we got to talk. I'm worried sick about Tony."

Ellie took in a deep breath and nodded. "Me too." Then she headed to the women's room. She pushed the door open and looked back to see Chet enter the elevator.

A few minutes later she ran into Cat coming in as she was leaving. "We wondered where you went. Then Dad said you were down here."

Ellie tried and failed to read Cat's expression as she continued, "Well? Are you going to tell me or do I have to imagine what just happened?"

Ellie sighed and wrapped her arms around Cat. "I'm not sure. But, I want you to know something. Your father was a good father. Hang onto that, okay?"

"I will. Mom, just so you know, while you were down here talking to Dad, we were all upstairs talking about both of you. We all approve."

"Of what?"

"Of whatever way you and Dad decide to be together or not be together in the future. We still love you both. Neither of you can change that."

Ellie let go of Cat and headed back to the sink to wipe away the new round of tears. She patted Cat on the shoulder. Then she headed to the elevator, leaving her daughter behind in the restroom. Once secure in the privacy of the empty elevator she shook her head and prayed again for Tony. *Tony—you have to get better. You have to live to see how your accident is bringing this family back together again.*

Chapter Twenty-Four

A gentle answer turns away wrath, but a harsh word stirs up anger.
(Proverbs 15:1)

Ellie pulled into the driveway at twelve-fifteen. Liam was busy making grilled cheese sandwiches. He asked no questions about Tony's condition. He listened politely, but with little real interest, when Ellie gave her report. After a few minutes, he asked, "How long do they think he'll be hospitalized?"

"I have no idea. He's not even awake yet. But they think he will be soon. Apparently all his injuries are ones that will heal with time, TLC, and some physical therapy."

"Well, that's a relief. Hope next time he's bright enough to put on a helmet. Or his parents have the moxie to make him wear one."

Ellie had thought the same thing, but decided this wasn't the best time to say so. She didn't know what to say in response, so she nodded and bit into her sandwich.

"Ellie, there's something I need to talk to you about."

"Okay. I'm listening."

"I want to be perfectly clear that I am not the solution to the medical bills this is going to rack up. I'm happy to support you—and I will through anything. But I didn't sign on to bail out your kids and their kids."

Ellie stared at him for a long time before she spoke. She realized she had her sandwich halfway to her mouth. She set it down and looked at him. She was trying to decipher what she saw in his face but couldn't read him.

"I don't think anyone even thought you should. They have their own insurance. I didn't marry you for your money. And I'm confident my children don't think I did either. But I do find it odd that this is what you want to talk about less than twenty-four hours after he was nearly killed in an accident."

"Well, I have to stay ahead of the curve. This wouldn't be the first time someone saw me and started seeing dollar signs. I just want to be clear. That's all. Anyway, maybe they ought to go after the driver of the car that hit Tony. He should have been able to steer clear of him."

"I really don't like the way this conversation is going. I'm getting a terrific headache from the lack of sleep last night and all the worrying about Tony. If you don't mind, I'm going to take a nap."

"Would it matter if I did mind?"

"You're joking, right? Trying to add a little levity to the situation?"

"Sure. Of course," he said backing down just a bit from his harsh tone of a moment before. "Sleep tight. Shall I wake you after a while?"

"Well, if I'm not up in time for bed, yes, sure, that'd be a good idea."

She tossed and turned for perhaps a half hour before she finally drifted off into a restless sleep. She was dreaming about something when she felt a hand on her shoulder. "Ellie, come on. It's time to wake up." She opened her eyes slowly and tried to remember where she was.

She was in her own bed. Liam was standing before her. It was bright daylight outside. Then it came to her. She remembered Tony and sat up with her feet over the side of the bed.

"What is it? Did they call? Is there news about Tony?"

"No, none of that. It's just that you've been back here an hour already, and I thought if you slept any longer you won't be able to sleep tonight. Besides, I need to go out and I thought you'd want to go with me. Maybe take a break from the hospital. I'm going to Hale's Book Shop."

The last thing Ellie wanted was to go with Liam on one of his excursions to the book store. The man could spend hours wandering up and down the aisles, "looking for inspiration," as he put it.

"Oh, Liam. I'm not really up for that. How about you drop me back at the hospital? I'll either get someone to bring me home or you can come get me when you're ready."

His frown told her he wasn't pleased with her answer, but he didn't challenge her decision. He just shrugged and waited for her to get up. They were quiet on the short ride to the hospital. She gave him a peck on the cheek and wished him well in his search for whatever he was researching today. "I'll call you if I get a ride home. Otherwise, I'll be in the ICU waiting room on the third floor."

"Okay. Good luck. Hope the little guy's doing better. Give my love to them all."

"I will," she said as she hurried toward the front door.

She had to walk past the gift shop on the way to the elevator. She went in to see if there was one of those helium balloons. Then she realized they might not let him have it in his ICU room. Finally she decided it was worth the chance. She bought the brightest one she could find with a big "Get Well Now!" imprinted on it. While waiting her turn to pay she spotted a row of journal type books. She picked up one with a photo of a beautiful garden on the front and back. It contained only blank pages. She remembered Elaine's suggestion from their breakfast—was it really just a few short hours ago? She walked out with the new journal book in her purse and the balloon floating high above her head.

Missy greeted her as soon as the elevator doors opened. "I'm so relieved to see you," she said as she folded herself into Ellie's arms.

"Has something changed? It's only been a few hours since I was here."

"Yes, and I don't know if it's good news or not. They want to do surgery—now."

"Surgery?! Why?"

"The swelling in his brain isn't coming down as fast as they want. They want to do something to reduce it."

Ellie sucked in a deep breath. Suddenly the balloon floating high over her head seemed ridiculous. As did the journal tucked in her bag. With a heaviness that felt like carrying concrete blocks she faced the reality that Tony might die, or worse, never come back to a normal childhood again. The thought hit her with a physical force. She forced herself to focus on Missy's panic-stricken face.

"Let's go sit down."

Though Missy and Ben hadn't attended worship services beyond an occasional Easter and Christmas Eve in years, Missy readily agreed when Ellie suggested they call Elaine. Ellie called Elaine while Missy called Ben to let him know his mother was there. Ben was on his way back to the hospital after delivering Erika to a neighbor. Ben and Missy had agreed there was nothing Erika could do for her brother and spending so many hours waiting was an unfair burden on her.

As Ellie had hoped she would, Elaine said she'd be there within the hour to pray with all of them before Tony's surgery. Next Ellie debated whether to call Liam. She realized she wasn't sure if she even wanted him with her. But she also didn't want to exclude him—he was her husband now. Tony was now part of his family too.

In the end Liam made the decision for her. "I'm really not comfortable in hospitals, Ellie. Besides, there's nothing I could do. I'll put in a plug for you from here. Call me when you want to come home."

She excused herself to the women's room after she hung up. She didn't want to let Missy see her crying. She had enough of her own stress to manage. Ellie was confused by her reaction. She was actually relieved Liam didn't want to be there. It freed her up to focus totally on Ben and Missy in their nightmare. Yet, she also felt let down and disappointed that Liam felt so free to focus on his discomfort when Tony's very life was on the line. She swept the doubts about Liam and their marriage back into the corner of her mind.

After a little cool water on her face and the warm blow dryer air on her hands she began to feel up to the long afternoon of waiting. *Thank God Elaine's coming.*

Something about the way in which Elaine talked to the nurses' station convinced them to let Elaine, Ben, Missy and Ellie all gather around Tony's bed. It all seemed so surreal seeing his miniature body lying limp against the sheets. The constant humming of the machines monitoring his bodily functions played like background music. There was also the constant background noise of phones ringing, medical staff conferring, other patients snoring, coughing, or moaning. An antiseptic smell permeated the area.

Elaine suggested they each gently lay one hand on Tony while she prayed. "Dear and gracious Lord, you gave Tony his life and now you hold his life in your hands. We ask that you guide the team that will soon cut into his frail physical body. We pray for patience in our time of waiting. We pray for hope for his loved ones who come to you now seeking help, hope, and restored health for this child. We know he is even more precious to you than to all of us. Into your hands we commend Tony's future. Thank you for being here with him and with us. Amen."

They stood together in silence for what seemed a long time, but in reality was only another minute or two.

Then Elaine gently suggested they return now to the waiting room so the staff could finish preparing Tony for surgery.

Time crawled in the waiting room. Elaine stayed with the family for another half hour and then excused herself after asking Ellie to call her as soon as they heard anything or Tony was in a recovery room.

The three tried to talk, but none had words to express their worst fears and deepest hopes. Talking about anything else seemed somehow disrespectful or inappropriate. So mostly they sat. Every once in a while Ellie would flip through a magazine, never actually seeing the words on the paper. Ben found excuses to wander off every twenty minutes or so. He'd come back with coffee no one bothered to drink; or a snack of some kind that no one wanted to eat.

At eight-twenty-seven a young man dressed in scrubs approached them. "I'm Dr. Steward. I helped with Tony's surgery. He's in the recovery room now. The surgery went very well. He's still not conscious, but we're hopeful the surgery will relieve the pressure. We're hoping he'll come around within the next day or so."

Missy and Ellie burst into tears of relief. Ben's eyes watered too.

"We're confident he's going to be okay, but it's going to be a long road back to health. I want you to make an appointment with Dr. Sharif. He's a neuropsychologist. Tony's likely to have some long-term neurological issues. He's also likely to have some psychological issues. Dr. Sharif can do an evaluation of his case now—before Tony even begins his recovery. That will lay the foundation for whatever comes up in the future."

He sounded so cool and removed . . . like he was discussing what might be showing at the theatre next weekend—instead of the future of a little ten-year-old child.

"What kind of things?" asked Ben.

"The brain is an amazing thing. It can store thousands of bits of information. But when there's been a trauma like this, those bits of information can get mixed up. His short-term memory might not be good. It could be temporary—or it might be something he'll have to deal with for the rest of his life. He might also have to relearn things like math or writing."

"What else?" asked Missy with more force than she'd intended.

"He might have impulse-control issues. He might become a bit difficult to manage. The part of his brain that should help him monitor his actions might be compromised. Look, at this point, this is all speculation. I'm just telling you what we've sometimes seen in patients who've had similar injuries. Dr. Sharif can help you sort through all this."

As he turned to leave, Ellie thought to ask, "When can we see him?"

"In about another hour or so. The anesthetic will start wearing off then. But don't expect him to be awake. That may take another day or so. You can call the nurses' station on Five. We're moving him into a Neuro ward when he leaves recovery. He should be there around ten o'clock."

CHAPTER TWENTY-FIVE

The heart of the discerning acquires knowledge; the ears of the wise seek it out. (Proverbs 18:15)

Ellie saw his feet first. She was staring at the floor of the waiting room near Tony's new room assignment. When the feet stopped in front of her, she slowly looked up to see Matt standing there in his Medic uniform. "I've been keeping track of Tony's progress," he explained. "I thought Grandma might appreciate a friendly face."

"Thank you. It's rough. I'm so scared."

Matt sat next to her and took her hands in his. "Of course you are. You'd be weird if you weren't. But he *is* in good hands. The best. He's young and resilient. I've seen kids with worse injuries go on to do amazing things."

"I hope you're right."

"Me too. So, where's the new husband?"

Ellie frowned. She wondered if Matt noticed it, but he didn't comment. "He's, well, he was here. But..."

Matt finished her sentence. "He doesn't do hospitals?"

"Yeah, something like that."

"Sadly, a lot of guys have that reaction. Especially men who are used to being in control of situations. The doctors have most of the control around here. It must be tough on you being here without him."

Ellie was surprised at Matt's assessment of the situation. He had just summed up what she had been thinking, but dared not say out loud—or even really to herself. The implications were too immense. She was still in "defend Liam" mode with her family and even with herself.

Matt continued. "He presents himself as a fairly confident man-about-the-world guy, so I suspect hospitals really challenge him." Matt laughed and added, "I could tell he was really pissed I knew you. If only he knew."

"Knew what?"

"Ellie, I feel I owe you an explanation. I had a wonderful time that night we went out to dinner. You have no idea how not in danger you were with me."

"What do you mean?"

"I prefer men."

Ellie was speechless.

"Did I shock you?"

"Yes, you did."

"Sorry. There's no good way to announce it. I figured you hadn't figured it out, and I wanted you to know. That's why I never called after that night. It was a fun, relaxing evening, and I needed that very much that night. So, thank you, Ellie—for just being you."

Ellie nodded and murmured, "You're welcome. Thank you."

"You remind me of my sister, who is, for the record, the only one in my family who is even speaking to me since I came out. Which is what I did about a week before I ran into you. You, dear Ellie, were like a breath of fresh air. You did me a world of good. And, also confirmed what I already knew. I prefer men."

"Why are you telling me this?"

"Let me count the reasons. One: This is a rotten break to have Tony here like this. I wanted to just stop by and give you a word of encouragement about him. Two: You are a very decent woman and I thought I owed you an explanation for why I never called. I felt like I had to say something."

Ellie stared at Matt but said nothing. Matt continued. "There's one more thing; I don't know if you're disappointed or not; but I am that

Liam can't—or won't—put his dislike of hospitals aside to be here for you. Seems odd to me."

Ellie had been thinking the same thing, but hadn't allowed herself to say so—even to herself.

"That's a lot to absorb. I need to go home now. It's been a hell of a day and I ache everywhere."

Matt responded, "I'm off duty now. How about I drive you home?"

"Thanks, but I don't think that'd be such a good idea. My son, Ben, will take me. I want to try to get him away from here for a few hours anyway. But, thank you, Matt. Thank you."

"You're welcome. Here's my card. Call me if you ever need anything. Anything at all."

"Okay," she said as she tucked the card in her purse.

CHAPTER TWENTY-SIX

I wait for you, O Lord; you will answer, O Lord my God.
(Psalm 38:15)

Ben drove Ellie home at nearly midnight. He was going back to the hospital to keep vigil with Missy but insisted that Ellie would be more help if she got a decent night's sleep. She tried but failed to get Ben to take a break himself. Actually, she was proud of him—and Missy. Tony had that going for him.

She walked into a dark house. There was one light on over the kitchen stove. Chipper woke up when he heard her. She was relieved to see a friendly face, even if it was on a dog. She picked him up and squeezed him so hard he yelped. She let him out for a minute and then sent him back to his bed with a biscuit for good measure. The house was quiet. Too quiet.

She heard Liam's snoring as she approached the bedroom. She quickly prepared for bed herself and crawled in next to him. He never even stirred. Though she was exhausted from the drama of it all, she couldn't fall asleep. She went through all her usual tricks to try—various mental images and memory games—but none of them worked. After an hour she gave up and got up.

Not knowing what else to do, she made a cup of Chamomile tea. This was becoming a regular habit. When it was ready she carried it to the den and folded herself into her favorite overstuffed chair. During the day she loved to gaze out the window of this room into her back yard. She'd planted flowers such that there was something of color nearly all year long. But in the night all she saw was her own reflection in the darkened window.

She decided this was as good a time as any to try using the journal she'd bought—was it really only a few hours ago? It seemed like a year had passed since her trip through the gift shop.

Here I am. Middle of the night and no sleep in sight. I'm so scared about Tony. I feel so helpless. Dear God, Please! Help him.

And me. I don't know what to do about Liam. Is this just adjusting to a new marriage? It wasn't like this with Chet at first—but I was so much younger then. Maybe I'm too wounded to love someone else. Maybe Liam's too wounded to let anyone love him. I am so confused. And so ashamed to be in this place. I don't know what to do or who to even talk to about it. But this can't go on.

Finally the tea's calming effect worked its way through her system and she began to feel drowsy. She was too tired to make the short trip to the back of the house and her own bed. Instead she moved from the chair to the couch and pulled the afghan off the back of it to cover herself. Within a few minutes she was sound asleep.

The next sound she heard was that of water running. She opened her eyes and tried to remember where she was. Once she realized she was on her own couch she tried to remember why. It all came back to her with a great heaviness. Tony. Liam. One so young and vulnerable. The other so much older and so confusing to her.

She stretched and got up. Liam was sitting at the breakfast table with the morning paper while the coffee was brewing.

Without looking up, he asked, "How's Tony?"

Ellie realized she wasn't sure she wanted to share any of the intensity of the last night with this man. If he didn't care enough to be there with them—or even put down his paper now—she wasn't sure he deserved to be included. As horrible as the situation was for all of them—it was also an event that was binding them together into an even tighter network of emotions and hopes they dare not speak aloud. It was like an initiation rite to be endured for the sake of being truly connected to one another. Though they didn't think about it, their willingness to endure the emotional agony was how one got into the inner core circle of intimacy with each other. Liam had opted out.

She settled on the short version. "He came out of surgery around eight-thirty and was heading into a room on the Neuro floor when Ben brought me home last night."

"What time did you get home?"

"Hmm, I guess right around midnight."

"Oh," he said without looking up.

"Liam, is something wrong?"

"Don't you think that's a bid of an odd question to ask given the circumstances?" His voice sounded hard and criticizing.

"I mean, is something wrong with *you*?"

"No, *I'm* fine. But *you're* not." He put down the paper and looked at her. "You've got to accept that you're married now. Of course, you're concerned about your grandson. However, he does have parents. Two of them. You don't need to be there around the clock like this. Maybe this is why Chet left you. Did you do this to him too? Or maybe you were hoping to see that Matt guy again. Was he there? Is that why you can't tear yourself away from the hospital?"

She felt like someone had just punched her in the gut. Before she could formulate any response he continued, "I'm not going to tolerate this, Ellie. You've got to make a choice. It's me or them. I didn't marry a tribe. I married you." His voice was getting louder and more intense. "I expect you to be a proper wife to me and show me the respect and attention I deserve."

She felt utterly alone and totally incapable of defending herself. There were so many things she wanted to say but lacked the courage and the energy to say anything. Though she willed herself not to do so, she began to cry. At first the tears came in a silent slow release over her eyes and down her cheeks. Gradually their intensity increased until she sat crying out all the fear and frustration of the past few days. The terror of possibly losing Tony for good or at least the good-natured happy-go-lucky little guy they all loved. All, except apparently, Liam.

Liam sat like a statue watching her cry as though she were some sort of science experiment unfolding in front of him. He offered no consolation either in words or gestures. He sat like a defiant child who'd just been told the cookie supply was being cut off.

Finally she pushed herself into a standing position and without a word headed back to the bedroom. The tears continued to flow along with the hot steamy water of the shower. She tried to force herself to think. But her mind was too battered from a combination of exhaustion and confusing emotions to respond.

When she was finally cried out she dressed and calmly walked back out into the kitchen where Liam was still sitting reading the paper.

"Liam, I don't expect you to understand what this has been like for me. How could you? You've had so little contact with family in your life. But if you insist on making me choose between you, whom I've known for less than a year, or my family that I've known for all of their lives and many years of my own life, I assure you, you will come out on the losing side of that choice. I'm going back to the hospital now. I'm going to pretend this conversation never took place. I'll be back in time for lunch."

And with that she grabbed her purse and walked out the door.

CHAPTER TWENTY-SEVEN

In God I trust; I will not be afraid. What can man do to me?
(Psalm 56:11)

As she had anticipated, Ben and Missy were still there. Both looked terrible. She convinced them to go home to sleep and spend some time with Erika who had to be worried and confused and needing her parents. She promised to stay until one of them came back.

As the elevator closed with them inside, she walked down the hall to Tony's room. She stood by his bedside a long time watching his chest gently rise and fall with each breath. He was still in a very deep sleep but at least he was breathing on his own. She offered up her prayers of gratitude for this step toward recovery. She stroked his reddish blond hair gently and thought about her own uncertain steps toward recovery.

My life is so different today than what I thought it'd be. Why did Chet really leave? Did I abandon him? I loved him. I truly did love him. I think I still do in spite of everything. I'm glad we got to talk. I do feel less awkward about it all now. But what about Liam? What have I gotten myself into? He treats me so well sometimes. Then he flips over and pulls a stunt like this morning. Does he have a point? Am I too focused on my family to make room for him? I am so confused. And what about Matt? Dear God, why has Matt suddenly appeared on the scene? To warn me? To validate my suspicions? I'm in trouble, God, and I have no idea what to do about it.

She heard footsteps behind her and turned to see Elaine. She was holding out two cups of hot coffee which she set down on the window ledge. Without a word, she patted Ellie's shoulder. Ellie was so relieved to see her that she started crying again. "This seems to be my best skill at the moment," she said as she used the back of her hands to wipe away the tears.

"There's been a lot to cry about around here," Elaine said and offered Ellie a hug which was gratefully accepted and reciprocated.

"Let's go sit in the waiting room and visit a bit. I don't think Tony will mind." She gently patted Tony's shoulder before she turned to leave.

In the waiting room Elaine said gently, "Talk to me. How's it going for my weary grandmother and newlywed friend?"

"Not well. Not well at all." Over the next half hour Ellie poured out the contents of her troubled and confused mind. Elaine listened without comment except to ask Ellie to repeat the words she couldn't understand either because Ellie was crying or speaking so softly.

Finally it was her turn to speak. "Ellie, as your pastor, I'm advising you to do what I know you already know—let God worry about Tony. You've all done all that you can for now. Of course you'll want to see him and be there for Ben and Missy. But Liam is right about there being others who can keep the vigil. Don't let this consume you. It won't help Tony and it will harm you. An hour or two a day is reasonable. Moving into the hospital—maybe not so much.

"Now, as your friend, making a mistake in misjudging the person you married isn't the unforgiveable sin. Maybe Liam can't accept the many interlocking relationships you've managed all your adult life. And maybe you have a finite capacity to make up for all the family life and love he didn't get that you did. If this isn't working out, it's okay to admit it and call it off."

"Is that what they teach pastors? To advise people with marital troubles to call it quits?"

"No. It's what I've learned on my own from watching many, many couples try to find a livable balance between him and her and the two of them together as a unit. Believe me; I think marriage is a very important relationship. Maybe the core relationship among mortals. Even more so than between parent and child or between sisters or brothers. I am all for marriage. But as one blunt colleague of mine puts it, 'It's a crap shoot.' We can do what we know how to do to stack the deck in favor of the relationship working. But actually, it's not the relationship that works or doesn't. It's the two people in it that have to make it work. And the odds are stacked against the couple that wants to get and stay married."

Ellie nodded but didn't speak. So Elaine continued. "It's no longer an economic hardship if a woman never marries. In fact, many women do quite well on their own. Marriage is no longer even considered the only way to produce and raise children. Now kids arrive through genetic engineering. They can be adopted by single parents or gay couples and some grow up with all sorts of combinations of adults in and out of their lives. I don't have the statistics, but I'll bet children living with their biological mother and father who were conceived without medical intervention are the minority in the population."

Ellie nodded again. "I feel so torn. I thought Liam was my second chance after whatever happened with Chet. I felt so good. It was so great to have someone want me and devote time and attention to me."

"And you feel foolish that maybe you walked into an emotional trap?"

"Yeah, I guess I do. Especially after people tried to warn me. I feel so stupid and foolish."

"People like Liam are desperate people. We all get lonely. We're designed for companionship. It's not good for man—or woman—to be alone. But we've done a very good job of disintegrating the social structure that provided companionship. We've taken the porches off the front of houses and built fortresses around us so neighbors hardly even know one another in many communities. We herd kids into massive school systems where overwhelmed teachers hardly even know the names of their students let alone anything about them personally. We've worshiped upper mobility as a career goal and moved families away from one another in the process. Most of us know more about fictional characters in movies and TV shows than we do about people next door or down the hall at work."

Ellie nodded. Elaine continued. "People like Liam only know how to try to stuff the hole where relationships should be by pulling in people and using them. Their pain is so deep and so wide that there's no room to think about what someone else may be experiencing. Their subconscious goal is to numb the alienation they feel by coercing a willing person to fill in that hole."

Ellie sighed. "And I was that willing person."

"Maybe. Don't beat yourself up too much. You were responding to a God-given urge to connect with someone. Liam was looking for someone to make the pain of loneliness go away. I tried my best to get him to open up a little about his losses when you both came for pre-marital counseling. I sensed then there might be issues too painful for him to discuss. You've tried. You've both tried in your own ways.

Maybe after all this with Tony calms down your feelings about Liam will too. But, if they don't—well, Ellie—if it isn't going to work out, it's okay to admit it."

"Actually, Liam and I have a lot in common," said Ellie with a hint of a smile now. "We're both concerned about Liam and how he's doing. The only difference is Liam is only concerned about Liam and I am pulled in a dozen different ways by the people I care about."

"Maybe so," said Elaine.

"So, now what do I do?"

"Take your time. Take very good care of yourself. Be careful. Be very careful. From what I've observed about Liam and people I know who seem to have his personality type, he can become very vindictive if he doesn't get what he wants or he feels threatened."

"Yeah, I've noticed that already."

"How are you financially?"

"Okay. But barely. I don't have enough to pay out thousands to an attorney if that's what you mean."

"Maybe it won't come to that. This might all blow over when you're not so worried about Tony. But if it doesn't, well, you belong to a community that loves you and it so happens we have a very good attorney who's a member. When you're ready, if you want me to, I can put you in touch with him. I'm pretty sure he could help you for a reasonable fee."

They talked a while longer and Ellie decided to go home instead of going back up to Tony's room. She sent a quick text message to Ben and slowly walked out to her car.

CHAPTER TWENTY-EIGHT

I was overcome by trouble and sorrow. (Psalm 116:3b)

For the next week time was an odd combination of both crawling along like a baby just learning how to move and racing by like a marathon runner. Tony gradually started responding. He woke up enough to nod his head when asked questions and seemed to know those around him. Sometimes Liam showed compassion by doing little things to help Ellie. Then he'd start pouting and behaving like a spoiled five-year-old.

Elaine continued to check in by phone every day and ended every conversation with an open invitation for coffee and ear time whenever Ellie wanted it. Matt came by once but didn't stop to talk beyond a quick inquiry into Tony's progress. Jerry offered to organize a family visitation schedule so there was someone at the hospital around the clock, allowing Ben and Missy to go home occasionally. Ellie took the eight a.m. to noon time slot. Since Liam still refused to come back to the hospital, it gave her time to read, journal, and reflect. Liam never again suggested she was going there to meet Matt. He seemed more focused on re-living his illustrious career by sorting through boxes of old files, letters, and reports. Tony was slowly improving. Life had settled into a new normal for the time being.

Ellie began to think she and Liam would be good together after all. *I guess the stress of all this really was just too much for him.*

Ten days after Tony's accident, Ellie returned to work at C.A.R.E. Though no one said anything to her, she sensed a difference in how people treated her. People were more cautious, more polite—as though she was fragile and had to be handled with care.

One day she overheard a couple of people saying how worried they were about her and debating how to respond. A new dance step had started: people offered to bring food and she quickly declined their offers. She insisted she was perfectly capable of managing her regular work schedule. She gave minimal answers to inquiries about Tony's progress. She offered no comments about life at home with Liam.

Late Friday afternoon Pete stopped by her office to wish her well for the weekend. Standing at the door with his hand on the knob, he turned and said, "Ellie, I've a group confession to make."

"What?"

"Most of us here have been talking about you behind your back. We're worried about you. Of course we expect you to be distracted and worried about Tony. Any normal person would be. But it seems there might be something else going on. I realize it's none of our business, but we all really are fond of you. Well, damn it, Ellie, are you alright?"

Ellie was so surprised by his awkwardness and bluntness that she decided maybe it would be a good idea to fess up to the reality she was trying to dodge herself.

"No, actually, I'm not. Tony's part of it, of course. But the worst part is Liam and how he's reacted. Or more accurately, has chosen mostly not to react. I think he's jealous of the attention Tony's getting. I can't come up with any other explanation for what I've experienced."

"I'm all ears." He moved back toward her desk and sat down again.

Ellie gave him a summary of the conversations about how Liam didn't expect to help out financially. And about how he complained about the time she spent at the hospital. She debated telling him about the weird conversation with Matt too, but then opted not to.

Pete sat without speaking for a couple of minutes, before finally asking, "Do you want me to go beat him up?"

"That is actually very tempting. But no, no thanks."

"Okay, then. Plan B. Ellie, I think you need to trust your instincts. I can see how you'd be a bit gun shy given the divorce from Chet after his mid-life meltdown or whatever. But, you are a very capable, mature, generous, healthy woman. If you think you're being treated badly, you are. And you don't have to put up with it. You don't have to undergo some sort of sick penitence for your failed marriage with Chet. What can I do to help you?"

What is this—the third person to tell me this? Is this how God works? Keep repeating the same message over and over until we finally get it? What is the message? Have I made a huge mistake here?

"You already have. It's very helpful to have someone validate that I'm not going crazy. But I will if I put up with this. I've been thinking that things will be alright once Tony's situation is settled. But, maybe that's wishful thinking. Maybe all this has just shown me the real Liam. I guess I'm going to be a twice-divorced woman. Imagine how proud Mom would be if she were still living. The thought terrifies me."

"I can understand that. But staying married because you don't want to admit defeat or own up to an error in judgment doesn't make sense. Love is supposed to enrich your life, not reduce it to a series of calm spots between battles. You sound diminished lately. Now I know why. I'm here for you in any way that's helpful."

"Thanks. Really. Thank you."

Saturday morning Ellie got up before Liam and made coffee. When he appeared in the kitchen she offered him a cup and offered to prepare breakfast. "You're not off to the hospital already?"

She couldn't tell if he was being sarcastic or surprised. By way of response she simply reiterated her offer to fix breakfast. A few minutes later they were sitting down to their plates of scrambled eggs, toast, sausage, juice, and a second round of coffee.

"Are you going to the hospital today?"

"Probably, later this afternoon. First I'm going to have lunch with Ginny."

"Who?"

"You remember, Ginny, from the writing class we took last spring."

"Why on earth would you want to do that?"

"Because she's my friend and with all that's happened over the past few months, I haven't seen or talked with her and I miss her."

"You just have to run off all the time, don't you? You just leave me any chance you get."

"Liam, this isn't about you. It's about me maintaining a friendship that means a lot to me."

"But I'm your best friend now."

"You are my husband. I still have friends. Marriage doesn't cancel them."

"You took vows. For better and for worse. Forsaking all others."

They argued for another fifteen minutes and finally Ellie said as calmly as she could manage, "You are free to interpret my having lunch with the good friend who got me to the class where I met you in any way you want. You'll have time to think about it while I'm having lunch."

With that she stood, cleared the plates, kissed the top of his head, and disappeared to the bedroom to dress for the day.

On the way to meet Ginny for lunch she drove into a park and pulled to a stop under the shade of a large maple tree. She called all three of her children to get updates on their situations. Tony was doing much better and was to start therapy on Monday. They'd start therapy in the hospital and if that went well, they'd send him home to continue treatments. He might even be able to go back to school in a few weeks, though they would probably need a tutor to work with him.

Cat and Jerry were making plans to take their family camping because the kids had a three-day weekend coming up soon. Bless them; they were taking Erika along for a few days of some child-size R & R.

Ike and Jodi were busy remodeling the upstairs of their old house between play rehearsals for Jodi.

Satisfied that her family was all accounted for and fending as best they could given the crisis with Tony, she headed to the restaurant.

Ginny's usual cheerful demeanor changed the instant she saw Ellie. "You're not well, are you?"

Ellie agreed but wondered if it was that obvious. What were people seeing in her that she was missing? Ginny tactfully waited until their orders were placed to ask what was going on. Ellie quickly filled her in on the nightmare that had been Tony's life recently. Then she was quiet. Ginny waited, but Ellie offered no additional information.

So Ginny took a guess, "Let me see. There's trouble in paradise. Liam didn't turn out to be the knight in shining armor after all."

"Apparently not."

Ellie poured out all her pain, doubts, dashed hopes, and confusion of the past couple of months. Ginny held her coffee mug with both hands midair and said nothing. When Ellie stopped Ginny asked, "So, does this mean you're going to leave him?"

"I don't know. I mean, it's only been six months. Shouldn't I give it some time? This situation with Tony has really been difficult. The honeymoon phase turned nightmarish pretty quickly after Tony got hurt."

"Ellie, not that marriage is a scoreboard—but how many votes have you gotten now that maybe this isn't in your best interest? Elaine, one. Matt, two. Pete, three. Me, four. How many votes do you need?"

"I feel so foolish. I had such high hopes. I was so crushed when Chet ran off. Then it felt so good to have someone want me again. Now I feel like I've been tricked or something—like a bait-and-switch sucker. Mostly I just feel weak and really stupid."

Ginny put her hand out to touch Ellie's but didn't speak for a moment. Then she whispered so softly Ellie had to lean in to hear her, "Follow your heart. It will always lead you to safety."

Ellie suspected Ginny was right. The problem was her heart wasn't sending out very strong messages at the moment. It was too broken. She was too exhausted from the tension of it all. Her mind refused to focus on any thought for more than a few moments at a time. For every decision she tried to make, a counter-idea pushed it aside. She was assaulted with "what if's" buzzing around her like mosquitoes in a swamp. She realized she didn't want to go back to her own home. It felt like it'd been taken over by some foreign invasion. She didn't want to go to the hospital. She just couldn't deal with the weight of the worry of Ben and Missy. She had nothing to give them.

When Ellie didn't respond, Ginny spoke again. "Why not take the afternoon off? Come to my house. Dan and I were going to go over to the West Side Market this afternoon. You can come crash at our place. You can take a nap; watch a movie; read a magazine. Do anything you want for yourself for a couple of hours. How's that sound?"

Ellie nodded and agreed that was the best option she'd had all week. They paid the check and soon Ellie was following Ginny the few blocks to Ginny's home. As she walked from the car to the house she put her phone on "Airplane Mode."

As Ginny and Dan were driving away, Ellie settled into their sofa with a copy of *Writer's Digest*. She decided she needed to focus again on the writing urge that had led her to the class where she met Liam. About half way through the first page of an article she closed her eyes. She woke up startled two hours later when she heard Ginny and Dan come in the back door. At first she couldn't figure out what they were doing in her house. Then she remembered she was in their house.

Dan asked her if she wanted to stay for dinner. She hesitated. "I think I really should go home."

"But you don't want to, do you?" Ginny asked.

She shook her head from side to side in agreement.

"Are you afraid?" Dan asked gently.

"More like gun shy. I never know what's going to set him off. I'm pretty sure he'll be in rare form since I've been gone all day. I just don't want to face it."

"Well, how about this. I'll call him and tell him we've kidnapped you and now we'll release you in exchange for him coming over here for dinner. He's not likely to assault you while we're around. Maybe some of my world famous grilling and a few beers will mellow him out enough to avoid a meltdown. How's that sound?"

"It sounds good to me. But, how do you . . . I mean why are you . . ."

Dan interrupted her before she could organize her thoughts. "How do I know what he's like?"

"Yeah, I guess that's what I was trying to ask."

"Ginny let me in on the reality that it might not all be wonderful for you at home right now. I was married to the female version of Liam for ten years. It didn't work. No matter what I did—or avoided doing—it was never the right thing to have done or to have left undone. People like my ex-wife—Sally—and Liam need help. But they usually don't get it because they are so convinced their problems are all caused by external factors beyond their control. But before we get into all that, let me call the chap and invite him over. We can talk while we wait."

A few minutes later Dan hung up the phone and gave the report. "Of course, he was stunned to hear from me. But he said he'd come. Even asked what to bring. I sent him off to buy a very particular brand of beer that will take him a while to find. I figure we've got an hour or so. I happen to have a few bottles of that beer on hand. Want one?"

Ellie gratefully accepted the glass with the full head of foam and settled back in one of the kitchen chairs. "Tell me more about Sally and how you handled life with her."

"First thing you need to get through your weary head is that you cannot control or cure the behavior. You can only decide if you want to continue to try to live with it or not. These people are really a challenge. It's easy to feel for them—when you're not trying to live with them. No one will think less of you if you decide this isn't what you bargained for."

"Really? Being divorced twice isn't going to raise any eyebrows?"

"Well, okay. Some will be quick to judge and come to wrong conclusions. But, Ellie, you don't need to commit yourself to a future of constant chaos and conflict because a few clueless people might think less of you for deciding not to do that."

"Hmm. Yeah, I see your point."

"For me it was like walking on eggshells all the time. I could never avoid the eggshells because she was constantly moving them. At first I tried to figure out what would make her happy and do lots of that. But she'd always find something wrong with what I did and criticize me for it. She'd get upset if I wasn't a mind reader. I was supposed to know she wanted to go out to eat. Or, if I suggested we go out, she'd have a meltdown because she'd spent all day planning what to cook at home. I couldn't win."

"I know that story. I used to think I knew how to cook. Liam seems sure I can't. He takes over everything I do in the kitchen. I never get it right. And if I just give up and let him do it all he complains that we're not a team and we're not working together."

"It won't always be like that. It'll get worse. He's on his good behavior now because he's still trying to court you and convince you that he's the solution to all your problems."

Ginny chimed in. "From what I've seen and heard, more like the source of them."

"He has his good points," defended Ellie.

"I know he must," agreed Dan. "All people do. But these people aren't wired like most people. They are so needy so deep inside that they really don't know what they're doing. Remember Jesus' words that fateful day, 'Father, forgive them, they know not what they do.'? Well, that goes double—no make that triple—for folks like Sally and Liam. They feel all out of control inside, so they try to control everything around them outside. And most of all they fear being abandoned—because they have been so often. I think it's a chicken-and-egg sort of thing on that issue. Are they paranoid about being abandoned because they have been, or are they abandoned because their paranoid behavior drives people away? Hard to know. But once the cycle gets started—well, it would have taken more patience and tolerance than I had to keep up with Sally."

Ellie sighed. "I see a lot of that in Liam. He's a dear man—when he's calm. But he can turn on a dime, and he can be really cruel and demeaning. Once he gets started I can't find an off switch to calm him down."

"Nor should you have to," said Ginny. "Look. We're all walking around wounded from something. But that doesn't give any of us the right to take it out on other people. It's not what happens to us in life that matters. It's what we do in response that counts."

They talked a few more minutes, then Dan got busy preparing the grill while Ginny started pulling things out of the refrigerator to make a tossed salad. Ellie went to the guest bathroom to freshen up.

When she came out Liam was just arriving. He gave her a hug and a kiss on the check and asked her how her day had gone. They spent the next few hours as a pleasant foursome talking about a range of topics from Tony's situation to the economy to the upcoming elections. Ellie felt safe, comfortable, content, and mystified as to why such moments had become such a rare treat in her life.

Chapter Twenty-Nine

Small is the gate and narrow the road that leads to life, and only a few find it. (Matthew 7:14)

The joy was short lived. Ellie followed Liam back to the house. She was barely in the door when his emotional switch flipped again from charming to complaining. "They don't like me. They just feel guilty for trying to come between us. You shouldn't have gone over there, Ellie."

"Liam, what on earth gives you the idea they don't like you? We were all laughing and joking and having a great time. Plus, we all love writing in some way."

"For a writer you sure can be dense sometimes. Don't you see— Dan is just trying to butter me up? I'll bet he wants to get me to reveal enough of my story so he can write something about it himself. You're too naïve. You can't trust some people. I've been around. I know these things."

"It must be so sad not trusting anyone."

"Well, people always give me a reason not to trust them. Including you. I thought you were different, but I'm learning I can't trust you either. If you're not running off to the hospital to see Matt, you're running off to give my secrets away to Ginny—who is probably telling them to Dan right now."

"I really don't think that's going to happen, Liam. For your information, Ginny didn't ask me any questions about your work. And you were there for all the conversation with Dan. They're new in town. They're looking for friends. I thought we all had a good time tonight. I'm sorry if you didn't."

How do I respond to this? Ellie thought and decided to say nothing more. Experience had taught her more words would only add more fuel to the fire of his perspective. Instead she touched him on the shoulder and tried to comfort him the way she would have comforted one of her children caught in an adolescent storm of swirling emotions.

A few minutes later they settled into bed and talked a few more minutes. Then Liam gave her a hug and a kiss and rolled over. He was asleep before Ellie could find a comfortable position. She tossed and turned a while and finally admitted tonight would be another date with Chamomile. As the water was coming to a boil she retrieved one of the sleep aid pills and washed it down with a glass of water.

Once she was settled in the sunroom she opened her journal and began to write. *Okay, God. It seems I have made a huge mistake here. It looks like the universe is lining up to tell me so. Elaine. Matt. Ginny. Pete. Even Dan. I don't want to be stupid or stubborn, but I really don't know what to do or where to start. He's in my house. How do I resolve this? What do I tell my kids? Where will I go? What will become of me?*

She put down the pen and tried to follow Pete's advice to do nothing. For the next few minutes she focused on her own breathing. She heard muffled sounds. Traffic on the street outside. Chipper snoring gently. The hum of the refrigerator. But mostly she focused on the rising and falling of her abdomen as she concentrated on breathing. Seven inhales. Hold for seven. Seven exhales. She counted the cycles on her fingers until she got to seven. Amazingly, she did feel calmer. Peaceful. Even hopeful. Though nothing had changed about her situation, she felt more prepared to face it.

She turned to a new page—that seems fitting she thought. Another new page in life. She made a list.

Things I need to do: Open a new bank account and start to stash cash.

It seemed only natural that she and Liam had merged their finances as well as their furnishings when they married. Now she understood why people sometimes insisted on pre-nups. Back to the list.

Pack an emergency suitcase and give it to Cat for safe keeping.

Tell Cat. And Ben. And Ike.

As she wrote she realized she'd made up her mind to leave Liam. Or rather, to try to get Liam to leave her. It was now a matter of executing the plan. She wondered when she should tell him about this plan. With a flash of absolute clarity, she knew the time was not right. She needed a team to help her, and she needed a plan for a place to go in case he became truly ugly.

Maybe it was the sleeping aid; maybe the Chamomile tea; or maybe the prayers—probably a combination of all three—whatever it was, Ellie felt as relaxed and calm as she could remember feeling since Ben's call about Tony's accident. This time when she crawled into bed she was asleep within minutes.

CHAPTER THIRTY

*I live . . . also with him who is contrite and lowly in spirit, to revive the
spirit of the lowly and to revive the heart of the contrite.
(Isaiah 57:15)*

The next few days were filled with a new way of life for Ellie. On the
one hand, she worked hard at spending time with Liam and keeping
life at home as calm as possible. She bit her tongue when he became
critical and went out of her way to do little things that she hoped
would please him. On the other hand, she was lining up time to talk to
the people she needed to help her end this union that had started not
quite a year ago. She still carried around a toxic level of guilt and self-
recrimination. She was constantly caught off guard by how supportive
and affirming people were toward her. People seemed genuinely more
concerned about her well-being than any lapses of sound judgment
she may have had.

As Tony made progress day by day, so did Ellie. She could actually
feel herself growing stronger and more confident. In some odd
symbiotic way Tony's improving physical health was progressing on
a parallel path to her improving mental and emotional health. *And a
little child shall lead them.*

As promised, Elaine had made arrangements for an attorney
who was a member at St. Luke's to meet with Ellie. Stanley Emerson
agreed to meet with her at her C.A.R.E. office. After she told him all
that happened over the past few months, he said he'd waive his usual
$2,500 retainer fee. He agreed to work out a repayment plan she could
start paying once the divorce was settled and she knew where she
stood with her finances. That was the good news. He also advised her
to start looking for another place to live.

"It will be nearly impossible to get Liam out of the house without
a very long and expensive legal battle. Once he finds out that you
want a divorce, he'll go hire a boatload of attorneys. Ellie, you need to
understand that his ego won't stand for him to lose. He'll do whatever
it takes to be the winner in this case. You will be the villain in the

story. You'll look like a self-serving gold-digger taking advantage of him for his financial assets. My advice? Find another place to live. It'll be easier to just give up the house than to get him out of it. Even if we are successful in evicting him, he'll always know where to find you. I worry about your physical safety."

"But he's never shown me any physical violence. It's all words."

"For now. One thing leads to another. Did you put his name on all your accounts?"

Ellie felt the old familiar flash of hot embarrassment. Reluctantly she nodded, "Yes."

Stanley sighed. "Okay. Well, I'll do what I can to get you a fair settlement, but I strongly recommend you be prepared to come out on the short side of this. Liam's personality types do well in court. It's an adversarial system. They're interested in winning. The court system is usually in favor of the ones with the most moxie and the most tenacious attorneys. I suggest you plan on settling for what you can get and don't fight him through the court. In fact, if you can do this with one attorney you'll come out way ahead."

Ellie felt utterly defeated.

"Ellie," he continued, "He doesn't do this on purpose. I suspect he really does care for you. He's just got an emotional handicap—like some people have physical or mental ones. I'm not justifying his behavior—but try not to take it so personally. He was emotionally handicapped long before you two got together."

So I have to choose between hurting him or continue to let him hurt me. Why? Why did I do this? Why was I drawn to him like a magnet to the fridge door? What's wrong with me? Though Ellie knew such questions really had no answers, she kept asking them anyway.

After the meeting she tried to focus on the work at the C.A.R.E. center. Mercifully it was a slow day, so it didn't matter that she wasn't really focusing or concentrating. Lynette stopped by and asked, "Anything I can do to help?"

"I wish you could. I'm afraid I've made a mess of things. I'm going to leave Liam. I just don't know how to tell him. Or when. Or what to do next."

"Wow. That's a heavy load. How do you figure you made a mess of things?"

"I should have waited longer. I should have asked more questions. I shouldn't have let my loneliness get the best of me. I should have listened to my family and friends."

"A lot of shoulds there. Maybe you took a chance—and gave him a chance—and it just didn't work out. That happens. Sooner or later we all make a mess of some kind. I've met a lot of people working here. I've never met one yet who didn't have some kind of a personal mess to contend with. I don't see any reason why you should be exempt from messes."

Ellie laughed. "If they gave out prizes for making messes, I think I'd qualify for one." Ellie gave Lynette the short version of Liam's jealousy and resentment about Tony's accident and her attorney's assessment of her options.

"Oh my. Ellie, my heart just aches for you. I'm so sorry this didn't work out. But tell me what you need."

"I need to figure out how come I keep making such a mess of things. What's wrong with me? Why can't I make a marriage work?"

"You did. For over thirty years."

"But I must have done something wrong to make Chet leave like that. And Liam? Why didn't I see the error of this before I married him? There's no fool like an old fool."

"Wow. You sure do know how to beat up on yourself." Lynette clasped and unclasped her hand several times before continuing. "You don't hold the patent on making a mess of things. I don't like to talk about this very much. But, sometimes, I feel the urge to talk about my messes to someone else, so they know they have company. Here goes."

With that she took in a deep breath and started talking. The more she talked the higher Ellie's eye brows raised and the farther her jaw dropped.

"When I was sixteen I was chomping at the bit to get out from under my mother's constant snooper-vision. She wanted to know where I was and what I was doing every minute. I really resented it. So, one day I decided I'd just have to lie to her. I told her I had a babysitting job after school."

"What I really had was an affair. With one of my high school teachers. He had a friend who traveled for work a lot and gave him the key to his condo. Mr. Watson—isn't that odd—I still call him 'Mr.' even though I slept with him—many times. He was twenty-five, married, and had a one-year-old baby at home."

"I didn't care. I believed him when he told me his wife was always pressuring him. It was like we connected. My mom was always on me about something, so I understood about feeling hassled by someone."

Ellie was stunned. "You?!"

"Yup. Me. Mercifully I didn't get pregnant. He broke it off right before summer vacation. I never knew why. But he didn't come back in the fall. Maybe his wife found out. Maybe the school administrators found out. I don't know."

"I was heart-broken. I wanted to lock myself up in my room and cry, but I couldn't because I couldn't let my mom know what had happened."

Ellie interrupted. "What happened then?"

"Somehow I managed to finish high school. I hardly dated anyone at all. None of the guys my age could hold a match to him. Then I went off to college. The college had a great career advisor. She was terrific. She seemed to sense I needed some extra care, so she found excuses to have me come to the office to help her with paper work."

"How'd that do any good?" asked Ellie.

"I started dropping hints about my little fling. She told me something that's stayed with me ever since, and caused me to change my major from education to social work."

"What did she tell you?"

"She told me we're all created in the image of God and we all manage to tarnish the image in some way somehow. Some of us do it out of rebellion like I did when I wanted to defy my mother's maternal instinct to protect me. Some do it out of ignorance and inexperience. Some by the poor choices they make that lead to disastrous consequences. We can ruin a life in an instant. It sometimes takes years and years to put one back together."

Ellie nodded, but said nothing.

"The important thing to know is that—just as God keeps creating—we get to keep re-creating ourselves. We can let our messes derail us. Or, we can figure out how to use them to help others when they mess up."

"When I was sixteen I was a self-centered, ungrateful daughter. I've long since seen the wisdom of my mother's ways. And, I spent many years mentoring pregnant teens. That's what led me to this job now."

Lynette paused, smiled at Ellie, and said, "Sounds like you might need a place to live soon."

"I have a place to live. But now I dread going there. How could I be so stupid?"

"Or maybe the question is 'How could you be so trusting?'"

"Isn't that just another word for naïve?"

"Maybe. But there's a need for trusting people in the world. The fact that others take advantage of them doesn't mean trust is a character flaw. It's taking advantage of people who trust that's the flaw."

"The really hard part is—I have fallen in love with him. I really do care about him."

"Caring is a good thing. But, as you surely know from working here with all these people—it's easy to let caring become enabling. We who love to help others too easily over-help."

"Yeah, I can see how I've done a lot of that."

"Seeing is the first step. We can't resolve problems we don't know exist."

"Well, I might need housing. I might also need to find another job with more income. I might need to go get in line and wait for my bag of groceries too."

"Trust, Ellie. I have a hunch God isn't done with you yet. My spare bedroom is available any time you need it." With that she gave Ellie a hug and left her to her thoughts.

CHAPTER THIRTY-ONE

In my anguish I cried to the Lord, and he answered by setting me free.
(Psalm 118:5)

Ellie's days were filled with indecision. She worried about Tony but now expressed her concern with a daily call to Ben or Missy and a visit or two a week to Tony. He was actually doing well. It was yet to be determined if he'd have the behavior problems the doctors had predicted. So far he was totally focused on the many games and other diversions that arrived at the house almost daily. It was like Christmas every day.

The start of the holiday season was fast approaching. Everyone seemed grateful for something else to focus on beyond Tony's condition. When Ellie wasn't worrying about Tony she was thinking about how and when to tell Liam she didn't want to continue the marriage. She was hoping they could at least get through the holidays together. However, she was lining up a safety net in case that wouldn't be possible.

She started moving a few things at a time to Lynette's home. She opened a new bank account and began putting what she could in it. She made duplicate copies of various documents and stored them in her office.

Next on the list of details to work out was Chipper. She couldn't imagine not having that dog's friendly companionship. Yet she realized if things got truly ugly, she'd have to leave in a hurry and she couldn't impose a dog on Lynette or anyone else. Or could she? She wondered if Chipper might not help Tony recover. That night she called Ben.

"You know, Ben, I've been thinking about when Tony comes home. Maybe Chipper could help him. He's great company. You should have seen him with Elaine's dad when he was dying. He's got a natural instinct that amazed us all."

"You'd be willing to let him go? I thought you loved Chipper more than any of the rest of us."

"You don't really believe that?"

"No, not really. But there have been a few comments about what that dog gets away with that none of us dared try when we lived with you."

Ellie laughed and continued. "You're just jealous. I had to make adults out of you. Chipper will always be a puppy at heart. So, what do you think?"

"Well, if you're willing, I think Chipper would be great medicine for Tony. The doctors are saying he might come home in another week or so."

"That is the best news I've heard all day. Okay. Let's try it and see what happens."

That weekend Ellie moved Chipper over to Ben and Missy's house. Erika was thrilled and wouldn't let Chipper out of her sight until her parents put their foot down at the idea of him sleeping on her bed with her.

Ellie was grateful to have that worry scratched off the list. Liam only muttered a few words when Ellie explained that she'd relocated Chipper to be with Tony.

The tension was starting to build, but remarkably, Liam seemed oblivious to it. Indeed, once she decided she was leaving, she no longer bothered to express her personal preferences or opinions. The fighting that had become part and parcel of daily life with Liam slowed to a peaceful co-existence. She felt deceitful living this double life. She knew this couldn't go on much longer, but she dreaded telling Liam of her decision.

The "Day of the Announcement" started out calmly enough. It was early November and they were having breakfast together. Ellie was telling Liam about how their family always took turns hosting Thanksgiving.

"The menu hasn't changed for three generations as far as I can tell. We just take turns hosting it. It's Ben and Missy's turn this year—but I thought we ought to offer to host it given what they've been through."

"I usually either skip Thanksgiving—or spend the day with someone from work. I'll do whatever you want, Ellie, for Thanksgiving." Then he grinned. "I have a special surprise for Christmas though. I booked us on a cruise for Christmas. We leave the twenty-third and return next year on the second."

Ellie knew she couldn't go, and that she had to say so now.

"Liam, why would you do something like that without even talking to me about it?"

"Why, because I wanted to surprise you of course."

"Well, you have. I can't go. Not this year."

"What do you mean you can't go? Can't you and I have a little time to ourselves?"

"We have. And we will again. I just don't want to spend the holidays away from my family. Especially not this year, not after Tony's accident."

Liam's expression instantly changed from one of excitement to near rage. "*I* am your family, Ellie. When are you going to get that through your thick head?"

"That's another thing I have to tell you, Liam. You are part of my family. But I still want to spend time with the other part of my family. I can't keep trying to juggle these two parts. I am so sorry— but this marriage wasn't a good idea. I don't want to be married to you anymore."

None of the many scenes she'd imagined might follow that announcement were what happened next. Liam said nothing for a long moment. When he next spoke he was blinking back tears.

"But *why*? Ellie, don't do this. We can make this work."

Ellie tried to explain all the random thoughts she'd wrestled with for the past few months. They all sounded weak and feeble to her. Finally she settled on saying only, "We don't live together well, Liam. This isn't working."

"It could if you could be a real wife to me. I can't compete with your kids. I had such great hopes for us. But you keep undermining them."

"Liam, I do care about you. More than I think you believe. I hoped you'd be grateful to have a family. I guess that's just the problem. I feel torn between what you want and what they want—no, not what they want—what I want with them. There's only one of me. I guess I thought I could make this all fit together—but I can see I was wrong."

After an exhausting hour of conversation, Liam finally asked, "I suppose you want me to move out?"

"One of us has to."

"Why? We could get divorced if your independence is so bloody important to you. But you don't have to move out. And I certainly don't intend to. In case you've forgotten, my moving in here was your idea. And my place is rented out. I don't have anywhere else to go."

Ellie was amazed at the sense of calm and determination she was feeling. Though she had no idea what would happen to her next, she was confident ending this was the right step to take.

"We can work out the details later. I do have a place to go. I guess today is the day I'll go there."

With that she retreated to the bedroom to start putting some things in a suitcase. Stanley had warned her to stay in the house as long as possible, but not to put herself in harm's way should Liam turn violent. Elaine had suggested Liam would be in shock for a couple of days. But when that wore off he'd likely become more angry than ever. Ellie had thought about how to handle this a hundred times. Now she was very glad she'd decided to put a few things over at Lynette's home—just in case.

She'd also already arranged a visit to Amelia. She'd stay there a week and see what happened next. With Thanksgiving just around the corner, she thought maybe a time-out might help them both. She was willing to postpone any final decisions until after the holidays. If that was agreeable to Liam. She'd have to let her children know and that was another conversation she was dreading. *One thing at a time. I have to wade through this mess one thing at a time.*

Liam was so stunned he didn't even protest when she brought her packed suitcase into the kitchen.

"Liam, I don't want to hurt you. Really I don't. I think we need a little time to both calm down and sort this out. I'm going to visit an old college friend for a few days. I guess you need some time to adjust to this. I've been thinking about this for a while, but I know it's caught you off guard. You can reach me by cell phone. When I come back we can talk about how to get through the holidays. I am touched with your offer to go on a cruise—but I'm just not up for it right now. I apologize if you think I've been putting you last."

She felt like a real heel, but she also felt confident she was doing the right thing. *I wonder if this is how Chet felt once he made up his mind to leave.*

Ellie would later look back on what happened next as an authentic miracle. She moved into Lynette's guest room until it was time to leave for her visit with Amelia. From there she called each of her children to let them know what she'd done. She expected them to be supportive—they had been so far. She had not expected the level of encouragement and affirmation each offered in their own way.

Cat's reaction was, typically, the most direct and blunt. "Well, Mom, I wouldn't like it if you told me, 'I told you so,' so I won't. But I will say, I had my reservations from the get go. Then when he just disappeared in the middle of the Tony crisis, I was really pissed at him and sorry for you. I'm not surprised, but I am sorry. What do you need most?"

"I think you just gave it to me, Sweetheart. I'm going to spend Thanksgiving with my old college roommate and her family this year. I don't think I can handle our usual gathering. I hope that's okay?"

"We'll miss you, but I think that's wise. It's going to be different anyway what with all the special needs for Tony right now. Let's get through this chapter and then plan a way to all do something special together later—maybe over spring break."

Ellie wept with gratitude. Then she called her other two children and got an abbreviated version of Cat's offer of support. Lynette was the perfect host. She invited Ellie to join her in the evenings but never pressured her to give up the solitude of the guest room. She offered just the right combination of companionship and space.

As anticipated, Liam called and sent several e-mails over the course of the next few days. Then there was an eerie silence from his end of what was left of the relationship. Unsure what to do next, she wrote him an e-mail inquiring what was happening.

Much to her amazement he called her to announce he was in Colorado. His daughter-in-law Grace had called because Liam's son was in a car accident. Although father and son had barely spoken to one another for several years, the accident shook loose a deep-seated desire to make amends. Grace called to ask Liam to come. And Liam went. He went and arranged to stay for several weeks. The issue of the holiday was resolved. Liam would spend them with his family. Ellie would spend Thanksgiving with Amelia and her family and Christmas with her own family. She was grateful for the time with Lynette and Amelia, but she wanted to be back in her own home and with her own people for Christmas.

Ellie returned to her own home, which now felt strange indeed with neither Chipper nor Liam there. The silence sometimes got to her, but she knew Chipper and Tony had become fast buddies. It gave her great pleasure to see the two of them together.

Liam called one night a couple of weeks before Christmas to try one more time to convince her to stay with him. "You'll never make it on your own, Ellie. You give away everything you earn and then some. You need me to take care of you. I've seen the light. My son's accident showed me what's important. Don't do anything until I come back. Please. Give me another chance."

Now Ellie felt like two invisible hands were gripping her on each shoulder and trying to pull her apart into two pieces. What if Ebenezer Scrooge's conversion wasn't just a fictional story? What if his son's accident was his Jacob Marley call to repentance? What if Ellie's announcement was like the Ghost of Christmas future warning Liam of his fate? Then what kind of a monster would she be to deny him this chance to change?

"I promise I'll think it over, Liam. That's all I can promise for the time being. Do you want me to put your son on the prayer chain at church?"

"Yes. Please."

"Consider it done."

For the next few weeks Ellie felt she was two people living side-by-side lives. Every day she'd get a call from Liam with an update on his son's condition. Then she'd oversee the dramas and desperation of clients at C.A.R.E. She was working a lot of overtime—partly because the colder weather made people more desperate, so the waiting lines grew longer. And partly because she wanted less time to re-think her decision and more time to be around friendly faces she knew and trusted.

She felt like a teenager asking permission to take the car as she made the rounds of her trusted inner circle of advisors. She talked one at a time with Ginny and Dan, Elaine, and Pete. They all told her basically the same thing. Pete said it best. "Yes, people really can and do change all the time. But that doesn't mean you should continue to try to live with someone who can make emotional turns on a dime and who wants to hold you responsible for his feelings and actions."

Ginny and Dan admitted they were really concerned about her, especially Dan. "Beware of the cycle, Ellie. You know this. It's just hard to apply it to your own situation. Romance, outburst, regret, romance. And on and on it goes. I don't like the way he's taken over control of your life. You're perfectly capable of managing your own life. Yes, maybe his son's situation has been a wake-up call to him. But I still think your instincts about leaving him are worth following."

"But I can't do this to him in the middle of a family crisis."

"Did you offer to go there?"

"Yes, and he said I didn't need to bother."

"Then what happened?" asked Ginny.

"Then he started complaining about how incompetent everyone was at the hospital. He even complained about Grace. I've never met this woman, but he used to think she was the only decent person in his family. He says she's not making him feel welcome."

"Well, at least he's consistent," said Dan. "It's always something with people like Liam. If there isn't a crisis, they'll create one. They need to be stressed out, and they need to make someone else responsible for it. It is a scary thing to have a son in the hospital. You of all people know that. If you stay with him, you'll have lots and lots of experience dealing with stress."

Liam's son was released from the hospital to a rehab center right before Christmas. It was estimated he'd stay there for the next eight weeks. Liam returned the first week of January and announced he wanted the divorce finalized as soon as possible. Ellie was surprised, but also relieved. He took charge of the situation by hiring an attorney,

writing up a settlement agreement that included splitting their real
estate back to the way it was before they married, and assessing Ellie
half the cost of the attorney fees. For good measure he added on the
cost of moving his things out of her home and off to Colorado. Suddenly
he and his son were best of buds and he needed to be there.

Ellie started to protest, but the words of her attorney rang in her
head, "Just say, 'Yes.' Don't try to fight him. In his world there's no such
thing as win-win. There's only room for one winner. He'll do whatever
it takes to make sure he's the one who wins."

When she reviewed the terms Liam was suggesting with Ginny
and Dan, Dan laughed. "Go for it Ellie. Don't worry about the finances.
We'll help you if you need help. But I suspect you won't."

She agreed to everything Liam's attorney requested. She signed
the papers in mid-January. The next day she drove Liam back to
the airport to return to Colorado. He planned to stay there through
both his son's recovery period and the required waiting time for the
divorce to be final. Ellie added Grace to her prayer list. She was sure
the woman would need all the prayers she could get.

The spring passed in a blur. Tony continued with physical therapy
and tutoring. He also focused on teaching Chipper new tricks. The dog
thrived on the attention, and Tony's confidence grew with each new
trick they mastered together.

Work at C.A.R.E. seemed to unfold as if on auto-pilot. Liam contacted
her only to inform her of the next step required in the divorce process.
Ellie moved through the days in a strange combination of relief and
curiosity about the future. She felt like a guest in her own life. She was
surprised to note that she did not feel lonely any more. Though she
was more alone than ever, she felt more at ease and comfortable in her
situation than she had in months.

One month short of what should have been their one-year
anniversary they were legally divorced. Each was now free to pursue
separate paths again. She got the call from Liam on her cell phone at
the beach. The same beach she'd gone to two years earlier for her first
solo vacation. Now the solitude mingled with the breeze, salt water,
and sand seemed like spending time with a trusted old friend.

Once again she had no idea what the next chapter would be, but
this time she had a new certainty that whatever it would be, she'd be

up for the task of meeting it and managing it—on her own. The Chet portion of her life seemed so long ago she sometimes actually had trouble conjuring up an image of his face in her mind. Liam seemed like a movie she'd watched with herself cast as one of the characters—interesting, but not real.

After that call she packed up her things and drove home. Much to her amazement she was singing as she drove along. The song that she let repeat again and again was Johnny Cash's "That Old Wheel—it's gonna roll around once more and when it does it will even up the score." Indeed.

Dan was right. Ellie was able to meet her end of the financial arrangements without borrowing money. Liam set up housekeeping in Colorado to be near his son. She saw on Facebook that he changed his status from "Single" back to "In a Relationship" less than two months after the divorce. When she saw it, she felt a surge of gratitude.

Chapter Thirty-Two

Dear children, let us not love with words or tongue but with actions and in truth. (1 John 3:18)

One day at C.A.R.E. when Pete was making his usual rounds, she confided that she still felt so foolish and confused about the whole Liam chapter. "Well, kiddo, you tried. It didn't work. You made a decision. And it appears the luck of the Irish was with you even if Liam was never really able to be there for you. Don't chew on it too much. Leave the chewing to the cows. They have more stomachs for it."

"But I feel like such a screw-up. I did something to ruin a perfectly good marriage that I really thought was as good as they get. And then I got all caught up in the world according to Liam and totally blew that one too."

"Ah, you have joined the ranks of the fallen. Doesn't feel too good, does it?"

"No, it sure doesn't."

"Lucky for you, you know your way to the well of the forgiven."

"What does that mean?"

"Ellie, we've all blown it. And none of us can ever get it right on our own. Here's how I see it. Life isn't really that hard. There are certain irrefutable realities. We get to choose if we believe in them or not. But their being real doesn't depend on our believing in them."

"And what are these realities, Oh Wise One?"

"There is a Creator and we are the created ones. So it makes sense to me that we would spend some intentional time getting to know the Creator—and checking in for instructions on how to best care for the creation. That's one. Two, we can choose to continue to be part of the problem God has to resolve—by insisting on having our own way and trying to control the world around us."

"Or?" asked Ellie.

"Or, we can admit we can't do it on our own, we need help, and hand ourselves over to accept the help that is offered. Some people call that repentance and salvation. I call it common sense," said Pete.

"How, exactly, does one go about doing that?"

"Elementary, my dear Miss Watson. That's the art of doing nothing I've been urging you to try. We intentionally focus on God by quieting ourselves, sitting patiently waiting, and trusting God knows what we need before we can put our longings into words. Call it prayer. Call it meditation. Call it whatever you want, just do it. It lets God know you're volunteering to be part of the solution."

Near the end of summer Ellie decided to take a second week at the shore. This time she wanted to practice Pete's "do nothing" therapy. Lynette told her if she'd visit an emergency relief center while there Ellie could count the time away as continuing education. Then the budget would cover her mileage. "I met a great woman at a conference last winter. I had hoped to go check out her center myself, but I just don't have time. It's more or less on your way. So you'd be doing me a huge favor if you'd check it out coming or going and let me know what you think."

Ellie played her favorite '60s CDs all the way to the shore, singing along and feeling like a hopeful young woman again. At the shore she spent hours each day watching the water lap the land. Sometimes she walked along it. Other times she just sat and watched. She greeted the sun each morning and waited for it to disappear over the horizon each evening.

In between she filled legal pads full of ideas she wanted to try to convert into short stories. She felt herself growing calmer and more confident page by page and day by day. A growing sense of hope for the future took root and grew deeper. By the end of the week she knew something very good was coming her way soon. She couldn't imagine what it would be. She wondered how she'd know when whatever it was unfolded. For the moment it was enough to just be—alone with her thoughts, her memories, and her hope for the future.

As requested, she stopped in to visit the Cecil County Relief Center on Route 40. Lynette had made the connection for her, so she was given the red carpet treatment. She spent a half day meeting and interviewing various staff members. The operation was impressive. She was glad she'd stopped. Now she had some new ideas to pass along to Lynette.

The songs that had accompanied her on the drive to the shore were her traveling companions on the drive back as well. *I can't believe how much has changed in just a couple of years. My life was so predictable before. And now—I hardly know from one day to the next day where I'll be. Or who I'll be with. Or what my marital status will be.* But now instead of such thoughts churning up the sludge of sorrow and regret, she found herself laughing at the situation. *Another chance to re-create myself. I certainly am light years away from boredom these days.* "That old wheel will roll around again," sang Johnny Cash.

"Yes, it will," she said out loud.

Chapter Thirty-Three

Weeping may remain for a night, but rejoicing comes in the morning.
(Psalm 30:5)

When Ellie returned to work Lynette invited her to lunch. She wasted no time getting to the purpose of the lunch.

"Ellie, I'm tendering my resignation as the Executive Director of C.A.R.E. It's been a remarkable fifteen years watching this grow from a few bags of groceries into the agency it is now. I'm so pleased with the progress. And I am so ready to not have to worry about it anymore. I plan to step down at the end of October. I've already spoken with the members of the board. We are all in agreement. We want you to take over."

Before Ellie could protest Lynette continued, "Please don't insult me by telling me you aren't qualified. I can tell from your enthusiasm about your visit to the Cecil County Center in Maryland you have what it takes. We all believe you are more than qualified. It will mean a pay raise, of course. There are some great continuing education events you can go to for training. The Board has set aside a few thousand dollars to send you to them over your first year. And, you can take as much additional time off before I go as you need so you'll be rested up and raring to go. Please, make my day. Say 'yes.'"

I thought I might have to resign, and here she's trying to give me a raise? God really does do amazing things. "Yes. Okay. I mean if you're really serious. Are you?"

Lynette laughed at her. "You'll be perfect for the job. I wanted to offer it to you months ago, but I didn't think I could while you were with Liam. I didn't think there would be any way you could give C.A.R.E. what it needed and keep up with Liam."

"Is this why you sent me to go tour the Maryland place?"

Lynette's smile confirmed Ellie's suspicion that she had been set up.

"But," Ellie said slowly. "I was thinking on my drive back that I really ought to do something with the writing I was working on when I was so suddenly interrupted by the Irish whirlwind."

Lynette nodded. "Hmm. Well, I can't lie to you—this job doesn't have a lot of free time built in. However, it does include a nice vacation package—four weeks a year to be exact—plus two for continuing education. And, the sources for stories are virtually without limit."

Ellie rolled the possibilities over for a couple of minutes. "I guess I could maybe work on a collection of feel-good stories about people who turned their lives around because they got a helping hand when life punched them in the gut. You know—inspirational little 'You can do it too' stories. *How to Re-Create your Life in Ten Hard Steps.*"

"I really like that idea. I'll bet you can get Dan and Ginny to help. It'll probably be a best seller. And it could be a money-maker for the center."

Now Ellie's mind was racing again. She was already imagining the clients she'd want to ask first for permission to share their stories. Ellie shook her head in disbelief at how yet more changes were swirling around her.

She'd been back at her desk an hour or so when Pete stopped by. He was grinning from ear to ear.

"I guess you heard?"

"Sure did. My prayers have been answered. You'll be great. I was hoping you might do me the honor of taking you out for a celebration dinner tonight. Any chance?"

"I don't know. Things are happening a little too fast for me. I haven't even unpacked yet from my trip to the shore. And I need to go reclaim Chipper from Tony. It's my turn to have him for a while." After Liam left, Ellie decided she had to time-share Chipper with Tony. The house was too quiet at night without him. Chipper quickly adjusted to the two-house arrangement.

"I think I can solve that problem. How about I give you enough time to empty the suitcase while I go pick up a picnic dinner? I'll come by for you around six, and we can go to Huntington for a picnic. Chipper can tag along. There's something I'd really like to talk over with you where we might have more privacy than here."

Ellie felt the familiar icy cold finger of panic start walking up her spine. "Is it about the new position? Is there some big problem I don't know about? Oh, Pete, maybe I'm not really qualified for this."

"Nonsense. Of course you are. I should have recorded the discussion at the board meeting when Lynette suggested you for the next CEO. Only it would have made your head so big we'd have to hire a carpenter to widen the doors around here.

"Actually," he said lowering his voice and stretching out his words, "it's a bit personal. I'd just be more comfortable talking about it somewhere other than here."

"Well, okay, if you're sure you're not going to tell me C.A.R.E. is being sued or about to run out money or anything horrible like that."

"I promise—none of that. Shall I pick you up around six then?"

"Okay. And we don't have to take Chipper. I'll leave him with Tony until tomorrow. He'd drive us nuts trying to steal the food off our plates. But if I had any gold stars you'd get one for offering."

Ellie couldn't remember when she'd last felt this good all over. She called Ben as soon as she got home to get a report on Tony, and to let them know they could keep Chipper one more night.

"Mom," Ben's voice sounded upbeat when he answered. "I think I owe you an apology. All those years I thought all your churchy religion stuff was fine for those who needed that sort of thing, but hardly anything I was interested in. But I have to admit—there must be something to the theory that prayer changes things. Tony is doing great. He's still got some work to do to get all his muscles going where his brain tries to send them. But other than that, he's a feisty pre-teenage guy. Today he gave us some back-talk. The normal stuff boys his age do to their parents. It sounded like music to me. It was all I could do to keep from hugging him for giving so much lip to Missy. She didn't even protest. She just started crying."

Ellie could relate as she felt a couple of her own tears break away. "Oh, Ben. Thank God. I am so pleased to hear this. As for the prayer business—I can't count how many people have told me they've been praying for him—for all of us."

"Would you mind if we joined you at church next week?"

When Ben didn't say more Ellie realized he couldn't see her nodding her head over the phone. "You bet. Is Tony up for a big breakfast after church?"

"I think so. He's eating non-stop again."

She was taking the laundry basket to the laundry room when she heard Pete pull into the driveway. On the drive along the lake to Huntington Beach he asked her questions about her visit to the Maryland Center. Then she told him about her ideas for turning the clients' success stories into a book that might inspire others and maybe make some money for the center in the process.

Pete laughed. "Spoken like a CEO—always looking for ways to generate financial support."

Over dinner he gradually became more quiet and withdrawn. Ellie suggested they put the picnic things away and go for a walk along the beach. Pete hardly spoke a word as they made their way down the beach and back again.

"Is there something wrong?" she asked him. "You said you had something to tell me and I don't think anything we've talked about so far required leaving the office to discuss."

"Yes, and no," he said. "Yes, something is wrong. Well there could be. I mean, I don't think anything's wrong yet—but that might change."

"Are you going for some mystery-man-of-the-year award?"

Pete started chewing on his bottom lip. "No. Ellie, I'm as nervous as a kid on his first date. I'm afraid I'm going to blow this. Sit down. I have to say this but I'm afraid to say it."

"Well, just spit it out. Whatever it is, I can't do anything about it until I know what it is."

"The problem is you. I don't mean you're a problem. Dear God, no. You're terrific. I so admire your spunk and your ability to bounce back. I think you must be half rubber. The problem is how I feel about you. I haven't felt like this for eons. I try not to feel the way I do because I remember feeling this way about my fiancé and those memories still make me wake up in a cold sweat sometimes."

Ellie started to speak, but Pete asked her not to just yet.

"I thought these feelings would fade. But they're only growing stronger. Then you got married to Liam, and I was relieved—for a while—because it was obvious nothing could ever develop between us while you were married to him. I felt like a real schmuck suggesting you leave him. I sensed it wasn't working out—but what I really thought was that you might be available again."

Ellie felt disoriented, like waking from a deep sleep and not knowing where she was at first. Pete continued. "Ellie, I almost didn't recommend you for the CEO position. Not because I didn't think you were qualified—you definitely are—but because there would be a problem . . ."

"Problem? What are you saying, Pete? You're confusing me—a lot."

"Well, damn it, Ellie, you're going to have to replace me on the board of directors. Immediately."

"Why on earth would I do a crazy thing like that?"

"Because, my dear Ellie, it would be a conflict of interest for the soon-to-be CEO of C.A.R.E. to be dating a board member."

"But, we're not dating."

"No, we're not. Yet. But I am so hoping we will be. Starting now—with this being our first date. Wouldn't this be a perfect first date? The moon's starting to make a reflection on the lake. The lake is become as still as glass. And we're together. God, Ellie, I know this sounds crazy—believe me I've told myself that it is crazy a hundred times. But this doesn't feel crazy—it seems right. It seems incredible. It seems like the way it's supposed to go."

"That ol' wheel, it's gonna roll around once more," said Ellie.

"What?"

"It's a song that's been stuck in my head recently. It's a Johnny Cash song about when love does you wrong and you're left alone and the price is high. But that's not the end. That ol' wheel is gonna roll around again."

Pete reached out for her hand. "I have been trying so hard to not be feeling all the affection and admiration I do feel for you, Ellie. Because I don't want to be hurt again and I for sure don't want to cause you even a second of hurt after what you've been through."

"But I can't pretend I don't feel this way anymore. I don't know what the future will bring. We might not be suited for each other at all. We might fight like cats and dogs. I know you've been hurt and confused. Me too. I know this is risky. But I'd like to travel with you into a very uncertain future. I'd like to be there as you take on your new position. I want to travel the unknown path up ahead with someone who is familiar with sorrow and setbacks but still has the gumption, the gall, the good sense to say 'Yes' to what life is offering her. I want to go forward with you—as your equal—your partner—and if you'll take another chance—even as your husband. Will you?"

More tears washed her cheeks. She turned to welcome the extended arms Pete held out to her.

"Okay, under one condition."

"And what might that be?"

"If we get married, we get married on the beach!"

Another New Beginning

DISCUSSION GUIDE

When the Love and Marriage Carriage Comes Unhitched

A Guide for Reflection and Discussions on Marriage and Divorce

Asunder takes the reader through the journey of Ellie, a middle-aged woman who is divorced and who assumed she was in a marriage that would last a lifetime. Losing a long-term mate due to divorce is one of life's most difficult transitions. The story is also about Ellie's process of recovery and moving on in a new direction. This discussion guide provides a resource for those who never expected to be divorced, but are. It is also a resource for individuals or groups who want to study the history and changing attitudes toward dating, marrying, and divorcing.

For people who are active in a faith community, divorce often brings with it the shame of having failed to live up to personal and faith community expectations that marriages last until death parts the couple. On the other hand, those who do have an active faith life and participate in a healthy faith community often also find great solace as they turn to the traditional resources of faith: prayer, study of Scripture, worship, fellowship, and encouragement from other members of the faith community. This guide is designed for people who do have such a relationship with a faith community, though it does not advocate any particular religious point of view. People of equally deep faith have radically different interpretations of the Bible and the appropriate application of biblical writings to modern thorny social and personal issues. This guide leans more to the wider end of the interpretive spectrum.

It is designed for both individual reflection and small group discussions on the themes and topics related to marriage and divorce found in *Asunder*.

The four sessions are:

Session 1: Love and Marriage Today: What Did You Expect?

Session 2: Marriage Through the Ages: What's Love Got to Do with It?

Session 3: Marriage and the Bible: Scripture Says What?

Session 4: When the Divorce Is Yours

One Guide—Multiple Uses

The guide is a resource for:

- Individual reflection and study

- Church adult study groups

- Book clubs

- Retreats

- Support groups for newly divorced people

- A Bible study based on marriage and divorce themes

The guide is not intended to replace the benefits of professional help to cope with the often painful and confusing raw emotions that frequently accompany divorce. It is intended to help individuals understand the phenomena of marriage and divorce in the broader context of history and modern society.

Since each marriage is unique, each divorce is a one-of-a-kind loss. Each person who experiences a divorce must find his or her own way through the many legal, financial, emotional, and social issues leading up to and following a divorce. This takes time. This resource is intended be a helpful companion on that journey.

Though each divorce is unique to the partners in it, there are emotions and experiences common among most divorcing people. Thousands of divorced people have found tremendous healing power in sharing both their struggles and progress within the context of a caring small group. This discussion guide is also designed for use in such groups.

Given the high divorce rate in recent decades, most families probably have at least one member who is divorced. This guide is also intended to help relatives and friends of divorced loved ones understand what that person is experiencing and perhaps gain a deeper understanding of how to accompany their loved one through this tough transition.

Wherever Two or More Are Gathered—
Outline for Small Group Discussions

The guide provides material for four small group sessions. Each session is geared to last from sixty to ninety minutes. The length will depend on how comfortable people are with one another and therefore how inclined they are to share their stories with the group. If possible, allow an hour and a half for each session, but don't worry if the group doesn't need that long. You may find you'll need more time in later sessions.

This outline provides a general process for each small group session. Adjust it according to the needs and size of the group. Six to eight people is an ideal size. If you gather more than eight people, consider breaking into sub-groups to make it easier for participants to explore and express their thoughts and feelings.

I. Gather (5 minutes). A psalm or other short inspirational piece is read aloud, followed by a minute or two for silent reflection.

II. Check-in (5–10 minutes/person). Each person in the group checks in with a brief update on their current situation. Others should refrain from commenting or interrupting.

III. Explore (20 minutes). Ideally participants will read each section before the group meets. If this is not the case, take turns reading the material for one of the sessions together. The material from that session is then discussed. Participants ask questions of themselves and each other, such as, "Do you agree or disagree with this? "Is this new information for you?" "Does this change any of your thoughts about marriage and divorce?"

IV. Ponder (15 minutes). Participants answer as many of the section questions as the group finds helpful. Or, they may prefer to address some of the chapter questions from *Asunder,* which are located at the end of this discussion guide. It may be helpful to have paper and pen available to jot down individual thoughts before sharing them with the group. If the group meets primarily as a support group, break into sets of two or three persons each for this portion of the meeting.

V. Plan ahead (5 minutes). Members of the group may talk about their plans for the coming week if they wish.

VI. Closing (5 minutes). If the group is part of a faith-based community, someone may offer a closing prayer, or people may gather in two's and three's to pray for one another.

On My Own—Outline for Individual Reflection

Use this general outline for individual reflection as often and for as long as it is helpful.

I.   Offer a prayer, asking God to provide what you need for yourself—and your former spouse. Remember, forgiveness is good for the soul. You don't have to like it. Just do it (5 minutes).

II. Read a psalm, one of the Scriptures at the beginning of each chapter of *Asunder*, or a passage from a inspirational resource. Read the selection through several times, reflecting on each phrase (15 minutes).

III. Review the questions for one of the *Asunder* chapters, located at the end of this discussion guide. Reflect on how they apply to your own situation. You may want to write about this in a journal (15 minutes).

IV. List ideas for things you can do today or as soon as possible to nurture yourself (5 minutes).

V. Name two or more people you could contact as soon as possible to talk with or get together, to socialize—not necessarily to process the divorce (5 minutes).

VI. Write out a prayer of your own using the TRIP approach: T = Thanksgiving; R = Regrets; I = Intercessions for others; and P = Plans for the day or next day (15–20 minutes).

Love and Marriage Today—What Did You Expect?

We grow up in a specific culture. Where we grow up determines what we learn about love and marriage, often without even realizing we are learning. Everyone everywhere is impacted by the institution of marriage. Getting married significantly and irreversibly influences the emotional development, for better or worse, of both people. Deciding not to marry, but rather to cohabitate, also has significant impact on what direction life moves.

Throughout the ages marriage has been the basic building block of all societies. The United States is no exception. The American Psychological Association reports that ninety percent of U.S. adults marry by age fifty. In recent decades there has been a sharp increase in the number of couples living together without getting married. It is becoming common for younger couples to live together first and then marry. A 2005 *USA Today* article reported over two-thirds of couples surveyed reported they lived together before they married (Sharon Jayson, "Cohabitation is Replacing Dating," July 17, 2005).

It is a relatively new wrinkle in the love and marriage department that so many couples feel no obligation to seal the deal legally. Once upon a not-that-long-ago time couples who lived together without benefit of wedding were considered to be living in sin. There are still faith communities who would use such labels for people, but the church seems to have less and less influence on the situation. Even Pope Francis was willing to marry a couple, with children, who had not previously been married.

Today couples choose to live as though married without the legal marriage license for many reasons, including:

- Having watched marriages so often dissolve in divorce, they decide there's no point in marrying.

- One or both have assets they wish to preserve from community property laws. This particularly applies to people who marry later in life. However, in some states couples who present themselves in public as a married couple are eventually considered common-law spouses.

- One partner wants to marry; the other does not. The one who wants the ceremony decides to stay in the relationship anyway.

- So many of their peers are already cohabitating with someone they conclude this is the natural thing to do.

While cohabitation is increasingly common and accepted, studies continue to confirm what disease researcher William Farr discovered in the nineteenth century: Marriage is good for your health. He compared the age of mortality rates for married people, never married people, and widowed people. He concluded single people died in undue proportions to those who were married.

Tara Parker-Pope summarizes Farr's research with the statement: "Marriage is a healthy estate. The single individual is more likely to be wrecked on his voyage than the lives joined together in matrimony." (Tara Parker-Pope, "Is Marriage Good for your Health?," *New York Times*, April 4, 2010.)

Parker-Pope goes on though to note that this depends on the state of the marriage union. A happy marriage is good for one's health. A stressful or contentious one has negative effects.

Marriage of course also has a direct and life-long impact of well-being on any children resulting from that union or living with the couple. Children both flourish and suffer as a result of the actions of the adults around them. Marriage always impacts more people than the two who choose to marry or decide to cohabitate without benefit of matrimony. This is no doubt why society has had so many rules and traditions around the institution of marriage through the ages.

The American Psychological Association researchers conclude a healthy marriage is good for the two individuals in the union, as well as any children they raise together. A stable nuclear family unit appears to still be the best option for maximizing a child's potential. Family and marriage therapist Gayle McAdoo notes, "Stability is the key. Any combination of caring adults who can create a safe and secure home life provides the children the best environment in which to grow up."

Stable marriages are also good for communities. Happily married people tend to make for healthier, more content, and more productive citizens than those who lack such a built-in support system. The institution of marriage is undergoing major renovations in the twenty-first century, but it's not going to disappear any time soon. Nor is the twenty-first century the first time in human history ideas about love and marriage have changed.

The traditional understanding of marriage being a union of one male and one female who choose one another and stay together until one of them dies is often considered the norm today. However, the reality is that people may have multiple marriages over the course of a lifetime. Families consist of multiple adults living together and raising children together. The possibilities include:

- Two biological parents

- Adoptive parents with or without contact with birth parents

- One biological parent plus a step-parent

- One biological parent plus a live-in significant other

- A single parent

- A parent or two, plus a grandparent or other relatives

- A same gender couple

- Grandparents or other relatives raising children of a relative

- Children living back and forth between homes of birth parents with on-going contact with four or more extended families.

These shifts in society's understanding of what constitutes a legal union between two people keep attorneys, judges, and social scientists employed. Not all people choose to be married. In parts of the world parents still arrange the marriages. In some cultures very young girls are married off to husbands old enough to be their fathers or grandfathers. Some groups still practice polygamy.

Though unions between adults come in many variations, the urge to merge one's life with another in a deeply intimate relationship remains an almost universal longing. No wonder so many novels, how-to books, plays, songs, operas, and movies focus on themes of love and marriage.

Regardless of our marital status, we cannot escape the impact of the institution of marriage.

Given that marriage is such an enormous part of life, it would seem logical that we'd want to put as much effort into preparing people for marriage as we do for their careers or driving on public highways. Sadly, our American culture often fails terribly in this regard. Young people generally learn more about driving a car than sustaining a marriage.

To be sure, churches sponsor courses and retreats designed to prepare couples for marriage and then to sustain a healthy marriage. Millions of couples have benefited from these efforts. However, in general, what we learn about love and marriage from our families and our American culture is often sadly insufficient.

Since the end of World War II social scientists and religious leaders have been bemoaning the alarming statistic that nearly one in two marriages ends in divorce. Obtaining a truly accurate divorce rate is tricky. Some marriages end in desertion rather than divorce. Some unions dissolve without ever being recorded in the marriage statistics.

Po Bronson, author of *Why Do I Love These People,* writes:

> *Divorce rates don't take into account social and economic events that can have a huge influence on both marriage and divorce rates. During the Depression, divorce rates dropped—because getting a divorce was too expensive. It was cheaper to just abandon a family—which men did. In World War II, there was a marriage boom as young men hurriedly married before they went off to war—and then a divorce boom as their stranger-husbands returned.*

(Po Bronson, *Why Do I Love These People*, Random House, 2006.)

Ultimately, the only divorce statistic most people really care about is the one that applies to them. Nonetheless, divorce is, thankfully, no longer the scandal it once was, and no longer a reason to shun or shame those who do divorce. On the other hand, no divorce statistic seems to deter people from marrying or living together as though married.

Cultural Images of Marriage

Cultural interpretations of marriage err in two ways. On the one hand, popular culture romanticizes the idea of marriage to levels no two human beings could ever sustain. No one human being can ever meet all the emotional, physical, mental, and spiritual needs of another. It simply is not realistic to think anyone ever could. Much of what is portrayed in romantic novels and movies is, frankly, hogwash. Such stories make for entertaining reading and viewing, but they are *fiction*, not reality.

Reality is sticking it out through thick and thin: being there in sickness, debt, doubt, disillusionment, discouragement, and conflicting ideas about how to do everything from loading the dishwasher to dealing with a teenager who is clearly headed down a very dangerous path.

Even the most motivated and mature couples are going to hit rough patches along the road of marriage. Life is messy. People have different ideas about how to approach the messes of life. So sometimes, a marriage gets sick. It needs professional intervention and time to heal and recover. Just as we'd expect someone seriously injured in a car wreck to need a lot of extra care and time to recover, so too marriages get to places where they need extra care and time to heal. The good news is that, in this day and age, we have a multitude of resources available to help.

On the other hand, much of modern society teaches that marriage is a prison, a trap, or a life-sentence of sacrificing one's own well-being to pander to the every whim of another. Much of our entertainment media seems to start with the assumption marriage is an optional status for those who want that sort of thing but hardly necessary any more in order to establish a family. Watch how current television shows portray marriage. It's hard to find a show that paints a positive portrait of marriage.

In summary, public attitudes toward couples are changing. In part this is because as an American society we've been wrestling with the legal definition of marriage and who is eligible to marry whom. The times, they are definitely a changing. The institution of marriage is complicated today. Yet, marriage and cohabitating couples remain a central foundation for society. All cultures in all times and locations have had some variation of marriage. This isn't likely to change any time soon.

Ponder

- What assumptions did you have about marriage as a child?

- What factors do you think gave you those ideas?

- What did you learn about marriage from the marriages in your own family?

- If you are or have been married, how did you and your spouse meet? When did you decide to marry? What advice did you get from family, friends, or any professionals you may have consulted? Was that helpful? Why or why not?

- Think of some popular television shows or recent movies. How is the institution of marriage portrayed in these shows?

Marriage through the Ages: What's Love Got to Do with It?

Marriage is nearly as old as human culture and predates recorded history. A staff-written article in the magazine *The Week* suggests marriage is around 4,000 years old. A Columbia University History Professor is quoted on the subject of traditional marriage: "Whenever people talk about traditional marriage or traditional families, historians throw up their hands. We say, 'When and where?' Different cultures evolved different rituals and customs around marriage." (Staff Writers, "How Marriage Has Changed Over the Centuries," TheWeek.com, June 1, 2012.)

The article continues to explain how in Western cultures marriage served primarily to preserve power as influential families merged with each other through marriages, or to acquire additional land, or to produce a legitimate heir. The article quotes Harvard historian Nancy Cott, "Until two hundred years ago monogamous households were limited to Western Europe and little settlements in North America."

By the time of Christ, marriage was a well established custom for the Hebrew, Greek, and Roman cultures.

Today people sometimes talk about the need to return to the biblical concept of marriage.

In order to have an accurate conversation about biblical marriage, we need to define which form of marriage is under discussion. The Bible references all of these:

- Patriarchy

- Matriarchy

- Polygamy (which is still legal in some Middle Eastern and African cultures, and still practiced, though illegally, by some in the United States)

- Monogamy

- Marriage among cousins (which was common in ancient societies and still is today in some closed communities; that is, those that have minimal or no contact with outsiders)

- Exogamy (marrying beyond one's own social structure which was common at the turn of the twentieth century when land-rich but cash-poor nobility in Europe courted daughters of wealthy industrialists in America in order to save their vast estates)

- Patriarchy plus concubines (how the ancient world dealt with infertility issues).

Though Scripture does not address marriage between two people of the same gender it does contain references to same-gender relationships. Such relationships have been known throughout history. For example, Baylor University Professor of Social Sciences Rodney Stark writes extensively about various homosexual relationships. He has authored over thirty books and numerous articles about life in biblical times. The fact there has been so much written and recorded about same-sex unions indicates this form of human love has been present for many centuries.

However, in ancient times marriage had little to do with love. It was about survival and economic prosperity, not love. Life in the ancient world was brutal. If the wild beasts who roamed everywhere didn't get you, war, pestilence, or famine would. In order to survive people needed to be part of a group. In order to ensure the survival of the species, people needed to mate. According to theologians Malina and Rohrbaugh:

> *Under normal circumstances in the world of Jesus, individuals really did not get married. Families did. Their wedding stood for the wedding of the larger extended families and symbolized fusion of the honor of both families involved. Divorce, then, would entail the dissolution of these extended family ties. In this very real sense, divorce represented a direct and unmistakable challenge to the family of the recently former wife and would likely result in family feuding.* (Bruce Malina and Richard Rohrbaugh, *Social Science Commentary on the Synoptic Gospels*, Augsburg Fortress Books, 2003.)

Marriage began as an economic necessity and stayed that way for centuries. As kingdoms and monarchies formed, marriage also became a political necessity—merging kingdoms. So a divorce had little to do with resolving the unhappiness of one of the parties and much to do with threatening the economic and political stability of two large extended families. The pressure to stay connected was enormous.

For much of history women have been considered property. They still are in some cultures. First they belonged to their fathers, then to their husbands. If neither of these men were available, they became the property of a brother. If that wasn't possible, the woman was in serious trouble. It was rare for a woman to own property or be able to function on her own away from a family unit of one kind or another. In some Middle Eastern cultures today a woman needs a letter of permission from a male guardian to travel independently of a male relative. As recently as the early 1900s in the United States the author's grandmother was denied a room for the night when traveling alone to visit her father.

Emotional well-being was not a high priority among our forbearers. It was hard enough to find enough to eat and raise at least a few of the children to adulthood. Emotional satisfaction was very low on the list of factors to consider. If a woman was incapable of producing an heir for her husband, he was easily granted a divorce in order to try his reproductive luck with another woman. Women were not granted the same privilege. It was generally assumed infertility was the woman's problem, not her husband's.

Thus, according to Stephanie Coontz in *Marriage, a History: How Love Conquered Marriage,* it was common for marriages to take place among cousins. Father Abraham married his half-sister, Sarah.

Polygamy was common for centuries. Not until the sixth and later centuries did monogamy become the norm in Western cultures. The church played a major role in insisting on only one wife per husband. However, Coontz contends that some of the well-entrenched European nobility wanted to continue the custom of having two or more wives. Even within the United States today there are a select few religious groups that believe polygamy is acceptable and even preferable. (Stephanie Coontz, *Marriage, a History: How Love Conquered Marriage,* Penguin Books, 2006.)

Marriages were still often arranged for political and economic gain. They were contracts between families—each providing one half of the new unit. The habit of posting notices of upcoming weddings was established in part to allow time to disclose an existing marriage that would preclude going forward with the intended one. We sometimes hear this line in movie wedding scenes: "If anyone knows why this man and woman should not be joined together in holy matrimony, let them speak now or forever hold their peace." That was the last chance for anyone who knew of an already existing spouse to let that information be made public.

Who had the authority to sanction weddings has also evolved. In the Middle Ages great political and theological debates were held to determine whether the Church granted nobility their authority to determine civil issues or the royalty granted the Church its authority. As the Church grew in influence in the Western culture, weddings were generally handled within the Church. However, as Europeans started migrating to the Americas before churches and clergy were available, this gradually changed. Lacking church officials to perform the weddings, people turned to the civil authorities to preside.

Today a faith community's religious leader may pronounce the couple husband and wife, but the legal documents testifying to the union are recorded and maintained in the county clerk's office. In Australia, the newly married couple does not greet wedding guests until all the legal documents are signed and witnessed by a representative of the government.

Interracial couples have probably always existed as one tribe or city-state would invade another. History includes many stories like that of Pocahontas, a Native American, who aided the earliest European settlers and later married one.

However, it wasn't that long ago that it was illegal in many states for two people of different ethnic backgrounds to marry. In 1664 Maryland enacted the first anti-miscegenation law (unions between two people of different ethnic heritage) in the United States. By the 1700s five states had such laws. Starting in the 1940s states started repealing such laws. (*International Encyclopedia of Marriage and Family,* 2003.) Then the Supreme Court declared such laws unconstitutional. (*Loving v. Virginia,* U.S. Supreme Court, 1967.)

Today bi-racial children are common. In urban schools one is as likely to see children with bi-racial heritages as children with two parents from the same ethnic background.

At various times in human history marriage was discouraged. Indeed, eventually some branches of the Christian church forbid clergy to marry. While many theological reasons for celibacy have been given, one of the primary reasons was that it was a better economic strategy to have unmarried priests and female religious servants. Children are expensive. Plus, children would inherit property, which the church hierarchy preferred to keep among the church's assets.

Zoar Village in Northeast Ohio is now a living-history museum that preserves the history of several hundred German Separatists who migrated there in 1817 to establish a religious colony of their own. They practiced celibacy from 1822 to 1829 because they needed the labor of every adult to get their village established. (Ohio Historical Society, www.ohiohistory. wordpress.com, April 4, 2015.)

The Industrial Revolution changed much of daily life in the Western world, including assumptions about love and marriage. The concept of marrying for love began to emerge in the 1700s but didn't really take hold until the 1800s. The Industrial Revolution made it possible for the masses to accumulate household commodities beyond what they actually needed just to survive. Men were able to earn enough to provide for their families. It became a status symbol for a man's wife to be a homemaker or socialite rather than an economic partner in providing for their family.

As recently as the early years of the twentieth century, a woman of middle or upper class status would quit working when she married. It was thought inappropriate for a married woman to be out working. The women who did work likely did so as servants in the homes of more well to do families or with their husbands in a family-owned business. Often the business was located in the same building as their living quarters.

Today the debate continues about how much of a woman's time belongs to her family versus how much to her employer, but it would be hard indeed to find someone who thought it improper for a woman to ever earn her own income. Men's roles are also in flux. It is no longer odd to find a father in the pediatrician's office with his new baby or toddler. Nor is it unusual for the father to be the primary care-giver at home while Mom is away at the office all day.

With all our modern emphasis on love, romance, and extravagant weddings, it's hard to imagine that marriage was once more of a business arrangement than a loving, mutually nurturing relationship.

Alvin Toffler wrote back in the 1970s that society would see what he termed serial monogamy. He predicted people will only be married to one person at a time; but will increasingly be married two, three, or more times over the course of their lives. His predictions have proven true for many in the twenty-first century. (Alvin Toffler, *Future Shock*, Random House, 1970.)

Changing Attitudes and Responses to Divorce

Laws around divorce have treated men differently than women until relatively recently. Generally divorce was the prerogative of the men, because women were considered property. In the United States divorce was rare until the twentieth century when divorce laws began to change. In earlier years courts were reluctant to grant divorces for anything less than extreme cruelty. Even under those circumstances, the religious leaders often advised the beaten spouse to bear it as part of their lot in this life.

This began to shift in the mid-1900s. Authors Vlosky and Monroe write of a sort of "divorce revolution" that took hold in the 1970s with the introduction of "no fault" divorces. (Denese Ashbaugh Vlosky and Pamela A. Monroe, "The Effective Dates of No-Fault Divorce Laws in the 50 States," Vol. 51, No. 4, *Families and the Law*, Oct. 2002.)

During the 1970s thirty-seven of the fifty states accepted no-fault divorce standards where previously one of the spouses had to prove grounds for divorce. Faith communities have discouraged people from divorcing because of the disruption it causes, especially for children. However, law or no law, people find ways to resolve unhappy marriages. Before the introduction of modern mass communication systems, the unhappy spouse would sometimes just leave. Today the wandering spouse can be tracked down, but that wasn't so easy before telegram, telephones, cross-continental railways, and other means of sharing information across state lines.

Whether leaving a marriage was legal or not, people found a way to call it quits. Eventually the laws caught up with the reality. For example, England's King Henry VIII battled with the church on this issue in the 1500s. He wanted to divorce his wife and take another. The church said "No." He responded by establishing his own church, the Church of England, or Anglican Church. In his church, divorce was allowed, especially for a king who desperately wanted a male heir to the throne.

In some ways the United States has come a long way in the response to divorcing couples. This is partially because divorce has become so common in Western culture. It would be hard to find a modern family that didn't have some divorced person within it. Some couples may experience their spouse as a life-long soul mate—but this is the exception rather than the norm. This wasn't even an expectation until relatively recently in the course of human history.

Fortunately we've moved beyond the days when people were coerced into staying in destructive and even life-threatening marriages. The pendulum seems to have shifted to the far extreme. Today people divorce for many reasons. Since the introduction of no fault divorces, people no longer have to give a reason beyond the marriage isn't working for them. In some classrooms children living with both biological parents are in the minority among the complex arrangements of step-parents, live-in partners, same-gender partners, and single parents.

Love and marriage relationships are still a fundamental part of the fabric of society. However, the ways people unite have changed tremendously through the centuries, and continue to evolve and change today.

Ponder

- How would you define a "traditional" marriage?

- List as many reasons as you can for why a person might choose to remain single.

- What do you think are the most important factors to consider when two people are thinking about marrying?

- What are the advantages of cohabitation over marriage? Of marriage over cohabitation?

- What would you consider to be valid reasons for ending a marriage via divorce?

- Think of five families you know fairly well. What do you know about the marital status of the people in those families?

- Do you know any couples you consider to be in a "non-traditional" relationship? What makes it so in your opinion?

SESSION THREE

Marriage and the Bible: Scripture Says What?

Churches often struggle with how to respond to divorcing members. Too often the response has been legalistic finger-wagging: "You made a commitment. You have to stick with it, no matter what." The Bible and what it says is often used as the justification for shunning and shaming divorced people. Because marriage is a universal human relationship, the Judeo-Christian Scriptures do have a lot to say about marriage. As noted in Session Two, Scripture identifies a wide variety of marriage arrangements.

Authority of Scripture

The Bible contains sixty-two references to marriage and another thirty to divorce. Old Testament references include data about various historical people and their families, the laws as handed out to the people by Moses, plus poetry and proverbs about the profound emotional connection between lovers. The New Testament passages are interpretations of Old Testament assumptions about marriage or divorce and practical advice from religious community leaders, particularly the apostle Paul in his letters to the new Christian communities.

Still, church communities struggle to know how to respond to divorcing members in a helpful way. Some members are denied participation in the church. In some faith traditions couples who divorce are excluded from communion. Some are forbidden to remarry—at least not in the church.

Some are scolded or advised to keep trying to make it work, even in situations of domestic violence.

Since the Bible is so often quoted in addressing the issue of divorce, it is useful to take a look at what Scripture really does say about marriage and divorce.

How We Read Scripture Matters

The Bible is not one book. It is a collection of sixty-six books—a library of wisdom. These books were written over a period of centuries— the last one being around 200 or so CE. They were written by different authors, to a variety of people, living in different places, for specific purposes. None of them were written to address life in the twenty-first century in the United States.

Biblical authors were influenced by the cultures in which they lived. The New Testament writings in particular were influenced by the Greek and Roman cultures. The Jewish people lived under Roman occupation at the time of the New Testament writings. The Greek culture also had a major influence on the thinking of people in that era. Much of what we read in Scripture was written to address the challenges of the Jewish/Christian communities living under those influences.

People of faith have approached the same Scriptures with radically different understandings about what they are reading and what the words mean. These different approaches to understanding and applying Scripture in modern times have led to more than a few conflicts between and within various faith communities.

Different faith traditions have very different understandings about what the Scriptures say and how to apply Scripture to social situations. The Bible contains legends, short stories, poetry, satire, and other forms of literature. All of these can reinforce great universal truths without being factually accurate. Different literary forms serve different purposes. We wouldn't expect to learn much history from a cookbook. We wouldn't expect a history book to be of much help in repairing a car. Each of these forms of writing is most beneficial when we accept it for what it is.

Additionally, any thorough study of Scripture must include studying the language in which the text was first written. None of it was originally written in English. Some texts have been translated from Aramaic or Hebrew into Greek and/or Latin before being translated into English. It's easy to lose the original intent in translation.

Only after careful study and research has been applied, do we dare make pronouncements about how to apply the text to today's thorny social issues.

Two Forms of Laws Contained in the Bible

Bible scholars refer to two forms of laws within the Bible. One form is normative or absolute laws, which are timeless and not subject to change with the shifting tides of human society. The Ten Commandments are these kinds of laws.

Casuistic or programmatic laws, which apply to a specific culture, time, or situation, comprise a second form of laws. For example U.S. citizens no longer expect to enforce biblical laws about how to treat slaves since as a society we finally concluded slavery is wrong. Yet the Bible contains references to treatment of slaves since slavery was common in biblical times.

Life Then and There

Life in the Middle East in the first century where Jesus did his teaching was about as different from life today in our North American society as it could be and still be on the same planet.

Back then:

- Men owned property, livestock, slaves, and their wives and children.

- Adultery was more a legal issue than a moral one. A man needed to be sure his sons, who would inherit his property, really were his sons.

- Additionally, forbidding adultery assured that a man had exclusive rights to his wife—his property. She was literally given to her husband by her father.

- Women could not own property.

- Women could not initiate divorce—for any reason.

- A man could divorce his wife for any reason and if he did, she could easily become desperate and destitute.

- A father chose a wife for his sons. Love was not the main issue; finding a suitable mother for future children and ensuring the family livelihood would thrive was more important.

- When a man left his family to start one of his own, he was leaving the security and support of his family system. Thus it was important that the bride be suitable to help him establish his own family and prosper.

The institution of marriage suffered in Jesus' time. Greek culture with its lax moral standards influenced society. Greek philosophy separated the physical from the spiritual. This led people to conclude it didn't matter what they did with their bodies, since the spiritual self was what mattered; or to ignore physical needs to pursue spiritual pastimes. The Jewish people were influenced by these negative attitudes toward marriage in the cultures around them.

The institution of marriage was further challenged because Christians, who were being persecuted in the Roman Empire, were less likely to marry. Single people could hide or leave more readily than people with family responsibilities.

It is against this backdrop that the author of Mark inserts the following exchange between Jesus and the Pharisees:

And standing up he (Jesus) went from there into the region around Judea and beyond the Jordan, and again crowds flocked to him. And as he was accustomed to doing, he again was teaching them. And the Pharisees coming up asked him if it is lawful for a man to divorce a wife, testing him. And answering, he said to them, "What did Moses command you?" And they said, "Moses allowed (us) to write a certificate of divorce and to divorce." But Jesus said to them, "For the hardness of your heart he wrote this commandment to you but from the beginning of creation he made them male and female. Because of this a man will leave his father and mother and shall adhere closely to his wife and the two will become one flesh, so that they are no longer two, but one flesh. Therefore what God has yoked together, let not man separate. And again in the house the disciples were asking him about this. And he said to them, "Whoever shall divorce his wife and marry another, commits adultery against her and if she, after divorcing her husband, shall marry another she commits adultery" (Mark 10:1-16, NRSV).

Assumptions about Marriage in New Testament Times

In the Mark account marriage has evolved in three phases: 1) The original intent that a male and female join together in marriage; 2) a period of compromise made necessary by the hardness of heart of the people; and, 3) Jesus re-introducing the original intent with a deepened ideal of marriage. Jesus taught that marriage was the original form of human fellowship.

The early church leaders who began to forge Christian doctrines after the time of Jesus taught that marriage is a continuation of the divine work of creation. (David Atkinson, "Marriage and Divorce," *Eerdmans Handbook to Christian Belief,* Eerdmans Publishing, 1982.)

As previously discussed, the Bible records several forms of marriage. Adultery was defined as having illicit sexual relations. A man, married or not, was only considered to be committing adultery if he had sexual relations with a woman who was either married or betrothed. The adultery deprived the rightful husband or betrothed to exclusive sexual contact with his woman.

In the Jewish culture a woman could be put to death if caught in an adulterous situation. Roman law limited the punishment to divorce, but the divorced woman forfeited the marriage contract money that her family had given to her husband. She was also denied the right to marry the person with whom she'd committed adultery.

Changes in Attitude in the New Testament

By the time of Jesus, divorce was so common women were reluctant to marry, though they often had little say in the matter. In the time of Moses a woman without a divorce certificate from her husband was abandoned. This is probably why Moses granted permission to divorce, in order to mitigate the situation. At first, a certificate was a simple statement written by the husband granting the woman permission to leave and marry another man.

As happens when more people get involved in a situation, the certificate process grew more complicated. Eventually getting a divorce certificate required the services of a skilled rabbi and an appearance in court where three rabbis and the Sanhedrin got involved in the process.

Jesus' teachings recorded in the New Testament were a change of the status of marriage and infidelity. Under early church teachings neither men nor women were free to have multiple partners; both were expected to limit sexual contact to within the marriage or to remain celibate.

Some of the earliest church teachers harbored rather negative outlooks on the institution of marriage. Consider St. Augustine (CE 430) who wrote, "I fail to see what use woman can be to man, if one excludes the function of bearing children." Or Justin Martyr (CE: 100-165) who believed, "We Christians marry only to produce children." (Robert Obach, *The Catholic Church on Marital Intercourse: From St. Paul to Pope John Paul II*, Lexington Books, 2009.)

In contrast to these negative impressions of matrimony, Jesus taught that marriage is a sacred relationship between partners, one that reflects God's divine love for humanity. If a divorced man or woman remarried they were considered guilty of adultery. This was a radical, new concept at the time.

Who Wants to Know, and Why

In Mark 10 the question about divorce is initiated by the Pharisees; not out of desire to know but to trap Jesus in some way. Jesus outsmarts them by tossing the question back at them, asking them what was commanded of them by Moses. They asked about what was allowed. Jesus asks about what is required. The Pharisees want to focus on what is legal. Jesus wants to focus on what is expected.

Then Jesus switches gears. He points out the only reason Moses conceded was because of humanity's refusal to accept God's plan for marriage. Moses was trying to keep some semblance of order and fairness in a situation that was eroding rapidly.

By referring back to the creation accounts Jesus focuses on the special sort of bond between a man and a woman in marriage that includes a coming together physically and spiritually. He and she form a third entity—they form a "we." God joins them together in this way, but each remains a free agent who can undo the union. Ultimately, it appears Jesus is not condemning divorce per se, but rather is elevating the importance of marriage and judging those who want to trade a current spouse in on a different partner.

What Does this Mean for Us Today?

Even though the sanctity of marriage was often corrupted in Jesus' time and some early religious leaders recommended staying single—Jesus taught that marriage is part of God's plan from the very beginning of creation. It was intended to be a gift to humanity. It still is.

However, humanity still struggles with issues of hardness of hearts and refusal to do things God's way. When this happens, divorce is a painful and sad commentary on our human inability to live up to God's hopes for us. David Atkinson writes in *Handbook to Christian Belief,* "A divorce, like an amputation, is the severing of what was once a living union. Indeed, the Old Testament word for divorce is related to cutting down trees, even chopping off heads." (David Atkinson, *Marriage and Divorce, Handbook to Christian Belief,* Lion Publishing, 1982.)

Ultimately, the most important commandment that applies to divorce or any other human setback is found a couple of chapters later. Again the religious authorities are trying to trap Jesus by asking about the laws regarding a brother's obligation to marry his deceased brother's widow so that she can produce an heir for the deceased husband. They want to know to whom she'll be married in the next life if she goes through all seven brothers without producing a child.

Jesus asks them: *"Is not this why you are wrong, that you know neither the Scriptures nor the power of God?"* Then he reminds them of the first and second most important commandments: *"You shall love the Lord your God with all your heart, and with all your soul, and with all your mind, and with all your strength. And you shall love your neighbor as yourself."*

Jesus concludes, *"There is no other commandment greater than these"* (Mark 12:24, 30-31, RSV).

A fair, love-focused study of Scripture does not condemn those who fail to sustain a marriage until the death of one spouse. Marriage is a gift. Divorce is a tragic loss of that gift. God is fond of giving second chances—and third, and fourth, and as many as it takes to restore us to a right spirit.

Churches have an important role to play in the realm of love and marriage, but it ought not be to condemn and exclude people who divorce. Rather, churches can be a source of preparation for marriage before the wedding, on-going encouragement and support after the wedding, and forgiveness and compassionate care when the union breaks under the strain of modern life.

Ponder

- What are your earliest memories about the Bible? Where did you first explore the contents of Scripture? Did what you learned comfort you or challenge and frighten you?

- What do you know about how churches have responded to people who get divorced? What do you think about those responses?

- What experiences have you had with Bible studies? What resources do you have for studying Scripture? What helps you understand the background, meaning, and application of Scripture?

- What reaction do you have when someone starts a conversation with the phrase, "The Bible says . . ."

- These passages shed light on the thinking about marriage in Old Testament times: Genesis 34 (entire chapter), Deuteronomy 22:13-30; Deuteronomy 24:1-5; and Deuteronomy 25:5-11.

- If you wish to study more about marriage from the New Testament era, these passages reflect the thinking of the earliest Christian leaders: 1 Corinthians 7 (entire chapter); Romans 7:1-3, and Hebrews 13:4.

SESSION FOUR

When the Divorce is Yours

In recent years some churches have begun offering divorce recovery workshops and seminars such as the thirteen-week Divorce Care program or the Love and Respect Seminars started by Emerson and Sarah Eggerichs. Many congregations provide care via their pastors or trained lay people. Some congregations offer organized social outings for single adults, sometimes organized according to various age groups (www.divorcecare. org, www.loveandrespect.com).

If you are one of the millions of Americans who have firsthand knowledge of divorce, you have probably learned that people around you often did not know quite how to respond to you. They may have wondered if they should ask you how you're doing or if they should give you space. They may not know if they should ever mention your former spouse's name in your presence. They debate whether to invite you to do things with them that you used to do as a foursome.

A divorce introduces a long list of lessons to learn that you probably never wanted to study. Your friends are probably struggling with how to be most supportive of you. Adjusting to divorce is a process that unfolds over a period of many months—possibly many years. Your friends and family members may not understand your swings in emotions. You may seem content and well-adjusted one day and then burst into tears for reasons you may not understand yourself, let alone know how to explain to anyone with you when it happens.

In today's society when marital bliss turns into perpetual hiss, some couples are quick to give up and head to the divorce attorney's office. Perhaps you were the one who just couldn't bear to continue in a relationship that was sucking the emotional life out of you. Perhaps you were on the receiving end of the announcement that your partner was leaving, for reasons that may not make any sense to you, no matter how long ago it happened.

People are freer today than ever to seek out lives of serenity and satisfaction in ways denied to previous generations. The down side of this is that this results in much confusion and many nasty fights about who gets what and who has what rights to decisions regarding the children. If you were married for many years and/or you have raised children together, there are many challenging issues to confront for years and years to come.

Responses to Expect When You Divorce

Often the response to the pain, humiliation, fear, and grief you may experience as you divorce will be silence. There will be no public announcement or mention in the prayers of the church. Many people learn about the divorce via the rumor mill. Rumor mills tend to be more rapid than accurate. Though you may be emotionally hemorrhaging, you likely will not receive the kinds of consolation provided when a spouse dies. When a spouse dies, people come around with cards and casseroles. When you divorce, people don't know what to do, so they often do nothing.

This inconsistent response to the death of your marriage can lead to terrible loneliness. First you lose your spouse and your anticipated future together; then in some cases, the support of family members; and in some cases even close friends. If you and your former spouse were active in a congregation together, one or both of you will probably drop out. This becomes yet another change generated by the divorce.

There are no easy answers for how to address this. Pastoral care helps. Professional counseling helps. Some congregations assign trained lay people to stay in touch through the loss and adjustment. This too can help. In recent years some churches have begun offering divorce recovery workshops and seminars such as the thirteen-week DivorceCare program (www.divorcecare.org).

Many congregations provide care via their pastors or trained lay people. Some congregations offer organized social outings for single adults, sometimes organized according to various age groups. Library and bookstore shelves are lined with advice books. Online book distributors offer literally hundreds of titles to consider. Online chat rooms provide a virtual community of other divorced and divorcing people. Be careful though as some of these postpone healthy recovery as untrained and unrestrained angry bitter people rehash the sins of their former mates with venom and hatred that may be understandable but won't promote healing.

Enterprising writers have crafted family ministry resources suggesting you and your estranged spouse participate in some faith-based ritual to acknowledge the divorce. While this seems like a potentially good idea, if you could work together well enough to pull that off, you probably wouldn't be divorcing.

It's understandable that church leaders, friends, and family don't know how to respond to people who are divorcing. You probably don't know yourself from one week to the next what would be most helpful to you. In the first painful months what most divorcing people want most is for the pain to go away.

Phases of Recovery

Divorced people can sometimes identify three phases they've experienced as they make their way through the recovery process: 1) He or she did this to me; 2) It was all my fault. I messed this up; 3) We undid this marriage together.

Phase 1: He/She Did this to Me

Common in the first phase of recovery is for you to believe your divorce was all your partner's fault. You might find yourself caught up in a whole lot of "if only" thinking. If only he/she would have or would have quit . . . Sadly, some divorced people remain stuck in this way of thinking. Though it's been fifteen years since Katrisha was divorced from Stanley, she still lists his many shortcomings to anyone who will listen.

Anger abounds and sometimes overflows the emotional banks that would normally hold it in check. The anger can cause considerable harm to your former spouse, your children, other family members, and innocent bystanders. Anger is a cover or bumper emotion, covering up the deep hurt beneath or behind it.

Like many who experience divorce, you may conclude divorcing is the most painful emotional event you've ever experienced. It is a wound that can take a very long time to heal. Divorce recovery coaches suggest it can take a year of recovery for every five years of marriage. Bitter tirades about your former spouse are understandable but can also drive away friends who want to be supportive, weary of the endless litany of the ex-partner's many character flaws.

The anger is understandable, but it needs to be managed in healthy ways. Otherwise, one risks the danger of being the subject of the next news report about the raw violence inflicted on a former spouse—with fatal consequences in some cases. Becoming the unwilling participant in a divorce can generate enormous feelings of betrayal and abandonment. However, acting out those angry feelings merely prolongs the healing process.

Phase 2: It Was All My Fault. I Messed this Up.

After months of blaming ex-husband Ralph, Samantha did a complete turn-around and began heaping coals of self-recrimination on herself. Ralph re-married two years after their divorce. She was still single and not dating five years later, convinced she must have been the problem in their marriage. Like some divorced people, you may come to the conclusion the divorce was all your fault, which is another phase in the recovery process. Perhaps you believe, "I must have done something horrible to drive him/her away."

This remorse, guilt, and shame can be self-destructive. It is not uncommon for divorced people to deal with their pain and doubts about their self-worth through addiction or other forms of self-defeating behavior. Trying to ease pain in these ways offers at best temporary relief. It often adds more misery to an already miserable situation.

Back in 1883 poet Ella Wheeler Wilcox pointed out that:

Laugh and the world laughs with you,

Weep and you weep alone,

For the sad old earth must borrow its mirth,

But has trouble enough of its own.

(Ella Wheeler Wilcox, *Pocket Book of Quotations*, Pocket Books, 1942.)

Tears have their place in the divorce recovery process. Tears help flush out the grief and sorrow that inevitably accompany the demise of a marriage. However, eventually, there comes a time to dry the tears and turn to a different form of companionship and social life.

Phase 3: We Undid this Together

Eventually, thankfully, most divorced people realize they both contributed to the death of their marriage—either through actions taken or actions not taken which might have made a difference. This realization is the third and final phase of recovery. However, people do not move through grief in neat linear phases. You may experience each of these phases many times over a period of years as you adjust to your new marital status.

You do not have to wait for your spouse to come to this same conclusion. Once you decide you each knowingly or unknowingly let the marriage change from one of mutual nurturing to one of distance and contention, you are well on your way to a happier and healthier future.

It is a blessing if you and your former spouse are able to eventually establish a friendly post-marriage relationship. This will be a great relief to your children, former in-laws, close friends, and others who struggle to know how to respond to the divorced version of the couple they'd known before.

However, both parties have to make the effort to be on friendly terms. It is impossible to do someone else's cooperating for them. Reaching a place of mutual respect and cooperation is the ideal goal. Some reach that goal; many others do not. You are only responsible for your part in that drama.

Divorced people who go on to live peace-filled lives have figured out a way to forgive with or without the participation of the former spouse. We cannot control how the other person behaves. We do control how we respond to whatever the other decides to do or refuses to do. Holding grudges is like sipping poison and hoping it will make the other person sick.

What to Do, What Not to Do

Friends often simply do not know what to say, so they say nothing. It is particularly difficult for close friends who remain fond of both parties and wish to avoid taking sides. For some the divorce decree is a long-awaited emancipation declaration. Friends wonder if this is the time to bring out the champagne and toast to new-found freedom.

For others the divorce decree feels like a death certificate for a life that ended too soon. Friends wonder if maybe they should hold a wake and wear black. Since only the two people in the marriage really know what happened, your wisest friends will proceed with caution before offering too many congratulations or too much sympathy.

The most helpful responses will likely come from friends who include their suddenly single-again friends in whatever social things they're doing. Being single again will probably be a jolt to every aspect of your life. Getting invited to events without worrying about even numbers of men and women present is a gift. God bless friends who invite conversation and take time—a lot of time—to talk through the confusing pendulum of your constantly changing emotions. Notes of encouragement, offers to listen and invitations to do things together go a long way toward mending a broken heart.

Moving On

Some divorce advice books and articles encourage dating, complete with intimate overnights—as soon as possible. Some even suggest sampling a variety of different bed partners. This is poor advice, primarily because spouses are not like cars that you trade in when you tire of one and need another one. Aside from issues of morality, such behavior doesn't allow your psyche or spirit time to recover.

Even if the divorce was in the best interests of both parties for reasons of emotional and physical well-being, there has been a major life transition. Your spirit needs a little time to catch up. Modern culture bombards us with constant noise and distractions. It is hard to find quiet places, but quiet spaces are exactly what your spirit needs to renew and recover. Just as bed rest is prescribed as part of the recovery process from major illnesses, so too is quiet time appropriate to recover from major losses. This doesn't mean you should drop out of life; but it is helpful to narrow the number of activities for a while to adjust to the many changes resulting from a divorce.

How long this takes varies from person to person. All human beings need some time to just be. "Just be" is very good advice for you as you learn how to be a separate human being again.

The divorce decree is not the end of the relationship. There are all sorts of emotional land mines up ahead to be navigated. When you married you formed a link that can never be completely undone. Until you die or develop complete amnesia, you cannot wipe out memories of experiences with your former spouse. The world is filled with all sorts of triggers that will bring the memories gushing up from your subconscious like the Old Faithful geyser.

Author Joan Didion describes how music, billboards, dates on the calendar, smells, and all manner of things set off the tears again in her first year of grieving the death of her husband and near death of their daughter. It is so for most divorced people as well. (Joan Didion, *The Year of Magical Thinking*, Alfred A. Knopf, 2005.)

There are decisions to make about how to handle the inevitable march of the calendar through holidays, birthdays, children's milestone events, and other life events that you once observed together. Does one attend while the other declines? Do you both go? Do you take turns? Where do new partners fit into the scheme of things? For older couples who divorce after decades of relating to the partner's extended family through weddings, births and baptisms, graduations, and probably a few funerals there is the sticky challenge of knowing whether and how to stay in touch with these people. Are all those relationships gone too?

All this has to be figured out day by day, event by event. It takes a very long time to sort it all out. If you do not take time to do this emotional sorting out, the chances of a successful future relationship with someone else are low. Attaching emotionally and physically to another person prematurely impedes the process and further complicates it.

Yet, divorced people can, do, and should move on. Moving on might well include marrying again. Or not. Either way, faith in God and participation in a caring community of faithful people can be an important part of that process. People really do need people.

The world is constantly changing. People either learn to adapt to the changes or suffer the consequences. Regardless of the reasons for the divorce, people do heal; but it happens in God's time. The reality is the odds were stacked against you before you said "I do."

Modern Culture Undermines Marriage

Modern culture undermines the institution of marriage in a variety of ways. Couples trying to navigate the rapids of marital hard times often do so in isolation from their families who might have served as shock absorbers during the turbulent times. Popular media is quick to mock marriage and slow to provide realistic examples of healthy marriages. Society generally takes a "don't ask, don't tell" attitude toward infidelity and promiscuity, until there's a political or economical advantage to shaming the wandering spouse in the public spotlight.

The modern work place typically puts corporate profit way ahead of family time, adding considerable stress to an already stressful situation. Exhausting travel schedules and insanely long commute times limit quality time together at home. So when a couple's marriage fails to match unrealistic romantic images, one or both figure they just got a bad deal and decide to trade this spouse in on another one.

There are three deal breakers that make sustaining a strong marriage extremely difficult. A marriage might overcome these, if *both* parties want to do so. They are:

- Addiction

- Abuse in any form

- Adultery

All these can be addressed and resolved. Maybe. The addicted, abusing, or adultery committing spouse has to admit there is a problem to be resolved. Too often the offending spouse thinks the only problem is that the other one is complaining about their behavior. Too often friends and even professionals blame the partner for causing the inappropriate behavior. It takes a tremendous amount of maturity to come face to face with our failures and admit we need to mend our ways. Since much of the emotional and mental condition that leads to addiction, abuse or adultery is an inability to maturely face life, this becomes a major stumbling block.

Later in Life Divorces

Divorce is rough at any age. When older couples divorce there are fewer years to regroup and put together a post-marriage life or start again with someone else. Sorting out who will get what from the many years of joined efforts reduces what may have been a civil relationship to calculated and often very bitter disputes about everything from the travel souvenirs to the dog.

When an older couple joins their lives they are operating without the foundation of years of shared efforts. They did not raise a family together or support one another's career efforts or navigate together their way through the many transitions of modern life. Each operates in a void of first-hand knowledge of what the other was like in decades past. The other's extended family of siblings and in-laws, adult children and their children, cousins, and long-term friends may or may not easily and readily welcome this new person into the family fold. It is not unlike the reaction of a physical body following an organ transplant.

Picking Up the Pieces

Only you can know what will help you recover, regroup, and move on after your divorce. The quality of your post-divorce life is in your hands. The worst thing you can do is spend the rest of your life resenting your former spouse or blaming yourself for being a less-than-ideal mate. Pick and choose from the suggestions below those that you think will help you move though the disappointment and pain to a new way of life in which you not only survive but once again thrive.

- Seek out a trusted friend and talk regularly about your changing emotions and challenges.

- Get professional help.

- Ask a pastor to guide you through a private service of confession and forgiveness.

- Participate in a divorce recovery program.

- Read your way through self-help books and magazine articles.

- Join a support group for divorced people or form one yourself.

- Write a letter to your former spouse (which you probably should refrain from mailing—at least for the first year).

- Join a new group that does things you enjoy—a new hobby or pick an old one you've let lapse.

- Redecorate your home if the divorce hasn't resulted in a move and you can afford to do so without piling up debt.

- Go on a few day trips or short overnight trips alone or with a group.

- Volunteer in a new venue where no one knows your story until you're ready to share it.

- Join a health club where you can meet some new people and get some exercise.

We live in a broken world. People do the best they can with what they've got, and sometimes that just isn't enough. But there is life after the death of a long-term marriage, and with enough time and self care, much of it can be very good.

Ponder

- If you've been divorced, what were some of the most difficult aspects of it? If you haven't been through a divorce, what do you think would be the most difficult aspect?

- What's the worst or least helpful thing anyone said to you following a major loss?

- What was the most helpful thing anyone said to you following a major loss?

- What are some of the most grace-filled things others have done for you?

- What helpful new insights about the institution of marriage has this study guide given you?

ASUNDER DISCUSSION QUESTIONS

You may wish to use the questions for each chapter of *Asunder* for personal study and reflection or with a small group of others who are struggling to adjust to being divorced. If your group is a book club the group leader may want to choose ten to twelve questions from the many listed here so the group can discuss *Asunder* in one meeting. Adult study group leaders may want to pre-select a few questions for each time the group meets.

As an alternative, groups may want to use the following more general discussion questions about marriage and divorce, in addition to the questions following the material in each of the four discussion guide sessions.

General Discussion Questions about Marriage and Divorce

1) What were your expectations about marriage when you were growing up? Did you expect you would marry? What did you think it would be like to be married?

2) Did anyone in your family divorce when you were a child? If so, what did the members of your family say about it?

3) Has anyone in your family been divorced and remarried? If so, how did the family respond to that situation?

4) How would you summarize the institution of marriage in the United States today?

5) What are some ideas you have about how friends or church members can be helpful to people experiencing divorce?

6) What changes have you observed in the way people today meet, court, and get together? What do you think about these changes?

7) What factors might indicate that someone was healing from a divorce?

8) What factors might indicate that someone was not healing?

9) How long do you think someone should wait to date after a divorce? Marry again?

10) What would you want to say to someone who was dead-set against their parents dating or marrying again?

CHAPTER BY CHAPTER DISCUSSION QUESTIONS

Chapter 1

1) Ellie discovers her wedding anniversary date triggers powerful memories. If you've been through a divorce talk about how you handled the first few anniversaries after the divorce.

2) If not, what are some special calendar dates that evoke powerful memories for you? How do you handle it when the memories switch from wonderful to painful?

3) Think about other significant dates that could be potential emotional landmines: birthdays, children's birthdays, anniversary dates of former in-laws or close friends the couple may have celebrated with before the divorce. What ideas do you have for the best ways to handle these occasions?

Chapter 2

1) Ellie turned to the water as a place to recover and find peace. Where are some of your favorite resting and renewing places?

2) Ellie admits she had bouts of doubt. Do you think this was typical? What would you want to say to someone who tells you they just aren't sure they believe all the "God stuff?"

3) Ellie's dreams were a source of both information and inspiration. Have you had particularly vivid dreams? Were they helpful to you? Comforting? Frightening?

Chapter 3

1) Ellie found refuge in her work at the emergency relief center. Has there been a time in your life when work helped you through a situation? In what ways did that help?

2) Ellie's pastor, Elaine Forbes, strongly urged her to seek professional help. Do you think that was appropriate? Why or why not?

3) How do you think professional help assists someone experiencing a major loss? What might you say to someone you think would benefit from such help, but seems afraid of it?

Chapter 4

1) Ellie experiences many changes after her divorce. Often one major life change starts a chain of other changes. Has that been true in your life? Explain.

2) The divorce led Ellie to more contact with her adult children. What words of wisdom would you give adult children regarding how to respond to the divorce of their parents?

3) Ellie was afraid the marriage of her daughter might also be in trouble. Do you think she was over reacting or not?

Chapter 5

1) At church Ellie is introduced to newcomers in the area and congregation. Think about how you first got acquainted with people who play a major part in your life now. Where do you see God's hand in making the introductions?

2) When have you surprised yourself at how you reacted to a new situation?

3) Ellie decided to keep her dream about writing from her family initially. Why do you think she was reluctant to talk about this?

Chapter 6

1) It is said birds of a feather like to flock together. Ginny and Ellie form a quick bond because they both have an interest in writing and have both been divorced. What common experiences or interests have helped you connect with others?

2) Women seem to naturally share their feelings and personal experiences with one another. Why do you think that is the case?

3) Ginny asks, "What's normal?" How would you define "normal?"

Chapter 7

1) Ellie is expanding her world and enjoying the new adventures. In what ways is your life today the way you thought it might be?

2) Some of the changes for Ellie are exciting; some are awkward and frightening. How do you handle the changes in your life?

3) Ellie took time to walk around her old neighborhood. Have you ever gone back through a home you once lived in? If so, what motivated you to do so and what was that like for you? Do you agree with the idea we can never go home again? Why or why not?

Chapter 8

1) How do you respond to people you haven't seen in a long time who don't know about a major life-changing event occuring in your life? How do you decide when and what to tell them?

2) Do you have any experience dating after the end of a marriage? If so, what were you feeling as you prepared for the date? Afterwards?

3) Neighborhoods (and all of life) are in constant change. How do you feel about the changes in your life and community? Is it progress or devastation?

Chapter 9

1) There isn't always a third party present in the break-up of a marriage. But often there is. What do you think is the best approach when you know a person is being unfaithful but you suspect their spouse is unaware?

2) To what extent should parents be involved in the work environment of their adult children?

3) To what extent should work colleagues get involved in each other's personal lives?

Chapter 10

1) Has your faith community been there for you in a time of crisis? If so, in what ways? If not, what do you wish had happened?

2) Divorce sets in motion a series of changes and losses. List as many as you can.

3) Ellie reports feeling like she might have died when Chet left her. Do you think she was being honest with herself or over reacting to the situation?

Chapter 11

1) A divorce often includes a move, change of job, change of church attendance, change of one's social life or other routines. How do you handle disruptions in your normal routines?

2) Pastor Trent (nicknamed Pete) encourages Ellie to try the "do nothing" therapy for a while. How easy or difficult is it for you to just "do nothing" once in a while?

3) Pete reveals what happened to his fiancé and how that led him to do the social ministry work he does. Have you been led down a certain path because of a tragedy that occurred to you or someone close to you? Discuss what happened.

Chapter 12

1) At C.A.R.E. some of the poorest clients are in a position to help those who are new to being poor. Does this surprise you?

2) Sooner or later we all find ourselves in a situation where we need help. How do you go about letting someone know you need help?

3) Ellie was finding healing and a renewed sense of hope through her work helping others. When or where have you experienced renewed optimism?

Chapter 13

1) Ellie begins to experience a panic attack at the thought of being all alone over the Christmas holiday. Have you ever had to be totally alone when you desperately wanted to be with someone—anyone? How did you handle it?

2) What do you think about Pastor Elaine's invitation to have Ellie spend the holiday with her dying father and family? Charity? Desperate need? Intuition? Amazing timing? Have you ever experienced that kind of perfect timing?

3) Ellie admits she was jealous of Pastor Elaine's mother because her husband died rather than divorcing her. What do you think about that conclusion? What might this indicate about her capacity to empathize with other people?

Chapter 14

1) It appears Ellie has turned an emotional corner and is moving out of her grief. How do you gage when you are recovering from some emotional blow?

2) Pete seems to enjoy a ministry of cookie-bearing and joke-telling. Do you think his approach is helpful? Why or why not?

3) What is your first impression of Liam? What do you think it was about him that attracted Ellie?

Chapter 15

1) Sexual intimacy is a core part of marriage; yet differing needs, interests, and drives often cause problems. How were you prepared for the sexual part of marriage? Who talked with you? What were you told? Was it helpful?

2) Ellie finds herself having a crush on Liam as if she were a teenager again. Do you think people are ever too old to re-experience those adolescent attractions? Why or why not?

3) Ellie seems to have many self-doubts about her sexual appeal and ability to respond. Today there seems to be a pill for every situation. Do you think had either Chet or Ellie been able to talk more openly and/or use medications their situation would have had a different ending? Why or why not?

Chapter 16

1) Ellie and Liam take their relationship from the dinner table to the bedroom, then away for a romantic weekend. What do you think about this? If she had called you for advice what you have told her?

2) Everyone has a life story. What do you make of Liam's?

3) Ellie wonders if Liam is her second chance at love and marriage. Do you think she's being realistic?

Chapter 17

1) Marrying Liam would change everything. What ideas do you have to suggest for how people who have been divorced approach dating and re-marriage?

2) If you have adult children, imagine telling them you're going to marry again, whether their other parent has died or you've been divorced. If you have parents in that situation, imagine your mother or father telling you they are remarrying. How do you think you'd respond to such an announcement?

3) Today quite a few people experience multiple spouses. Do you think it realistic to still anticipate people will stay married to just one partner their whole life? Why or why not?

Chapter 18

1) Even as Ellie prepares to tell her adult children about Liam and their plans to marry, she still harbors feelings of affection for Chet. What do you make of that?

2) Why do you think Ellie was so nervous about telling her children about Liam?

3) How much should a parent confide in adult children regarding their personal love lives and plans?

Chapter 19

1) Ellie's daughter wastes no time questioning Ellie's judgment in deciding to marry Liam. Why do you think Cat decides to do so?

2) Relationships with extended family can be a major source of painful, conflicted emotions. What do you think is the proper approach between divorced spouses and their former spouse's extended families?

3) Ellie has doubts about this new relationship. How do you think she should respond to these doubts?

Chapter 20

1) Pastor Elaine seems to have some concerns about this new relationship. How do you think she should handle her reservations?

2) Before they leave their honeymoon Liam is asking Ellie to make a major change in her life. What do you think of this?

3) Deciding where to live is a major crossroad for later-in-life new relationships. What factors would you want to consider if you wanted to either have someone move in with you or you decided to relocate to another home?

Chapter 21

1) We naturally get attached to our stuff. Deciding what to keep, what to store, and what to let go are difficult decisions for some people. Why do you think this is so?

2) Life seems to be settling into a new normal for Liam and Ellie. Yet there were many adjustments to make. What would be your top priorities if you had to start a new life with a new significant other added to your existing immediate family?

3) How do you think Liam is adjusting to his new family life?

Chapter 22

1) A crisis tends to bring out the best and worse we have to offer one another. How would you describe the reactions to Tony's coma on the part of Ellie? Liam? Chet? Shirley?

2) It seems as though Ellie wants to turn the clock back to before Liam and Shirley entered the scene. Why do you think she might want to do that?

3) Ellie is starting to second guess the wisdom of marrying Liam. Again she experiences deep, conflicting emotions. Do you think this is typical in a second marriage? Why or why not?

Chapter 23

1) When a man and woman unite in holy matrimony they establish some chords that cannot be broken, not even by death or divorce. What do you think is pulling Chet and Ellie back together at the hospital?

2) Hospitals are places for healing. Do you think the dialogue between Chet and Ellie brought about a new level of healing for either of them? Why or why not?

3) What do you make of Ellie's brief exchange with Cat in the hospital restroom following Ellie's first private conversation with Chet since the divorce?

Chapter 24

1) Liam seems more concerned about the health of his finances than the recovery of his step-grandson Tony. What does this tell you about Liam?

2) The need for Tony to undergo surgery opens up another tender topic—different assumptions and beliefs about the role of God, church, and prayer in such situations. How do members of your family discuss or avoid discussing faith issues?

3) Ellie goes through the waiting without Liam. Do you think this was more a relief or disappointment to her?

Chapter 25

1) What impact do you think it had on Ellie to learn that Matt is gay?

2) What impact do you think it had on her to have Matt validate her own feelings about Liam that she'd been hesitant to express?

3) What do you suppose Ellie was telling herself after Matt left?

Chapter 26

1) Have you developed the journal habit? If so, is it helpful to you in processing things? If not, do you think it might be helpful at times?

2) Ellie is now torn between two worlds—the hospital world that takes on a life of its own and the world of being a newlywed. How do you think she's handling the transition back and forth between them?

3) Do you think Liam has a valid point about Ellie's priorities?

Chapter 27

1) Marriage in the modern world has radically changed women's roles and options. Ellie is wondering if she's made a huge mistake in marrying Liam. Do you think so? Why or why not?

2) What do you think about Pastor Elaine's summary of marriage today?

3) What do you make of Pastor Elaine and Ellie's assessment of Liam's personality? Have you known people like him? If so, what was that like for you?

Chapter 28

1) When Ellie's C.A.R.E. Board member Pete becomes the third person to suggest Liam's response to grandson Tony's bike accident is not appropriate, Ellie wonders if this is how God communicates with us when we need to make an adjustment in our lives. How have you experienced God nudging you to make a change in your life?

2) Ellie confides that she fears she may be a twice-divorced woman and it terrifies her. What do you think she should do about her second marriage?

3) Ellie confides in Pastor Elaine that she feels weak and really stupid for getting into a second marriage that appears to be failing. How do you think people end up in relationships that don't work out well?

Chapter 29

1) Liam suffers from a mental condition known as borderline-personality-disorder, often resulting from unresolved abandonment issues in early childhood. What do you think is the role and responsibility of a person who marries such a person?

2) Ellie has some painful decisions to make and tries to find solace and solutions through prayer. How do you decide what to do when you don't know what to do?

3) She makes her decision and swings into action. How do you prepare for a major transition in your life when you are the one who initiated the change?

Chapter 30

1) Ellie discovers that the people in whom she confides her plans to leave Liam are more concerned about her than critical of her decisions. Does this surprise you? Why or why not?

2) Ellie's attorney advices her to plan on losing her home and coming out on the short end of the divorce proceedings. Why do you think this is his advice to Ellie and what do think of that advice?

3) Ellie is shocked to hear Lynette, her boss, confess to an adolescent affair with one of her teachers. Lynette says she only uses that chapter of her life to help other people through their messes. What opportunities have you had to use what you thought was a colossal failure to help someone else?

Chapter 31

1) Liam tells Ellie he can't compete with her children and their families for her affection. People with grown children and families who marry later in life often run into these difficulties. How do you think older adults should handle resistance from their adult children who object to their marrying again?

2) Liam seems a changed man after spending time with his son again. Do you believe people ever can really change their basic personality? Why or why not?

3) In the end Liam took charge of the divorce arrangements and Ellie kept her home. What potential disasters in your life had a happier resolution than you anticipated?

Chapter 32

1) Pete sums up his theory about our relationship with God for Ellie. Do you agree with his conclusions? Why or why not?

2) What have you been taught about the nature of prayer and how God responds?

3) Ellie discovers that while she still has a lot of unresolved questions about the future, she finds herself laughing at her situation. How do you account for this change from distress to optimism?

Chapter 33

1) Ellie thought she would have to resign her position at C.A.R.E. and instead is asked to become the CEO of it. What unanticipated experience of grace like that have you experienced?

2) The offer of the new position immediately gets Ellie's creative ideas flowing again. What situation might energize you with new-found creativity?

3) Pete proposes. Ellie accepts. Are they crazy? Brave? Foolish? Hopeful? All of the above?

Kathryn Haueisen (pictured) was born and raised in Ohio where she fell in love with Lake Erie and writing. Her writing career was launched when *The Plain Dealer* (Cleveland) bought an article she wrote as a journalism class assignement. Since then she's written dozens of magazine articles and four non-fiction books. She is a graduate of Bowling Green State University and earned a Master of Divinity at Wartburg Theological Seminary. This is her maiden voyage into fiction. A Lutheran minister, she lives in Houston with her husband Tom Brandino.

Amanda Faucett Photopgraphy Houston, Texas

The Rev. Haueisen is available for speaking engagements. Contact her at www.howwisethen.com or through Blue Ocotillo Publishing, www.blueocotillo.com.